A Palette
for Murder

**The Aurora Anderson Mystery Series
by Sybil Johnson**

FATAL BRUSHSTROKE (#1)
PAINT THE TOWN DEAD (#2)
A PALETTE FOR MURDER (#3)

Praise for the Aurora Anderson Mystery Series

PAINT THE TOWN DEAD (#2)

"Plenty of charming characters, red herrings, labyrinthine twists and turns and brushes with death before you can even begin to guess whodunit. *Paint the Town Dead* is a cleverly crafted mystery full of secrets and intrigues that kept me guessing till the end."

– Connie Archer,
Author of the Soup Lover's Mystery Series

"Johnson paints characters with a folksy charm that makes them feel like family...Color me a fan!"

– Diane Vallere,
Author of *The Decorator Who Knew Too Much*

"Rory is definitely a quirky character; she has the ability to draw the readers in so that they want to follow her through her adventures."

– *Suspense Magazine*

"The plot thickens and becomes more entangled as Rory pursues all and any possible angles [to catch the killer]. Many intriguing complications arise during this search for the truth. An easy to read mystery with an amateur female sleuth who is a very likeable and believable character."

– *LibraryThing*

"Rory finds herself needing to uncover the truth of a friend's shocking death as everyone else seems satisfied with the easy answer. She's willing to risk friendships, and her own life, to chip away to reach the unvarnished truth. Paint the Town Dead is an engaging mystery set amidst a painting convention and showcases the complexity of relationships when a tragedy strikes."

– Christina Freeburn,
Author of *Masked to Death*

FATAL BRUSHSTROKE (#1)

"Johnson has penned a charming mystery filled with colorful characters, clever plot twists and unexpected surprises that will keep you guessing whodunit right until the end. A rewarding read and a refreshing debut."

—Hannah Dennison,
Author of the Vicky Hill Mysteries Mysteries

"Johnson has an assured, steady hand in creating complex plotlines in *Fatal Brushstroke*. Readers will definitely want to revisit Vista Beach in Aurora's next outing of investigating."

– Naomi Hirahara,
Edgar Award-Winning Author of *Murder on Bamboo Lane*

"A fun and fast-paced romp with plenty of suspense and intrigue, colorful characters, infidelity and family secrets. *Fatal Brushstroke* is sure to please cozy readers, especially those who love crafts mixed with murder."

– Sue Ann Jaffarian,
Author of the Ghost of Granny Apples Mystery Series

"Enjoyable, fun and entertaining...Aurora is a strong character you immediately feel like you have known her a lifetime...I love books that keep you reading late into the night and for me this is one of them great books."

– *Shelley's Book Case*

"The strength of the book, as in most good cozy mysteries, lies in the main character...The book really poses the question, within a well-written cozy, is nature or nurture more important in what a person becomes?...This underlying story makes this an interesting choice for book clubs to discuss."

– *Examiner.com*

A Palette for Murder

An Aurora Anderson Mystery

Sybil Johnson

HENERY PRESS

A PALETTE FOR MURDER
An Aurora Anderson Mystery
Part of the Henery Press Mystery Collection

First Edition | January 2017

Henery Press, LLC
www.henerypress.com

This is a work of fiction. Any references to historical events, real people, or real locales are used fictitiously. Other names, characters, places, and incidents are the product of the author's imagination, and any resemblance to actual events or locales or persons, living or dead, is entirely coincidental.

Trade Paperback ISBN-13: 978-1-63511-141-5
Digital epub ISBN-13: 978-1-63511-142-2
Kindle ISBN-13: 978-1-63511-143-9
Hardcover Paperback ISBN-13: 978-1-63511-144-6

Printed in the United States of America

To Project Egypt,
for always being there.

ACKNOWLEDGMENTS

When you send your work out into the world, you never know what its reception is going to be like. A big thank you to everyone who has taken the time to tell me they enjoyed Rory's previous adventures. It means the world to me.

To Project Egypt, the greatest group of friends one could have, *dw3 ntr n=tn*. Your friendship and support over the years has meant a lot to me.

To Erin George, Rachel Jackson and everyone else at Henery Press, thank you, thank you, thank you. Your advice and support are much appreciated. I'm proud to be one of the chicks in the hen house.

To the talented Stephanie Chontos, thank you for the wonderful cover art that's graced all three of my books. I raise my paintbrush to you.

A special thank you goes to Lia Biscoe for starting me on my decorative painting journey all those years ago.

And, finally, to my husband, Steve, thank you for supporting me in my writing endeavors.

Chapter 1

The sun beat down mercilessly on the residents of the quiet Los Angeles County city of Vista Beach, in the grips of an August heat wave that showed no signs of cooling off.

Rory Anderson closed her eyes and sighed contentedly as cool air washed over her head. Just a few more seconds, she told herself, and she would be ready to get back to work.

"What are you doing?" a voice behind her said.

Rory took her head out of the freezer compartment of the side-by-side refrigerator and turned to face the back door, where Liz Dexter peered through the screen into the kitchen of the single-story stucco house.

Rory unhooked the latch on the screen door and ushered her best friend inside. "It's hot, and I'm desperate. I can only shed so many clothes. Go on, try it yourself."

Clad in shorts and a tank top, the petite woman gingerly poked her head in the freezer. A smile slowly spread across her face. "Wow. That is nice."

"Too bad it's not a walk-in." Rory glanced at the thermometer on the wall. Eleven thirty and already eighty-five inside. When it was this hot, her brain refused to function. She didn't envision getting any more programming done right now. The final tweaks to her conferencing software would have to wait until right before the test run that evening. "I wish it would cool down. I can't work in this heat. Not even an ocean breeze to cool off the house in two whole weeks. I'm almost at the point of installing central air."

"You'd be better off buying more fans or one of those portable units if you can find them. All the air conditioning companies in the area are booked solid. A lot of Vista Beach Realty's clients are on waiting lists, including two of mine. By the time they get around to you, the temperature will have dropped and you won't need it anymore."

"It's times like this I wish I had an air-conditioned office to go to instead of working at home."

"I'm practically living at mine these days." Liz closed the freezer door. As she walked toward the kitchen table, her foot brushed against a small trash bag leaning against the legs of a chair. Empty soda cans spilled out onto the tile floor. She bent down and stuffed them back into the bag. "Looks like you have recycling to take in. Or are these for that homeless friend of yours, the one who hangs out near the pier? What's his name?"

"Kit. It's about time for me to head downtown to give them to him. I promised I'd drop them by today." Rory crinkled her face in worry. "I hope he's doing okay in this heat. He seemed fine when I saw him three days ago, but it's so hot in the sun."

"We can check on him on our way to the mall."

Rory blinked several times and stared blankly at her friend. "The mall?"

Liz put her hands on her hips. "Did you forget about shopping for a new outfit? We're still on for tomorrow night, right?" Her eyes narrowed. "You're not going to chicken out on me, are you?"

"Don't worry, I'll go out with this mystery man you've set me up with." Rory glanced at the thermometer once again. The temperature had risen an entire degree in the short time they'd been talking. "It's ridiculously hot in here. Let's go. We can grab some lunch while we're out." Leaving the fan in the front room running and the windows in the back of the house open, Rory tucked her phone in the pocket of her khaki shorts and grabbed the bag full of cans before they headed out the door to her friend's car.

A block from the beach, Liz turned into a city parking lot and pulled into a space overlooking the ocean. They fed the meter and joined the throng headed down the hill toward the pier. A family pedaled by on the street beside them toward the bike path that ran along the beach, parents on a tandem followed by three helmeted kids on individual bikes.

A head taller than her friend, Rory walked beside Liz as they looked both ways and crossed the path at the base of the pier before stopping to take in the scene before them. Trash bag filled with empty soda cans in one hand, Rory brushed beads of sweat off her face with the other as her gaze swept the area from the benches that lined the length of the pier, facing out toward the beach and ocean, to the nearby cafe that served drinks and snacks. Two people stood in line waiting to place their orders. All of the plastic chairs at the tables that surrounded the hut were filled with customers, none of them the man she was looking for.

"I don't see him. Now I'm really worried. He's always here on Friday. He hangs out on a bench on the pier. That one right there." Rory pointed to the concrete bench closest to them now occupied by a middle-aged couple watching a volleyball game in progress on the beach below.

"He could be working. He picks up odd jobs now and then, doesn't he?"

"He said he would be here. He always keeps his word."

"Maybe it got too hot for him and he moved indoors. Isn't there a cooling center near here?"

"I forgot about that. Let's check it out."

The two walked the short distance to the community center where two rooms had been reserved as a place where residents could escape the abnormally high temperatures and spend the day in an air-conditioned space. They entered the emergency cooling center, poked their heads inside one of the rooms, and scanned the tables and chairs scattered around the area, looking for Kit.

"Granny G's here." Liz nodded toward a table on the far side where Rory's seventy-five-year-old neighbor sat with three other gray-haired women, playing cards. "I guess she doesn't have air conditioning at her place either."

Mrs. Griswold looked up from the cards in her hands and waved at the two of them. Rory waved back. "I don't think anyone on my block does. It's not very common." She made a second pass over the tables and chairs in case she'd missed Kit the first time. "He's not here."

After looking in the other room, they walked to the nearby library where the homeless man often hung out. When they couldn't find him there either, they headed back to the beach. They were almost at the pier when frenzied barking reached their ears.

"That bark sounds familiar. I think it's Buddy, Kit's dog. Sounds like he's on the beach. That's weird. Kit knows dogs aren't allowed on the sand. He never takes Buddy there." With long strides, Rory hurried toward the steep flight of stairs that led from street level down to the sand, forcing Liz to jog to keep up.

From the top of the steps, Rory stared down at the crowded beach where a golden retriever, leash trailing behind, was running back and forth between the water and a group of sun worshippers lying on beach towels. As she watched, a man dressed in a white polo shirt and red swim trunks hurried over and tried to grab the leash, but the dog evaded him, growling when the lifeguard got within three feet.

Rory and Liz ran down the stairs, kicking off their flip-flops at the bottom, and headed toward Buddy and the man. Rory's feet burned as she walked as fast as she could across the scorching sand, heels sinking in with every step, making progress slow. Halfway to the water's edge, she called out the dog's name.

As soon as the retriever heard her voice, he stopped barking and ran toward her.

"This dog yours?" the lifeguard said when she was within earshot.

"He belongs to a friend. I'm worried about him. If Buddy's here, he must be close by." Rory bent down and addressed the dog. "Where's Kit, Buddy? Is he in trouble? Show me."

Seeming to understand, the dog raced toward the water, leading them to the shady area underneath the pier. As they followed, making faster progress once they reached the packed sand, Rory spotted a bicycle leaning against one of the rough concrete posts that supported the pier. White plastic bags full of belongings dangled from every available space on the bike, obstructing her view of the area in front of the post. As she got closer, she spotted bare legs on the sand.

The three of them hurried forward and found a man with a closely cropped beard wearing shorts and a t-shirt sitting against a post, his sandal-clad legs extended out in front of him, waves lapping onto the nearby shore. A sizable lump on his head and a gash on his forearm, he didn't respond when Rory called out to him. With his nose, Buddy nudged his companion's right arm.

While Rory and Liz stood nearby, concerned looks on their faces, the lifeguard knelt down next to Kit, placing his hand on the other man's arm.

"Sir, can you hear me? Are you all right? Can you tell me what happened?"

At the lifeguard's touch, Kit batted his hands as if he thought he was being attacked. Rory released her hold on the trash bag filled with cans and dropped down onto her knees on the sand on the other side of him, next to the dog. She held Kit's flailing arms until he quieted down.

In her gentlest voice, she said, "It's me, Rory. We won't hurt you. We're here to help. Can you tell us what happened? Who did this to you?"

With his last bit of energy, Kit mumbled something, but even when she put her ear close to his lips, all she could make out was "Zoe" followed by a long pause and "find." Then he slumped down and closed his eyes.

Unable to get any further response out of Kit, the lifeguard borrowed Rory's cell phone to call for help, then directed Liz to wait near the steps down to the beach for the ambulance to guide the paramedics to the spot underneath the pier.

"Help will be here soon, but we need to cool him down now," the lifeguard said to Rory.

Under his direction, she borrowed towels from nearby sunbathers and dipped them in the ocean water. She'd barely placed them on Kit's overheated body when a bright yellow truck with the word "Lifeguard" written on the side in red lettering drove across the sand and stopped halfway between the water and the steps. Its two occupants leapt out and, after consulting with their colleague, cleared a path from the stairs to the water's edge, holding back the group of curious onlookers who had gathered on the sand. People leaned over the railing on the pier and stared down at the commotion on the beach below them.

An ambulance screeched to a halt in the parking lot at the base of the pier moments later, and Liz led the EMTs to Kit. Before long, the man was strapped to a board in the back of the truck and driven across the sand to the base of the steps. Between the paramedics and lifeguards, they hauled him up the steep stairs to the waiting ambulance. A uniformed police officer spoke briefly to the two groups before Kit was whisked away.

Buddy tried to follow, but Rory held tightly onto his leash and spoke soothingly to the retriever.

The uniformed officer headed across the sand toward Rory and Liz. After introductions had been made, Officer Carr said, "Are you the ones who found him?"

Rory nodded. "How is he? What did the paramedics say?"

"Did someone hit him?" Liz asked.

"Looks like he was in a fight, all right. He has a pretty nasty bump on his head. I'd say it happened fairly recently. Plus he's dehydrated." The officer looked sympathetically at the two women. "Don't worry, your friend's in good hands," he said in a reassuring voice. "They'll do everything they can for him. What can you tell me about him? We didn't find any ID in his pockets."

"I don't know his full name," Rory said. "Everyone calls him Kit. He never wanted to talk about his past, and I didn't want to pry."

Carr made a notation in his notebook. "How did you two meet?"

"He pushed me out of the way of a car that ran a red light and almost hit me. That was about a month and a half ago." Rory shuddered when she thought back to the SUV that had come within inches of mowing her down in the middle of a crosswalk. "We started talking afterward. I've seen him at least once a week since."

The officer whistled. "Lots of distracted drivers out there. I see it all the time. Sounds like you were lucky he was around."

"I know." If it hadn't been for the homeless man's quick action, she would have landed in the hospital or worse.

He looked over at Liz who was standing nearby, petting Buddy. "What about you, ma'am? Do you know anything about this Kit?"

"Wish I knew something that would help. I've seen him around town, but I've only exchanged a few words with him."

"Did you two see anyone nearby when you found him? Maybe someone talking to him or walking away?"

Rory thought back to the discovery, mentally retracing her steps from the stairs down to the beach across the sand to the water's edge. "Not really. Just the lifeguard and those guys." She nodded toward the beachgoers ten yards away who had now returned to their sunbathing. "The dog was barking and the lifeguard was trying to grab his leash, but no one was anywhere near Kit." She glanced at the beach in the opposite direction. "Not that I could see, anyway. From where I was standing, though, I couldn't see the other side of the pier. Whoever hit him could have walked under the pier across the sand on the north side and blended in with the crowd."

"Was he conscious when you found him? Did he say anything to you?"

"Barely. He mumbled a name. Zoe, I think. There were a couple words before that, but I couldn't make them out. I could hardly hear him. I might be mistaken about the name."

Officer Carr kept taking notes.

"Do either of you have any idea who this Zoe is? A relative, maybe?"

Rory and Liz both said no.

"What about his phone?" Rory said. "Was it in his pocket? Maybe her number's in it."

"Or at least emergency contact info," Liz said.

"He has a cell phone?"

"I've seen him use one. An old flip-phone model."

"We didn't find anything on him. This his stuff?" He nodded to the bicycle leaning against the post. "Maybe his wallet and the phone are in there."

Rory handed Buddy's leash to Liz, who kept the dog occupied while the other two searched Kit's belongings. Neither of the items they were looking for were in any of the bags. The only thing of interest Rory found was a picture of a clean-shaven younger version of Kit with a woman about his age. From the pose, Rory suspected she was his girlfriend or wife. She turned it over. "Me and Zoe" was written in a scrawl across the back. "This is the name he mentioned. At least now we have a face to go with it." She handed the photo to the officer.

"Do either of you recognize her?"

They shook their heads.

"I'll take this, ask around. Someone might know something." He ran his hand through his hair. "Poor guy. I always feel sorry for anyone who lives on the streets. It might be warm and relatively safe here at the beach, but it's not like having a comfy bed to go home to every night."

"Before you leave, can we take a photo of it? We can ask around ourselves, see if anyone recognizes her. She might know about Kit's medical history. I couldn't tell the paramedics anything when they asked," Rory said.

"Good idea." The officer held the photo while they took a picture of it with their smart phones. "Does the dog belong to him? Do you want me to call animal control? They'll put him in a shelter until Kit gets better."

Rory and Liz exchanged glances.

"That's okay," Rory finally said. "We'll take care of him."

"That's fine, but remember, dogs aren't allowed on the beach. Better take him somewhere before someone complains. You know where the animal shelter is, right? I don't want to see him running around town."

Rory nodded. "Don't worry. We'll make sure he has a home. What are you going to do now?"

"We'll do our best to catch the son of...um...the person who hit him. Let me know if you remember anything that can help. Thanks for your time, ladies. If I need anything else, I know where to find you." Officer Carr headed toward the group sunbathing nearby and began questioning them.

Rory knelt down on the sand, wrapped her arms around the golden retriever's neck, and placed the side of her face against his. "Don't worry, Buddy," she said softly. "Everything will be okay. Your pal is in good hands."

Chapter 2

"What are we going to do with him?" Liz nodded toward Buddy. "You're not really planning on taking him to the animal shelter, are you?" she said, the horror unmistakable in her voice.

Rory buried her face in the retriever's fur before standing up. "I don't like the idea of his going to the pound any more than you do. We need to find him a temporary home. I could take him, but I'm worried he won't be happy with me. He's used to constant companionship."

"And I've got a condo that doesn't allow dogs." Liz tapped her chin. After a moment of thought, her face brightened. "I've got it! I just sold a house with a big backyard to a client. Double lot in the eastern part of town. I hear they're looking for a second dog. Buddy will need someone to play with." She handed the leash to Rory so she could make the call.

"Make sure they know it's only temporary."

Liz nodded in acknowledgement as she scrolled through the contacts in her cell phone until she found the number she was looking for. After a brief conversation, she hung up and turned to her friend with a smile on her face. "All set. They're happy to take care of him."

"Do we need to give them money for food? He's a big dog. I bet he eats a lot."

"They said not to worry about it."

"That's generous of them." Rory handed the dog's leash back to Liz.

"They're generous people. They'll take care of whatever he needs, bath, food, vet."

"His fur's pretty clean. Kit must have bathed him recently. I think he usually takes him in the restroom and cleans him up."

Liz looked down at the golden retriever who sat obediently by her side. "Well, Buddy, you've got a new home waiting for you and a new friend to play with. Don't worry, though, it's only temporary. You'll see your pal as soon as he's well enough."

The dog looked up at her and barked his approval.

"While you take care of Buddy, I'm going to stash Kit's things at my place. They'll be safe there." Rory glanced back at the bicycle still propped against the concrete post, piled high with so many bags the wheels and handlebars were barely visible. "That's probably everything he has in the world."

"I don't know if the bike will fit in my car."

"It'll fit in mine, but it'll take me a while to go home and drive back here. I don't like the idea of leaving his stuff unattended for that long." Rory thought about it for a moment, then called her mother on her cell. Less than five minutes later, she'd arranged to store the bicycle at her mother's store within walking distance of the pier. "We'll have to postpone our shopping trip."

Liz waved away the comment. "This is more important. We have plenty of time."

"Tonight's the software test, and I have some work to do before then. Is tomorrow morning okay?"

"Sure." Liz picked up the trash bag filled with empty cans. "Let me take care of the recycling. That bike is enough for you to deal with."

While Liz led Buddy to her car, Rory wheeled the heavily laden bicycle across the sand on the north side of the pier until she found a spot where the beach was level with the bicycle path. She paused to wash her feet at the shower at the edge of the sand, then put on her flip-flops and traveled along the path and up the hill toward Main Street. The bags banged against her leg as she climbed. Half the people she encountered took one glance at the bike with its mountain of plastic bags and frowned, the other half avoided looking at her altogether. She ignored them and concentrated on pushing the bike up the steep incline. At the top, she paused to catch her breath.

After the short break, she continued her trek, turning into the alleyway that ran behind her mother's tole painting and scrapbooking supply store. She rested the bike against the wall before unlocking the back door of Arika's Scrap 'n Paint, calling out to her mother as she walked from the back room through the empty classroom out onto the sales floor where Arika Anderson was talking with a slender woman clad in a vibrantly colored dress that flowed around her ankles. Arika stood next to the cash register while the owner of Beach Healing and Acupuncture stood on the other side of the counter. A paper bag rested on the surface between them.

"...will improve your health by leaps and bounds. You and Swan will feel years younger in no time," Willow Bingen was saying as Rory entered the room.

"Are you and Dad okay?" Rory's chest tightened at the thought her parents might be sick.

Arika waved away her daughter's concern. "We're healthy as horses. No need to worry."

The charm bracelet on Willow's wrist jingled as she pushed the paper bag across the counter. "Maybe you can convince your mother this is what she needs."

Rory opened the bag and sniffed. Cinnamon, ginger and a smell she didn't recognize filled her nostrils. "What is it?"

"Tea. My own special blend. You should try it. Never too early to worry about strengthening your immune system."

Arika plucked the bag out of Rory's hand and pushed it back across the counter. "I appreciate your concern, but we're feeling fine. I don't know where you got the idea we weren't." She turned toward her daughter. "You brought the bike?"

"It's in the alley."

Arika led the way into the back room with a sigh of relief that was short lived when Willow followed them, keeping up a nonstop monologue on the healing properties of herbs.

"Lord help me," Arika muttered in an exasperated tone.

Rory glanced over at Willow, but the woman seemed not to have heard the comment.

"You can put it over there." Rory's mother pointed toward a spot in the back corner of the combination storage room/office. "There should be enough room for it."

Rory wheeled the bike inside and set it in the space carved out for it. "Thanks for doing this, Mom. I'll come get it later with my car."

"Not necessary. It can stay here as long as needed."

Willow wrinkled her nose in disgust. "I'm surprised at you, Rory. Walking around town with a bike that looks like that. You can't even ride it with all those bags hanging on it. Why do you need them, anyway?"

Rory struggled to keep the anger out of her voice. "It belongs to a friend of mine who's in the hospital."

"Homeless." Willow nodded in satisfaction, pleased with herself that she'd recognized the truth. "When I moved here, I didn't expect to find so many homeless in such a wealthy community. The good weather attracts them, I suppose. The city should do more about them though. Thieves, that's what they all are, thieves. I'll have to have a talk with—"

Arika raised her voice and turned to her daughter. "Do the police know what happened?"

"Police?" Willow said. "Why are you talking to the police? Did your friend attack someone?"

Rory bit her lip to prevent herself from saying something she would regret. She turned her back on Willow and addressed her mother. "Looks like Kit was hit over the head and the heat got to him. I'm going down to the hospital to check on him soon. He was in pretty bad shape."

"Do the police know who did it?" Willow asked.

Rory shook her head.

"We'll have to wait until he regains consciousness. He was pretty out of it when we found him."

"Probably got into a scuffle with someone over who could panhandle where," Willow said. "Men and their dogs. One and the same, squabbling over territory."

"What about relatives?" Arika asked. "Are the police notifying them?"

"I don't know if he has any or if he even wants them to know where he is. He did mention a name though. I think he wants me to find her." Rory brought a photo up on her cell phone and showed it to her mother. "Have you ever seen her? Her name's Zoe."

Arika stared at the photo.

"No one resembling her has come into the store. What about you, Willow? Do you know her?"

The woman barely looked at the phone's screen before shaking her head. "Haven't seen her around town." She glanced at her amber bracelet watch. "I'd better be off. I have a client coming in soon. I'll leave the tea, no charge." She placed the paper bag on the desk. "If you want more, remember my store's just a few doors down."

As soon as Willow left, Arika sighed with relief and threw the tea in a trashcan. "She was getting on my nerves."

"Are you feeling okay? You're not sick again, are you?"

Arika patted her daughter on the arm. "Everything's fine. That was in the past. I'm back to normal now. Willow's just trying to drum up more business for her store. She's been making her way down the street, giving away samples of her 'special tea' to everyone." She pointed at the bicycle. "Maybe there's something else in Kit's belongings that will tell us how to find Zoe. Did you check everything?"

"Wouldn't hurt to look again." They searched each bag. In one, they found toothpaste along with a toothbrush and tiny bars of soap with a local hotel's name on it. In several others were a pair of clean but well-worn jeans and a handful of t-shirts—one for every day of the week—tennis shoes, socks and clean underwear. A bag of laundry rounded out the clothes. Rory set it aside to take home to wash.

She checked the flyleaves of the two books she found, hoping Kit's full name was inside, but nothing was written on the pages. Tucked in with the books was a paper bag that contained a half-eaten sandwich, an apple, and a slip of paper with a Bible verse written on it.

Arika stared at the bag in her daughter's hand. "That looks like one of the lunches from the church. You know who might know something? Reverend Paulson. He talks to a lot of the men and women who stop by for the weekly lunch giveaway. Maybe he can tell you more about Kit and give you a lead on Zoe."

"That's today, isn't it? The food is pretty fresh. He must have gotten it earlier. I'll check with Reverend Paulson on my way home. If Kit got his lunch before someone hit him, they might have seen something. Maybe he got into a fight at the church."

After returning everything except the bag of laundry to its place on the bike, Rory said goodbye to her mother and headed out the door.

Chapter 3

When Rory rounded the corner onto Seashell Lane, she spotted a dozen men and women waiting patiently by the side door of the church she and her parents attended. A volunteer stood just inside the door, handing out lunch bags to the line which extended into the neighboring parking lot.

She walked around the building and entered the church complex through another entrance, making her way down the familiar hallways past the sanctuary to the community room, where she found Reverend Paulson in the kitchen area, elbow deep in water, washing dishes.

When the minister spotted her, he smiled, rinsed the last dish and put it in the drainer. "Come to help out? I'm sure we can find something for you to do." He wiped his hands on a dishtowel.

"Not today. I actually need your help. I think this man was here earlier. His name's Kit." She showed the minister a photo she'd taken of Kit and his dog the week before followed by the one of the younger version of Kit and the woman. "Do you know how I can find her? Her name's Zoe."

He peered at the photo on the phone's screen. "I've seen him around, but not the young lady. Is something wrong?"

"I found him hurt on the beach today. Before he was taken to the hospital, he asked me to find her. At least I think that's what he wanted. He was a little incoherent."

The minister leaned against the sink and frowned in

concentration. "He's a regular. I don't know much about him. I don't have as much time to talk with everyone as I would like. If he's who I'm thinking of, we haven't exchanged more than a dozen words in the time he's been coming here. Maybe one of the volunteers knows more." He waved his hand in a come-with-me gesture and headed through the community room to a nearby storeroom where a middle-aged woman was checking supplies off a list. "You know Kit, don't you, Victoria?" he said to the woman. "Was he here today?"

"Sure was. Came and got his lunch at eleven on the dot like he always does. Why?"

"He's in the hospital. He asked me to find Zoe for him." Rory showed her the picture.

"I don't recognize her." Victoria frowned. "That's too bad. When he was here earlier, he was coughing a bit, but I didn't think anything of it. I guess it was more than just a cold. He never mentioned anyone named Zoe, sorry."

"Did you see him get into a fight with anyone?"

"No fights, not today."

"Are there many?"

"We get the occasional scuffle, but overall everyone's pretty nice to each other."

Rory and the minister checked with the other volunteers, but no one could tell her anything she didn't already know. After Reverend Paulson promised to call if he found out anything, Rory walked the rest of the way home and picked up her car for the short drive to the hospital. At the information desk, a volunteer checked the computer. When she couldn't find Kit in the system, she made a phone call before she handed Rory a visitor's badge and gave her directions to his room.

Rory bought cheerful flowers in the gift shop, then took the elevator to the appropriate floor. Inside the hospital room, a nurse was checking the patient's IV. When Rory knocked on the door, the woman turned and smiled.

"Is it okay if I visit for a while?" Rory asked.

"Sure. You're the first person who's stopped by." The nurse crossed the room to the doorway. "He's in and out right now, but I'm sure he'll welcome the company."

After the nurse left, Rory placed the flowers on a table where Kit could see them and know someone was thinking about him. She dragged a chair over to the side of the bed and sat down. In her gentlest voice, she said, "Kit? It's me, Rory." She waited for a response, but the man's eyes remained closed. Even though she didn't know if he understood, or even heard, anything she said, she continued talking to him. "Just wanted you to know all of your things are safe. My mom's taking care of them at the store. And Buddy's okay too. Good people are looking after him. He's got a yard and another dog to play with."

As soon as she mentioned his dog's name, Kit's eyes fluttered open. "Buddy?" he said in a hoarse voice.

"That's right. Buddy's safe. He's with a family not far from here. On Paskowitz. They're going to take care of him until you get out of here. How are you doing? You gave everyone quite a scare. Do you remember what happened?"

Kit stared at her as if he was having trouble understanding the words coming out of her mouth. He squinted and looked around the room. "Where am I?"

"You're in the hospital. We found you underneath the pier. I'm afraid I haven't had any luck finding Zoe. Is there anyone else you want me to call?"

"Where did you hear that name?"

"You said it right before you passed out. You asked me to find her...didn't you?"

"No, you misunderstood." He turned his face away from her and stared at the wall. "There's no one."

She placed a slip of paper with her cell phone number written on it on the table next to his hospital bed. "I'm leaving my phone number. If you need anything while you're here, call me."

Before she could say anything else, someone knocked on the door. "Can I come in?" a deep voice said.

Rory turned to find a handsome man standing in the doorway. Her heart skipped a beat, as it did every time she saw him. She smiled and gestured for him to come inside. "Kit, this is Detective Green. Are you feeling well enough to answer questions?"

He nodded, a wary look in his eyes.

The detective took a flip-top notepad out of the inner pocket of his suit. "That's quite a lump you have on your head. Do you know how you got it?"

Kit touched the bandage on his forehead as if realizing for the first time something was wrong. "I'm not sure."

"Did someone hit you?"

"Hit me?" He touched the bandage again, then shook his head and winced. "I'm sorry, I don't remember."

"What's the last thing you do remember? Take your time."

Kit frowned in concentration. "I got my lunch at the church like I always do on Friday. This is still Friday, isn't it?"

Once he got confirmation, he continued, "I ate half the sandwich, I think, then Buddy and I walked down to the beach. Buddy. Where's Buddy?" He looked in confusion around the room and called out to his dog, his voice getting louder and louder with each call.

Rory told him over and over again his dog was in good hands, but the news didn't seem to sink in.

As his agitation grew, the nurse appeared in the doorway and looked sternly at Rory and Detective Green. "I think that's enough for now. He needs his rest." She shooed them out the door and into the hallway where they stood out of sight of Kit.

Rory listened as the nurse calmed her friend down, then turned to the detective. "I hope he'll be okay. Did the doctors tell you anything?"

"The head injury isn't serious. He was severely dehydrated when the paramedics brought him in. And he's running a slight fever, but no one seems overly concerned about it. He should be out of here in a day or two."

Rory sighed in relief.

"Thank goodness. Maybe he'll remember more after his fever's gone."

The detective touched her arm in a reassuring gesture. "We're doing everything we can to find out what happened. Have you thought of anything more? Something you didn't tell Officer Carr?"

"No, not a thing. There were a lot of people on the beach, but no one who looked suspicious."

"He might not have been hit there. We're looking into the possibility he was in a fight somewhere else and walked down to the beach afterward." He put his notebook back in his jacket pocket. "Why didn't you tell me about the car that almost ran you down?"

"Oh, you heard. Everything happened so fast. I didn't really have anything to tell, and I wasn't hurt so I decided not to file a police report."

"I'm not talking about filing a report. Why didn't you tell *me*?" He shook his head in exasperation. "Next time something like that happens, don't be afraid to call me."

Rory smiled to herself at his concern for her wellbeing. "Okay, Detective, but there won't be any need for a call like that."

He cocked an eyebrow. "With your track record? And why don't you start calling me Martin. We've known each other long enough."

"Okay...Martin. I forgot to thank you for visiting my mother when she was in the hospital. She really appreciated you and Mel stopping by."

"I'm glad she's better."

"How is Mel, anyway? She hasn't been into the store lately."

He looked at her, a puzzled expression on his face. "She moved back East to go to med school. Didn't she tell you?"

Rory shook her head. "So soon? She was talking about becoming a doctor, but I didn't realize she'd started school. I thought she was planning on staying in the area. Are you two...?"

Detective Green shook his head. "We decided it was better to stop seeing each other. We're still friends though."

"Oh." Rory stared at her feet, avoiding his gaze, embarrassed that she hadn't known and that a tiny part of her was glad he was single again.

An awkward silence surrounded them until he finally cleared his throat and said, "I was wonder—" His phone chimed, indicating the arrival of a text message. He frowned at the display. "I'm sorry, I have to go. I hope your friend gets better soon." As he headed down the hall, he called over his shoulder, "Stay out of trouble."

Rory hummed to herself as she walked toward the nurse's station to leave her phone number in case Kit needed anything and wasn't able to call himself.

Chapter 4

"Thanks a lot for helping me test out this software. There's nothing like a real-life situation to iron out the kinks." Rory smiled at the woman with blonde hair styled in a short bob in the chair beside her. The two sat side by side in Dawn Ogden's dining room that evening, staring at a computer screen on the table in front of them.

"You're helping me out. If this class works out well, I'll buy your software and schedule several more," Dawn said. "I love working at Arika's Scrap 'n Paint, but this is what I want to do full time."

"I can't thank you enough for running the store when my mom was sick." Rory's eyes misted over when she thought of her mother's recent illness, a nasty bacterial infection that had laid her up for over two weeks.

"I was happy to help. Arika's like a mother to me." Dawn patted Rory's hand. "I know how worried you were."

Rory blinked away the tears and smiled. "Are you ready to start the test run?"

Dawn checked over the painting supplies on the table. Brushes, two-ounce bottles of acrylic paint, palette paper and a water basin were laid out in front of her. "All set."

Rory talked the painting teacher through starting the conferencing software, and soon the two of them were looking at themselves from a window that filled a quarter of the screen. A few more taps on the keyboard and, moments later, two more windows popped up on the display. Liz's smiling face appeared in one while a thirty-something woman wearing glasses showed up in the other.

"Hi!" Liz waved at the two of them. "That was pretty easy."

"Can you both hear us okay?" Rory said.

Liz gave them a thumbs up while Teresa Mut nodded and spoke but no sound came out of her mouth.

"Could you speak up, Teresa?" Rory said.

The woman adjusted something on her end. "Sorry. I can hear you fine. I accidentally turned off the sound."

"Are we ready to get started?" Rory asked.

A knock came from Teresa's screen. "Excuse me. Let me just get that." She got up and disappeared from the computer display, returning moments later with a plate of food.

"Teresa, are you in a hotel? I didn't mean for you to go to any expense for this." Rory gave her a worried glance.

"It isn't costing me a thing. I know one of the owners. I do a lot of weddings here. He's letting me use the room for a few hours. It's a mini-vacation for me. I can't concentrate with the kids around. Breaks like these keep me from going crazy."

With three kids between the ages of two and seven, the woman probably welcomed any break she could get. Teresa doted on her "monkeys," as she called them, but Rory suspected they and her wedding-planning business ran the woman ragged.

"Let's get started. You all have your cheat sheets, right?" Rory waved a piece of paper in front of the camera, a document explaining the software features she sent to all the test participants earlier in the week.

After they all nodded, Dawn put up a photo of the finished piece she was demonstrating that evening onto the screen. Once she verified that the jpeg appeared on each of the student's displays, Dawn pointed the camera at a piece of poster board where she'd already painted a circle in a medium shade of blue. "You get that 3D effect in trompe l'oeil projects using a combination of shading, highlighting and adding cast shadows. Today I'll teach you how to transform this plain circle into a ball using the first two techniques. First, let's review the proper way to load your brush."

Rory sat back in her seat and watched as the teacher demonstrated. She took notes of changes to make to her program, occasionally interrupting to make sure the students were seeing everything on their ends. Dawn had finished shading the circle and was about to demonstrate highlighting when the doorbell rang. She looked up briefly, then continued her explanation.

When the doorbell sounded again, Rory looked at Dawn and said, "Do you want to get that? We can wait."

"Ignore it. They'll go away."

She had barely said the words when the doorbell rang once again, more insistently this time, followed by a pounding that drowned out the question Teresa was asking. A shrill voice that seemed vaguely familiar called out Dawn's name.

The painting teacher looked toward the entryway in annoyance. "I'd better get that. Sorry about this. I'll be right back."

While Dawn took care of her visitor, Rory asked the others their opinions of the software. As they talked, Rory heard the murmur of voices in the background. She tried to ignore the conversation in the next room, but when the voices grew louder and louder she couldn't help overhearing the words "never" and "forgive."

"Now, pumpkin..." the shrill voice said.

"Don't call me that!" Dawn's voice was the angriest Rory had ever heard it.

"Okay, okay!"

Looks of concern came across all of their faces. Rory stopped in mid-sentence and turned her head toward the front door.

"What was that?" Teresa said.

"What's going on?" Liz craned her neck as if she could poke her head through the screen and see into Dawn's home.

"I have no idea." Rory leaned back in her chair, but furniture blocked her view of the front door.

"Turn the camera so we can see."

Liz made a swiveling motion with her hand.

"Wouldn't help," Rory said. "There's a bookcase in the way."

She put her finger to her lips to indicate the other two should stay quiet and strained to hear the muffled voices coming from the other room. "I think she's talking to Willow. I'll be right back."

Rory tiptoed across the dining room toward the entryway. She peered around the doorway in time to see Dawn say "You have no right" and shove a protesting Willow out the front door. Rory hurried back to the computer and whispered, "That was Willow all right. Dawn just pushed her out the door."

"Really?" Liz and Teresa said in hushed voices.

"Any idea what they were talking about?" Teresa asked.

"It was more like arguing. Nothing I heard made sense to me. I have no idea."

"Teresa, Willow's a friend of yours. Any idea what's going on?" Liz asked.

The woman shook her head. "No clue. Willow took one of Dawn's classes not long ago. Everything seemed fine between them then."

The door slammed shut.

"Shh! She's coming back," Rory said.

When Dawn slid into the chair moments later, her face was pale but composed.

"Everything okay?" Rory asked.

"Sorry about that. Just a misunderstanding. Nothing to worry about. Now, where were we?"

As Dawn continued where she left off, Rory couldn't help wondering why the painting teacher was arguing with one of her students and what had gotten the normally placid woman so bent out of shape.

After the test run was over and she had a list of changes to make to the software, Rory met up with Liz for a late dinner. They were walking back to Liz's car in the restaurant parking lot when Rory's phone rang. She frowned as she listened to the woman on the other end of the line.

"Is everything okay?" Liz asked.

"Kit left the hospital."

"They discharged him already?" Liz unlocked the car door and slipped into the driver's seat of the black Lexus sedan.

Rory curled her long legs into the passenger seat. "Not exactly. He got dressed when they weren't looking and walked out the door."

"No one stopped him?"

"They didn't notice until he was long gone. There were emergencies on the floor."

"Maybe he went to see Buddy."

"All I told him was the name of the street where the family that's taking care of him lives, not the house number. I suppose he could have gone there to see if he could find him."

"Easy enough to find out." They drove over to the eastern part of the city, stopping in front of a craftsman-style house on Paskowitz Lane. When no one answered the front door, they headed toward the backyard, where they heard dogs barking and children laughing. Liz called out as she opened the gate. Lights lit up the expanse of grass where two golden retrievers were playing fetch with a grade-school-aged boy and girl. Buddy bounded up to Rory and barked. After she gave him a quick pat on the head, the dog raced back to his canine companion.

A woman smiled as she walked toward them. "Come to visit Buddy?" She held her hand out to Rory. "We haven't met. I'm Bethany."

Rory shook her hand, murmured her name followed by "nice to meet you" and nodded toward the dog. "He seems to be doing well. Has anyone stopped by looking for him? His owner left the hospital."

Surprise with a tinge of disappointment came over the woman's face. "They discharged him already?"

Liz shook her head. "He left against the doctor's advice. We thought he might have come looking for his dog."

"No one's been by. He's not dangerous, is he?" Bethany cast a worried look at her kids, who were running around the yard with the two dogs.

"No, we just want to make sure he's okay," Rory said.

"I'll call you if he stops by." She clapped her hands and called out to her children. "Okay, play time's over. Off to bed." As her kids put away their toys and headed inside, Bethany said over her shoulder, "I hope you find him. Let me know if there's anything I can do."

Rory and Liz went out the way they came in, carefully closing the gate behind them. Next stop was Arika's Scrap 'n Paint, where Rory let herself in the back door of the closed store. Kit's bicycle and all his possessions were still in the same spot and didn't appear to have been touched. They drove slowly down the streets of downtown Vista Beach, past the library and the church, but saw no sign of him.

Finally, Liz said, "It's too dark. He could be sleeping anywhere. We'll have better luck in daylight."

Rory reluctantly nodded her head in agreement. They ended the day disappointed and worried they hadn't found Kit but determined to continue the search the next morning.

Chapter 5

Saturday morning dawned as hot as ever. Rory and Liz searched everywhere they could think of for Kit but didn't find him. As Liz drove the short distance to the mall, the two talked about that evening's double date.

"You still haven't told me his name." Rory fiddled with the radio, hopping from station to station in search of music that appealed to her.

Liz swatted her hand away and turned off the radio. "All you need to know is he's new in town, taller than you, and cute. I'm not saying anything else. You know what happened last time."

"I was not stalking that guy!"

"No, you just looked him up on the internet and drove by his house. Twice. You freaked him out."

Rory folded her arms and slumped down in her seat. "I wanted to know what I was getting into. I don't like blind dates."

"Trust me. This one's a keeper. Besides, I checked your horoscope. Today's an auspicious day for starting a new relationship."

"You know I don't believe in astrology."

"Just wait until tonight. You'll see."

Rory tried on a half dozen dresses, but none of them seemed right. While Rory waited in the dressing room, Liz scoured the sales floor for more possibilities, returning with a royal blue halter-neck dress. "Try this one."

Rory slipped the sleeveless dress over her head. It hugged her body, its flared skirt hitting several inches above her knee. She stepped out of the dressing room.

Liz motioned with her hand. "Turn around."

Rory slowly rotated so her friend could see the dress from every angle.

Liz nodded her head in satisfaction. "That's it. This is the one. That shade of blue really makes your eyes pop."

Rory tugged at the hem. "You're sure it's not too short?"

"It's perfect for you. With your height and long legs, he won't know what hit him."

When Liz dropped her off half an hour later, Rory headed up the path to her front door. She sighed and shook her head when she saw the white circle lying on her front lawn. She walked across the grass and bent down to pick up the collar. She didn't have to read the words engraved on the silver charm attached to it to know who it belonged to. She'd lost track of how many times she'd found the collar on her lawn since Willow moved into the neighborhood six months ago. Sekhmet, the woman's chocolate Abyssinian cat, delighted in shedding it every chance she got. Rory always returned it to her neighbor only to have it end up back on her grass a week later.

Holding the collar in her hand, Rory headed inside to drop off her purchases, then walked down the block past Mrs. Griswold's house to the Tudor-style home on the other side. When she reached the front door, faint music reached her ears. She rang the bell and knocked several times.

When no one answered, Rory headed around the corner through the open gate to see if Willow was in the back of the house and couldn't hear her. The music grew louder as she made her way down the side of the house toward the backyard. When she rounded the corner, she found the French doors leading into the back of the house ajar and a window wide open, its screen propped against the wall underneath it. A sense of foreboding washed over her, and a voice inside her told her to run away, but she shook it off, walked up to the French doors and knocked. When no one responded, she poked her head inside and called out in a loud voice, "Willow, it's Rory. Just bringing back Sekhmet's collar. Can I come in?"

She waited a moment, but when she heard no movement or answering call from inside the house, she opened the door wider and stepped inside. Classical music surrounded her as she looked around the open room. To her left a couch and chairs sat facing a fireplace. The wood floor extended into a large kitchen on the right side of the room. On an island in its center were partially cut up vegetables on a cutting board. The half-dozen pendant lights suspended from the kitchen ceiling were on even though it was the middle of the day and enough light streamed through the windows to make them unnecessary.

Rory furrowed her brow in worry. She called out again as she walked into the kitchen area. As she made her way farther inside, she discovered a half-dozen drawers open, papers and kitchen tools scattered across the oak floor. Her gaze shifted to the far side of the kitchen, where feet peeked out from behind the large island. She hurried across the room to find her neighbor lying on her side on the floor, legs curled up toward her head.

Rory bent down to feel for Willow's pulse, but stopped when she saw the knife sticking out of her chest. The collar Rory held in her hand dropped to the floor. She staggered, reaching for the granite countertop to steady herself. She closed her eyes and willed herself to breathe slowly.

When she'd calmed herself down, Rory opened her eyes, glanced at the body once again to make sure she wasn't imagining it, pulled her cell phone out of her pocket and, for the third time in the past five months, called 911 to report finding a body.

Once she recovered from the shock of finding her neighbor, she retrieved the collar from the floor and stuffed it into the pocket of her khaki shorts. Rory took a deep breath and steeled herself to look at Willow's body again. The woman's colorful dress, the same one she'd worn the previous day, was bunched up around her knees. Something gold peeked out from under the fabric. Without thinking, Rory reached down to pick it up, but caught herself in time. The police would want to see the scene exactly as she found it.

Her gaze swept the room from the open window past the ransacked drawers, finally landing on the counter where a butcher block knife holder sat, one of its slots empty. The handles of the others in the set matched the handle of the knife in Willow's chest.

Her neighbor must have been in the middle of cooking, stepped into another room for a moment and returned to find the intruder inside her house. Rory shuddered at the thought of the confrontation that must have followed.

A reddish stain on the floor caught her eye. Rory stepped forward to find a bloody shoeprint on the wood floor. She examined the bottom of her sandals to make sure she hadn't accidentally stepped in blood. Satisfied the partial print wasn't hers, she was bending down to study it when she heard a noise behind her. A male voice said, "Ma'am?"

She turned to find a uniformed officer standing in the doorway. She explained the situation to him, then pointed down at the spot on the floor. "That footprint's not mine."

The officer looked at the area she was pointing to. "Noted. The detective is on his way. He'll want to speak with you. Why don't you wait for him outside."

They'd just stepped onto the lawn when crime scene personnel arrived. After instructing her to stay in the backyard, the officer left her to secure the front of the house.

As Rory paced the area, a glint of white caught her eye. She crossed the lawn toward the unknown object. One of Willow's business cards lay on the grass next to a row of shrubs. Under one of them she spotted a credit card.

Bending at the waist, she bent down to look through the nearest shrub. Parting its leaves, she spotted the strap of an embroidered bag. She had her head in the bushes, reaching down for the object, when she heard a cough behind her. She turned to discover Detective Green staring at her, eyebrow cocked, an amused expression on his face.

"Playing Nancy Drew again?" he said in his deep voice.

Rory pictured him looking at her butt sticking up in the air and blushed. "Did you see these?" She pointed at the cards. "And I think that's Willow's purse in the plant."

"Interesting." He bent down to look at the place she'd indicated. "Don't touch anything. I'll have someone collect it all. Wait over there." He pointed to the other side of the yard. "I'll be back soon." He led a man with the words "Coroner's Investigator" written on the back of his jacket into the house.

Rory moved over to the open window and peered inside the kitchen. A woman was systematically going through the room, bagging evidence, while a man applied powder to various surfaces looking for prints. The coroner's investigator stooped down to examine the body, disappearing behind the island. Detective Green squatted on the floor near Willow's feet. He must have sensed her staring because he turned to look in her direction, shook his head and with a flick of his hand, shooed her away.

Rory backed away from the window, moving to one side so he couldn't see her, and examined the screen that was resting against the wall. She moved from window to window in the back of the house, finding them all closed with their screens intact. The intruder must have removed the screen from the one open window and entered the house through it.

Moments later, the detective returned to the backyard and pulled out his notebook. "Tell me how you found her."

He took notes as she explained about the collar and her attempt to return it. He showed her a plastic evidence bag. "Any idea what this is?"

Rory peered at the bag. Inside was a tiny golden sun. She knew she'd seen it before, but it took her a moment to figure out where. "That's from Willow's charm bracelet."

"Bracelet?"

"Wasn't she wearing it? She never took it off."

"Expensive?"

"It was important to her. Not sure how much it was worth to

anyone else. She wore other jewelry too." She pictured Willow's hands and wrists in her mind. "An amber ring and a bracelet watch. Amber too, I think. I don't remember seeing them on her. Are they missing too?"

He made another notation in his notebook. "Would you recognize them if you saw them again?"

Rory considered the question. "I think so." She pointed to the open window. "Do you think the intruder came through the window and left through the door?"

"That's one theory."

She thought about the article she'd read in last week's *Vista Beach View* about a rash of burglaries occurring in a neighboring city where the thief entered through windows and screen doors left open because of the heat. She wondered if the crime wave had finally spilled across city lines.

"Do you think it's the same people?"

He tilted his head inquiringly.

"As the burglaries mentioned in the newspaper."

"Perhaps."

"So it was a burglary gone wrong," she said softly.

"Or someone wanted it to look that way. Did you notice anything suspicious last night?"

"Is that when she died?"

He remained silent and waited for her to answer.

"Nothing I can think of. I was holed up in my house working late. I'm far enough away I don't think I would have heard anything anyway."

"No strange noises or cars on the street?"

"I didn't hear or see anything." Rory nodded toward the Mission-style house next door. "Mrs. Griswold might have. You should ask her."

"Thanks for your time. Go back to your house. I'll stop by if I have any more questions. And no talking to the press."

"If you see the cat, could you let me know? Someone needs to take care of her."

"Don't worry. We'll look around the house for her," he said before heading back inside.

Rory stepped to one side and peered through a window into the kitchen. The detective glanced over and mouthed the words "Go home" when he spotted her through the glass. She hurried around the corner along the side of the house. As she reached the front yard, a cab pulled up, stopping in the middle of the street behind the crowd that had gathered. The officer Rory met earlier held up the tape so she could duck under it. Neighbors tried talking with her as she made her way toward her house, but she waved away their questions.

Dressed in a suit, a young man about her age shouldered his way through the crowd and approached one of the two uniformed officers stationed near the edge of the property. He started to duck under the tape, but the officer held him back.

"Let me through."

"I'm sorry, sir, but you'll have to stay behind the tape."

"But I live here. I have a right to know what's going on."

"If you'll wait right here, sir, I'll get Detective Green for you."

Rory stopped on the edge of the crowd beside the hedge that separated Willow's property from Mrs. Griswold's and waited to see what would happen. A rustling noise attracted her attention. Rory stepped backward and looked around the hedge, where her seventy-five-year-old neighbor was leaning against the shrubbery, clippers in hand, ear pressed against the foliage. Rory cleared her throat. As soon as Mrs. Griswold heard the noise, she clipped a few imaginary sprigs off the perfectly shaped hedge.

With a jerk of her head, Rory motioned for her neighbor to join her. Together they peeked around the barrier between the properties and watched the scene play out before them, ready to duck behind the hedge at a moment's notice. As they watched, Detective Green emerged from behind the gate with the officer who'd gone to get him. While the officer began clearing out the spectators who'd gathered, the detective walked over to the young man and motioned for the other policeman to let him through.

"Are you in charge? Where's Willow? Has something happened to her? I have a right to know. This is my home."

Rory remembered seeing him periodically on the street, but hadn't realized he lived there. She glanced over at her neighbor and raised an eyebrow in a question.

Mrs. Griswold nodded and mouthed the word "sometimes."

"What's your name?" Detective Green took out his notebook.

"Lance. Lance Paladin."

"You live here? Are you related to Ms. Bingen?"

"She's my girlfriend. What's going on? Willow?" Lance took a step forward, calling the woman's name over and over again, his voice becoming more and more frantic. He turned to the detective. "What's happened to her? Was she taken to the hospital?" His eyes opened wide when he noticed the coroner's van. "Is Willow...? She's not...? Oh, God, no."

"If you'll just calm down, sir, I'll let you know what's going on. Take a few deep breaths," Green said in a soothing tone of voice.

As he slowly breathed in and out, the franticness left the young man's eyes and he no longer seemed ready to collapse.

"Let's talk over here." The detective led the man to a wood and wrought-iron bench that sat on the lawn at the edge of the property away from the street. Mrs. Griswold and Rory crept along the hedge until they thought they were abreast of the bench. Rory raised on tiptoe and peeked over the foliage. The detective and Lance sat less than three feet away. She glanced down at Mrs. Griswold and gave her a thumbs up, then returned her gaze to the two men.

"I'm sorry to tell you that Ms. Bingen was killed sometime last night."

"No, no, no, that can't be! You must be mistaken."

"A neighbor identified her."

As if sensing someone was watching, Detective Green glanced at the place where the two women hid. Rory froze, afraid she'd been discovered, but he gave no indication he saw her. She ducked down and huddled with Mrs. Griswold against the plant, peering through gaps in the hedge, and listened to the rest of the conversation that drifted over the barrier. From her vantage point, Rory could only see the end of the bench where Lance sat.

"I can't believe she's gone. I told her not to leave the windows on the ground floor open even if it is hot."

"Was that something she did a lot? Leave the windows open?" the detective continued.

"She left one open upstairs and one of the kitchen windows open every night. She felt it was too stuffy otherwise. She thought it was okay since they're both at the back of the house. I kept telling her she should get an alarm system, especially since I'm not here all the time, but she said there was no need." Lance buried his face in his hands. "This is all my fault. I should have insisted."

A pause, where Rory assumed the detective was waiting for the man to recover, then the questioning continued.

"You're away a lot?"

"I live here half the time. I have an apartment in Hawthorne."

"Trading up," Mrs. Griswold murmured so only Rory could hear.

"I see," Detective Green said. "Is that where you were last night? In your apartment?"

"You don't think I had something to do with this?"

"Just gathering information."

"I was in San Diego on business. Flew out Thursday and came back today. My flight landed an hour ago."

"Can anyone verify that?"

"The taxi driver who dropped me off here. Check with the airline, the hotel, the people I met with. They'll all tell you I was there." He gave the detective the flight and hotel information as well as the names of the people he'd done business with.

"When did you talk to Ms. Bingen last?"

"Yesterday afternoon. I called her between meetings. Everything was fine."

"She didn't mention anything unusual? Someone following her? Anything like that?"

"No, she never said anything to me."

"Are there any relatives we should notify?"

"No, she had no one. Can I go inside, pick up a few things?"

"Not while we're processing the scene. I'll let you know when we're done. Here's my card if you think of anything else. Do you need a ride to your apartment?"

Lance took the detective's business card. "No thanks. My car's parked on the street."

As soon as the conversation ended, Mrs. Griswold and Rory stepped to the front of the lawn and stood next to a flowerbed, pointing at a rose as if they'd been talking about gardening the entire time.

Lance stopped to unlock the door of a Mustang parked in front of Mrs. Griswold's house. He put his suitcase in the trunk and slammed it shut, then glanced in their direction. A thoughtful look on his face, he walked toward them.

"Mrs. Griswold, right? And you're Aurora. No, Rory?"

They nodded their heads in acknowledgement.

"How are you doing, young man? So sorry for your loss." Mrs. Griswold extended her hand in sympathy. "Is there anything we can do for you?"

"I was hoping I could talk to you both."

"Of course. Why don't we go inside. I made iced tea from a lovely Governor Gray tea my grandson brought me from his recent trip to South Carolina. It's the only place in the U.S. where tea is grown, you know." She looked significantly at Rory. "Albert's still single. And looking."

Rory and Lance followed Mrs. Griswold up the walkway through the front door of the Mission-style house into the cluttered living room. While the older woman went into the kitchen to get the tea, the other two settled onto a couch upholstered in a flowered fabric reminiscent of the eighties.

"You found her, didn't you?"

Lance sat with his elbows on his knees and stared down at his clasped hands.

"Did the police tell you that?"

"I saw you leaving the house when the taxi dropped me off. I wondered what you were doing there. When I found out Willow was...gone and the police told me a neighbor identified her, I realized they wouldn't let anyone behind the tape unless..."

"...I'd found her."

He sat up straight and looked at her. "How, how did you find her?"

"Sekhmet left her collar on my lawn. I went to return it." She dug the collar out of the pocket of her shorts and handed it to him. "I forgot all about it. Here."

He held it in his hands and stared down at it with the ghost of a smile on his face. "She's always shedding it. Don't know why Willow kept on putting it back on. The cat obviously doesn't like it. I've lost track of how many times someone returned it to us." He frowned. "What about Sekhmet? Someone needs to take care of her. Did you see her in the house? The police wouldn't let me inside so I couldn't check on her."

"I didn't see her anywhere, but you know how cats can hide. I didn't get the chance to look through the house, only the kitchen." Rory clamped her mouth shut, afraid she'd said too much.

"Is that where you found Willow? In the kitchen?"

She looked down at her hands, unsure what to say.

"Please, tell me what you saw. Do you think she suffered?"

"I don't think the police would want me to talk about it." And you really don't want to know what she looked like, Rory thought.

He looked at her with pleading eyes. "Please, I need to know."

She shook her head, reluctant to talk about the gruesome scene. "You don't want that, believe me. You're better off not knowing."

"Why don't I give you my number. If you see Sekhmet, could you let me know?"

He was putting his phone number into her cell phone when Mrs. Griswold entered the room bearing a tray with ice-filled glasses, a pitcher of tea and a sugar bowl. She raised an eyebrow as Lance handed the cell back to Rory.

"Just getting his number so I can keep him updated on the cat," she hastened to explain.

Mrs. Griswold sat down in an armchair and poured the tea. They sipped in silence until she finally said, "You've had some shocking news. How can we help?"

"The police aren't telling me anything. They won't even tell me how she died. I have a right to know what happened," Lance said.

"I can't tell you much. I didn't find her." Mrs. Griswold looked at Rory and raised an eyebrow in a question.

Rory shuddered when an image of the knife protruding from Willow's chest popped into her mind. When she shook her head without saying anything, Lance turned to Mrs. Griswold and said, "What about you? Do you know anything? Willow told me you're the Neighborhood Watch block captain."

"The lights were on in the house when I found her," Rory said. "It probably happened after dark. When did Willow usually eat dinner?"

"Late. Why are you asking? Is that when it happened, when she was cooking dinner?"

Rory kept quiet, sure she'd said too much this time.

"Did either of you see anything last night? Anyone lurking around the house?" Lance said.

Rory shook her head. "My eyes were glued to the computer screen until I went to bed."

Mrs. Griswold sat back in her chair and placed her glass on the side table next to her. "Nothing I would call unusual. I'm not sure I should say anything else until I talk to the police."

The color drained from his face. "She was seeing someone else, wasn't she? You can tell me. It's okay. I've known there was something going on for a while."

"I'm sure it's nothing. They're just friends."

Rory looked from one to the other. "Who are you talking about?"

"The chief," Mrs. Griswold reluctantly said.

"As in Vista Beach Police Chief Marshall?"

The older woman nodded.

"He stopped by last night. He didn't stay long. I'm sure it was all aboveboard. Probably knew you were out of town so he was checking on her."

"A lot of good that did," Lance said.

"When was this?" Rory asked.

"Around eight. I heard the chimes from the Catholic church a few blocks from here."

"Nothing else?" he asked.

Mrs. Griswold hesitated for a fraction of a second before shaking her head.

Lance set his glass on the coffee table and stood up. "Thanks for your hospitality." He turned to Rory and said, "You have my number. Call me if you see Sekhmet. I'd like to know she's okay."

Rory nodded her head. After Mrs. Griswold showed him out and they finished their iced tea, Rory loaded everything on the tray and carried it into the kitchen at the back of the house. The room's windows faced the backyard and Willow's property next door. While the older woman washed, Rory dried.

As she worked, her mind wandered to the relationship between Lance and Willow. There must be twenty years' difference in age between the two of them. She wondered what had attracted them to each other.

As if reading her thoughts, Mrs. Griswold said, "It's the sex."

"What?"

"That's what keeps them together. Can't beat it with an older woman. We know what we're doing."

Rory almost dropped the glass she was drying. She opened and closed her mouth a few times, unsure how to respond. Mrs. Griswold kept on washing dishes and putting them in the drainer, oblivious to Rory's discomfort.

"I don't mean to criticize, but he did just lose his girlfriend," she said. "You shouldn't throw yourself at him like that, pretending to get his phone number so you can tell him about the cat. You can't be that hard up."

"But, I didn't...I wouldn't..." Rory sputtered.

Mrs. Griswold gave her a knowing look and continued with the dishes. "I didn't want to say it when Lance was here, but Chief Marshall visited Willow a lot. At least once a week."

"How long has this been going on?"

"A while. Not sure they were having an affair though. He didn't stay long enough, if you know what I mean."

Rory was hanging the wet towel on the rack when they heard a shout outside. They both looked out the window to see a woman in a tank top and flowered leggings with a crimson streak in her black hair scrambling over the stucco wall separating the two properties. When the woman landed on the ground, she crouched down and looked wild-eyed around her as if looking for a place to hide.

Without skipping a beat, Mrs. Griswold opened the back door and silently motioned for Veronica Justice to come inside. The reporter for the weekly newspaper, the *Vista Beach View*, raced across the lawn through the door and sat down at the kitchen table, a little out of breath. Mrs. Griswold grabbed a broom and stepped out onto the patio. She'd barely started sweeping when a uniformed officer poked his head over the wall.

Rory's neighbor paused and looked inquiringly at the officer who, after a quick look around the yard and down the side of the house, shrugged his shoulders and disappeared into Willow's backyard.

As soon as he dropped out of sight, Mrs. Griswold came back inside. She returned the broom to the nearby closet and stood in front of Veronica. "Now, young lady, explain yourself. Tell me why I shouldn't call that officer over and tell him you're here. What were you doing next door?"

Beneath lids painted with vibrant eye makeup, the reporter looked at her and said, "My job."

Mrs. Griswold raised an eyebrow. Veronica sat back in her chair and folded her arms in front of her chest, revealing a long scrape on her right forearm.

"You're bleeding." Rory nodded at the scratch.

"Am I?"

Veronica looked down at her arm.

Mrs. Griswold took a first aid kit out of a nearby cupboard. While she cleaned and bandaged the wound, Rory sat down at the table and said, "Why were you running? Did you disturb the crime scene?"

Veronica's nose ring quivered as she shook her head. "I was just looking around."

Rory's eyes narrowed. "The police didn't invite you in, did they?" She couldn't see Detective Green letting a reporter from the local newspaper wander around the crime scene, especially after he'd specifically warned Rory about talking to the press.

"Not exactly." Veronica winced as Mrs. Griswold slapped on a bandage. "I sort of popped over the fence from the property on the other side. No one was home," she continued a bit defensively. "I was careful not to disturb anything in Willow's backyard."

"So why was that policeman chasing you?" Mrs. Griswold asked.

"Stop ganging up on me." Veronica turned to Rory. "You were there. You found the body, right? Tell me what you saw." She pulled a small notepad out of the tote bag she used as her purse.

"How do you know that?"

"I overheard one of the officers talking to another. They were marveling at how you keep on finding bodies. How you're a regular Jessica Fletcher. Three of them in five months. Kind of suspicious is what they thought."

Rory groaned inwardly. Not this again. "I have nothing to say. You're going to have to find out through official channels. How did you even know about Willow?"

"Please! There are police cars on the block and crime scene tape around the house. That's a pretty big hint."

"But how did you know there was police activity on this street in the first place? Your office is downtown."

"A source told me they saw a bunch of police cars on the block so I popped by for a look-see. With that crowd outside, it wasn't hard to find out who lives in the house. Look, I'm just trying to report the news, keep the police honest."

"I'm sure they'll tell you what they can, when they can."

"Will they?"

Rory studied her, sensing she knew more than she was saying. "What do you know?"

"You can read all about it in the paper."

"But that doesn't come out until Thursday. That's almost a week away. Wouldn't it be old news by then?"

"Check the paper's website. I'll have an update before then. I might even talk about it on Vista Beach Confidential," Veronica said, referring to her blog where she reported on happenings around the city.

"What aren't you saying?"

"I'll give you a hint. Not everyone liked her business practices."

"What do you mean?"

"Check VBC or the paper's website." She closed her notepad and stuffed it in her bag.

Veronica thanked Mrs. Griswold, then slung her tote bag over her shoulder and headed toward the front door. As Rory watched her walk away, she frowned and wondered what the reporter had found out about Willow and if it had anything to do with her untimely death.

Chapter 6

As soon as Rory stepped inside her house, she cautiously moved from room to room in the twelve-hundred-square-foot structure, checking for any signs of an intruder. She breathed a sigh of relief when everything appeared undisturbed.

She jumped when her cell phone rang. She laughed at herself, pulled her phone out of the pocket of her shorts and sank down onto the sofa.

"Just wanted to let you know I might be a little late. I'm showing a client a couple houses and they're not here yet," Liz said. "Don't worry though, we'll still have plenty of time to work on your makeup."

"I'm not sure I'm up to going out tonight." Rory couldn't see herself making small talk with someone she didn't know after the day's gruesome discovery.

The hum of background voices filled the silence as Liz digested the comment.

"What happened? You were fine with it this morning. Do you need me to take you to the doctor? Or are you worried about Kit? You've done everything you can. Don't worry, Dashing D's on the job. He'll find him."

"It's not that." Rory took a deep breath. "I found Willow today. Someone killed her."

"Wispy Willow's dead?" Liz's voice rose briefly then fell to a whisper. "You didn't find her in your garden, did you?"

Rory shivered as she recalled finding the body of her painting teacher in one of her flowerbeds five months before. "Not this time. She was in her kitchen. Looks like she surprised someone breaking into her house."

Liz sucked in her breath. "That's horrible. How did they get in?"

"Through an open window in the back. At least that's what Det—Martin thinks. There was a screen propped up against one of the kitchen windows."

"It's Martin now, is it? Is that why you don't want to go tonight? Have you forgotten he's got a girlfriend?"

"They broke up."

"When did this happen?"

"Not sure exactly. He told me about it when I saw him at the hospital yesterday."

"And you didn't tell me?"

"I figured you already knew. You always know everything before I do."

"I'm slipping." Rory could almost hear her friend shaking her head in disbelief. "I think you should still go tonight. It'll be good for you. Keep your mind off today. And, if there's someone running around the city breaking into houses, I don't like the idea of you being home alone. At least I have a condo with a security system."

"I can't run scared. The police are patrolling the neighborhood. I'll make sure I close the windows before I go to bed."

"It's only dinner. We don't have to stay out late."

Rory sank farther down into the sofa cushions and thought about what Liz had said. Getting dressed up might be a good thing for her. Better than sitting at home by herself, thinking about what she'd found two doors down and wondering if the intruder was going to break into her house next. "I did buy a new dress. Hate for it to go to waste."

"Good," Liz said. "I'll come over as soon as I finish with my client."

After she hung up, Rory settled down at her desk to work on

her conferencing software. Her mind kept wandering so often that a change that should have taken only a few minutes stretched into half an hour. Every time she heard a noise outside, she got up to see what had caused it, but it was only the usual neighborhood sounds: cars coming and going, dogs barking, neighbors walking by.

She abandoned her software and turned to her weekend cleaning chores. By the time Liz arrived, the place was neat and tidy and she'd changed into her new dress.

Rory settled into a chair in the kitchen while Liz laid out her supplies on the table. She was finishing up the eye makeup and deciding on the lipstick color when Rory's cell phone chirped, alerting her to a new post on Vista Beach Confidential.

An article titled "Landlord from Hell?" had been posted moments before. It began, "When Willow Bingen bought the old Walker building downtown six months ago, she promised her tenants everything would stay the same. But the owner of Beach Healing and Acupuncture soon changed her tune..."

"What are you doing? I can't finish your makeup with your head bent down like that."

"You've got to read this."

Rory showed the screen to Liz, who took the phone and pored over the post.

"Looks like Willow was adding a CAM provision to her tenant's leases," Liz said.

"I didn't even know she owned the building next to my mom's. What's a CAM provision?"

"Stands for Common Area Maintenance. It requires a tenant to pay a share of the operating expenses of the building. They weren't happy about the change."

"She couldn't just add it, could she?" Rory asked.

"When a lease is up for renewal, everything's up for negotiation." Liz placed the phone on the kitchen table out of Rory's reach and went back to work. When she finished, she stepped back, cocked her head and studied her friend. Nodding her head in satisfaction, she handed Rory a mirror. "You'll knock his socks off." She was putting away her makeup supplies when Rory's cell crowed. Liz glanced down at its display and pushed the phone across the table. "It's your mom."

After a short conversation, Rory turned to Liz. "Do we have time to make a quick stop before we head to the restaurant?"

"I think so. What's up?"

"Mom's worried about Dawn. She called in sick today and now she's not answering her phone. Mom's stuck at the store and wants us to make sure she's okay."

"Dawn seemed fine last night."

"Maybe it's one of those twenty-four-hour bugs. Let's go."

They grabbed their things and headed out the door. A short time later, Rory eased her car into a parking space in front of the Spanish-style house she'd visited the previous evening.

Liz peered through the passenger window. "Looks pretty quiet. Do you think she's home?"

"Her car's in the driveway."

Rory led the way up the path to the front door and rang the bell. When no one answered, she walked to a nearby window, cupped her hands around her eyes and peered inside at the living room. A pale face stared back at her from the other side of the glass. Rory yelped and jumped back. She'd just finished describing what she'd seen to Liz when the front door opened and Dawn poked her head out.

"Sorry, I didn't mean to startle you. I didn't hear the bell." She covered her hand with a tissue and coughed. "Did you need something?"

"Mom sent us to check on you. You didn't answer your phone so she got worried."

"I was sleeping so soundly, I guess I didn't hear it ringing. Tell your mother I'm feeling much better. I want to be one hundred percent for work on Monday, so if you'll excuse me, I'm going to lie down on the couch and get some more rest."

Rory was in the middle of saying "Let us know if you need anything" when the front door closed.

"That was a little abrupt, wasn't it?" Liz said as they headed back to the car.

"She's probably one of those people who wants to be alone when she's sick." Rory turned the key in the ignition and drove to Big Wave Steak and Seafood in downtown Vista Beach, where they settled down at the bar to wait for their dates to arrive.

Rory took a sip of her ginger ale. "Doug's coming, right? Which one is he?"

"The doctor who works at that clinic in Hawthorne. You met him once when he dropped me off at your place."

"Oh, right."

"You don't remember him, do you?"

"You have so many boyfriends. How am I supposed to keep track?"

"At least I'm getting myself out there. Yours is a doctor too."

Rory glanced nervously at the time on her cell phone. "Where are they?"

"That's them now."

Liz pointed her martini glass toward the doorway, where two men stood, one a foot taller than the other. The taller one had a backpack slung over his shoulder with a red rabbit's foot hanging from a zipper pull. She waved them over.

The taller one held out his hand to Rory. "Hi, I'm Tripp. Tripp Keating. I believe you're my date for the evening."

Rory looked into eyes that twinkled when he smiled, the bluest ones she'd ever seen. She took his hand, holding it a moment longer than necessary, and stammered out her name.

After all the introductions had been made, the hostess led them to their table. Rory took a seat between Liz and Tripp. They made small talk as the waiter distributed the menus and filled their water glasses.

When a waiter delivered a steak knife to a neighboring table, Rory's mind flashed back to the knife sticking out of Willow's chest. She bent her head to study her menu. "Definitely not the steak," she murmured to herself.

Tripp gently touched her arm and leaned toward her. "Are you okay?" he whispered. "You look like you've seen a ghost."

Rory placed her menu on the table. "I'm fine. I think I'll have the Caesar salad." She gave him her brightest smile. "Liz tells me you moved to town recently. Where were you before?"

"Africa. I do some work with Doctors Without Borders. I've been to Central America, Africa, all kinds of places. Wherever I'm needed, really. This is one of the rare occasions I'm back in the U.S. I hope to make it more permanent this time."

"That sounds interesting. What's your specialty?"

"I'm a trauma surgeon, but right now I'm working at a local clinic with Doug." He nodded across the table at Liz's date. "There's a real need for good low-cost medical care in a lot of places, even here in the States."

"Do you have family nearby?"

"No, but I grew up in a place similar to this. Surfing's a hobby of mine so I decided this would be a good area to hang out for a while. A friend introduced me to Reverend Paulson at Good Samaritan church. He's letting me stay there in exchange for doing odd jobs."

"Good Samaritan? My parents and I go there. I don't remember seeing you."

"I've only been in town a few weeks. I usually hang out towards the back during the service, but Reverend Paulson convinced me to join the choir, so I'll be front and center tomorrow morning. I'll be sure to look for you. But enough about me. Tell me about your job."

Rory was telling him about her freelance software business when the waiter came to take their orders. During dinner, Tripp regaled them with stories of his travels while Doug talked about the clinic where they both worked. "Did you hear about that murder on Seagull Lane?" Doug speared a piece of his blood-red steak. "That's your street, isn't it?" he said to Rory. "Were you home?"

Rory averted her gaze as he popped the piece of meat into his mouth. "I'm not supposed to talk about it."

"Why not? Wait, did you find the body? What is that, your third?"

"Doug!" Liz said.

"What? Everyone in town knows she has a habit of finding bodies. It's been in the paper."

"Doesn't matter. It's not proper dinner table conversation."

A faint cock-a-doodle-doo sounded from Rory's clutch, saving her from having to say anything else. She checked the display on her cell phone. "Sorry, I have to take this." She headed outside to answer the call. When she returned to the table five minutes later, a chastised Doug apologized.

"Bad news?" Liz asked.

"They found Kit. He's back in the hospital."

"A friend of yours?" Tripp asked.

Rory explained how they'd found the homeless man on the beach.

"I think I've met him at the church," Tripp said. "He comes and gets lunch there on Fridays, right?"

"That's right." Rory put her napkin on the table and stood up. "I'm sorry to cut this short, but I need to go to the hospital to check on him. I had a good time though."

"Would you like me to go with you?" Tripp asked, concern in his voice. "I can interpret doctor-speak for you. And they might tell me more than they would you."

"That would be nice," Rory said.

"You'll have to drive though. I don't have a car."

"How do you get around?" Liz asked.

"Public transportation, mostly, and I have a bicycle."

"Go," Liz said. "We'll take care of the check. I'll get a ride home from Doug."

Rory smiled her thanks, then she and Tripp headed to the hospital. Along the way, they talked about Kit.

"Do you know anything about his background?" Rory said. "He never wants to talk about his past with me."

Tripp leaned back in his seat and stared out the window. "I've only had a few conversations with him. All he wants to talk about are books. Can't get enough of them. I tried to find out more, believe me, but I haven't been here that long. It takes time to build up trust. Maybe someone else knows him better."

They lapsed into silence that lasted until they reached their destination.

Before long, they were standing by Kit's hospital room, waiting for the doctor to finish his examination. Rory peered into the room. A steady beep came from a monitor that displayed Kit's vital signs while an IV pumped what she assumed was an antibiotic into his unconscious body. From where she stood, she couldn't tell if the numbers on the screen were good or bad. She was just happy not to hear the shrill sound of an alarm.

When the doctor came out of the room, he greeted Tripp like an old friend. They stood off to one side and discussed Kit's condition while Rory ventured inside the room and stood by the bed. She closed her hand around his and gently called his name so he would know someone was there. No response other than a slight fluttering of his eyelids. She said his name again. This time his eyes opened fully for a moment. He smiled and seemed to recognize her before he closed them again.

Rory squeezed Kit's hand and stepped out into the hallway where Tripp now stood by himself.

"It's not good," he said. "Let's talk over here." He led her to a row of chairs in the hallway a few doors down. As soon as they were seated, he got straight to the point. "I won't sugarcoat it. He's picked up a nasty infection. Between that and the blow to his head, it's not looking good."

"I thought the head injury wasn't a problem."

"Head injuries are tricky. Sometimes a problem shows up later. That's why we like to monitor patients for a while."

"They can help him, can't they?"

"They're doing everything they can." He took her hand and squeezed it. "He's getting the best care possible. Why don't I give you my number in case you have any more questions."

After exchanging phone numbers, they walked out the front door of the hospital. Rory silently vowed to find Kit's family. She couldn't heal him, but she could make sure he was surrounded by loved ones if the worst happened.

Chapter 7

The next morning, Rory slipped into the pew next to her parents moments before the church service was about to begin. Tripp waved at her before taking his place with the rest of the choir at the front of the sanctuary. She smiled shyly and waved back.

Swan Anderson leaned toward her, his gaze focused on Tripp. "Should I have a talk with him, man to man?"

"Dad!" she said in a hushed voice.

Arika gave her husband an affectionate smile and gently swatted him on the arm with her program. "Swan, stop torturing your daughter. The service is about to start."

"Just trying to help," he said, a twinkle in his eyes.

The minister walked to the front, and the congregation rose for the opening hymn.

Rory smiled up at her father who, at six foot three, was three inches taller than she was. She sang along with the choir, occasionally casting a glance at Tripp, wondering if he'd enjoyed their date as much as she had. She stood oblivious to the world around her, unaware the hymn had ended until her father gently tugged on her arm to remind her it was time to return to her seat.

She blushed and sat down, embarrassed to be caught daydreaming in church. From then on, she focused her attention on the service, bowing her head with the rest of the congregation when Reverend Paulson prayed for the sick, mentioning Kit by name. As they all stood for the next hymn, she caught movement out of the corner of her eye. She turned her head slightly in time to see Dawn slip into a pew across the aisle. The woman's face was pale, but her walk was steady and she seemed to have recovered from her illness.

After the service was over, Rory wended her way through the crowd gathered on the patio near the church entrance looking for Dawn, but she was nowhere in sight. In the parking lot, Rory spotted her standing next to her car, shaking her head at Detective Green. Moments later, he closed his notepad and left her leaning against her car.

Rory headed across the parking lot. "Are you okay?" She touched Dawn's shoulder. "What did Detective Green want?"

Dawn looked up, her face paler than Rory had ever seen it.

"Here, sit down." She led her to a stone bench on the sidewalk next to the parking lot. "Tell me what's going on."

"You've got to help me."

"Are you feeling worse? Do you want me to take you to the doctor?"

"I'm not sick anymore. It's that detective. He thinks I did it."

"Detective Green? What does he think you did?"

"Killed Willow."

"Why would he think that?"

"I was there the night she died."

"At her house?"

"I found her body. What am I going to do?" Dawn buried her head in her hands.

Rory patted her back a few times and waited for her to recover. Dawn took a deep breath and sat up, then turned to Rory and laid a pleading hand on her arm. "Please, help me."

"I'll do whatever I can, but I'm not sure what's going on. Tell me from the beginning."

In fits and starts, Dawn explained how she'd gone to Willow's house late Friday evening, and when the woman didn't answer the front door, she'd gone around to the back and discovered the body in the kitchen. "I didn't kill her, I swear."

"Why didn't you call the police?"

"I don't trust them. I saw what they did to you when you found that body in your garden."

"You must have realized they'd find out you were there."

"I thought I was careful. I wiped off everything I touched, or I thought I did. I stepped in some blood and didn't realize it."

That explained the bloody shoe print near the body, Rory thought. "I can see why they're suspicious."

"I didn't do it. Now they want my DNA."

"Is that what Detective Green was talking to you about just now?"

Dawn nodded, then took a tissue out of her purse and dabbed her eyes. "I'm not giving it to them. I won't be railroaded. You have to help me. You know what it's like to be accused of murder when you're innocent."

Rory cast her mind back to April when the police had suspected her of killing her painting teacher. She'd been proved innocent in the end, but she cringed every time she thought of how frightened she had been. She didn't want anyone else to go through anything like that. "I'm not sure what I can do," she said hesitantly.

"Ask around. You solved those other murders. Aren't you friends with that detective, the one you saw me talking to?"

"You could hire a private investigator. I can give you a name."

"Can't afford it. I'm barely getting by as it is."

Rory studied the woman's hopeful face. Rory's heart went out to her, and she remembered how comforting Dawn had been when her mother was sick.

"Okay, I'll see what I can find out. No promises though. And you've got to tell me everything."

"Of course. What do you want to know?"

"Why did you go to see her?"

"We had a bit of a dust-up. You remember, she stopped by my place when we were testing your software." After Rory nodded, Dawn continued, "It wasn't anything major, just a stupid argument about one of my classes. She was trying to tell me how to teach. Got my back up, you know."

Rory nodded, thinking of how fond Willow had been of giving unsolicited advice.

"After our argument, she sent out an email to the students in one of my classes, saying some changes should be made. I give everyone a class list so they can contact each other, establish a painting community, not so they can criticize people."

"What sort of changes did she think you should make?"

"She said I was too old-fashioned in the way I teach. Said I should use an overhead projector during class instead of using a poster board for my demonstrations."

"Is that why you decided to do the online courses?"

"I was planning on starting them anyway." Dawn took a deep breath. "I couldn't get the argument and the email out of my head, so I stopped by her place that evening to have it out with her. Sure, I was mad, but I didn't kill her!"

"Doesn't seem like much of a motive. Is that it?"

"A neighbor saw me knocking on the door, and, to make matters worse, my cell phone puts me in the area around the time Willow died. Eleven p.m. She must have been killed right before I got there. I was planning on stopping by her house earlier, but I had errands to run. If I hadn't had things to do, I might be dead now too." Tears trickled down the woman's face.

Rory hugged her until she stopped crying.

"Thanks." Dawn took a tissue out of her purse and blew her nose. She gave Rory a faint smile. "Thanks so much. I don't know how I'll ever repay you."

"I haven't done anything yet."

"Promise me you'll try. That's all I ask. You're my only hope."

After Rory assured her she'd do what she could, Dawn headed back to her car.

Rory was thinking about the conversation, sorting through everything in her mind, when a shadow fell over her. She looked up to find Detective Green standing in front of her, a serious expression on his face.

"I'm sorry to bother you at church, but duty calls."

"I understand. I saw you talking to Dawn earlier."

"Ms. Ogden's a friend of yours, right? Are you two close?"

"I'd say so. Why do you ask?"

"I'm checking on her movements over the last few days. She said she saw you Friday evening. What time was that?"

"She didn't do it, you know. Kill Willow. She's not that kind of person."

He merely stared at her and waited for her response.

"She was helping me test out my conferencing software. We started around seven thirty and finished a little after nine."

He jotted something down in his notebook. "Anything unusual happen during your test?"

Rory stared down at her khakis. She didn't want to get Dawn in any more trouble, but she couldn't lie to the police, especially not to someone she considered a friend. She squared her shoulders and looked up. "Willow stopped by in the middle of the test, but I couldn't hear what they were talking about."

"Was it friendly?"

"Like I said, I couldn't hear more than a few words, nothing that made sense to me, but the tone of their voices was a little...sharp."

"So they were arguing?"

"You could say that."

"Did she and Ms. Bingen have a lot of issues?"

"Not any more than anyone else. Willow could be...controlling. She liked to butt in to everyone's lives."

He raised an eyebrow. "Yours too?"

"Not yet." But it was only a matter of time, Rory thought. "Dawn was stupid, not telling you she found Willow, but she couldn't have done it."

"How can you be so sure?"

"I just know." She studied him. "What happened to the burglary-gone-wrong angle?"

"We're investigating all possibilities." He snapped his notebook shut and put it back in the pocket of his suit. "I think your friend's holding something back. If you have any influence over her, get her to tell us everything she knows. It's better we find out from her rather than someone else. Thank you for your time."

As he headed toward his car, Rory stared after him, wondering if Dawn really was holding something back. She shook her head and began mentally planning her next move. Now that she knew approximately when Willow had died, she could question her neighbors to see if they'd seen anything. Hopefully, one of them could tell her something that would clear Dawn's name.

Chapter 8

"Dawn wants you to investigate, huh? Where do we start?" Liz said over the speaker on Rory's cell phone.

Rory sat in her desk chair and typed as she talked. "I was going to ask my neighbors if they saw anything that could help, but now I'm not so sure. If the police had found anything that pointed to someone else, they wouldn't be focusing on Dawn."

"What about Granny G?"

"She saw Chief Marshall visit Willow that night."

"*Our* Chief Marshall? What was he doing there?"

"Willow's boyfriend thinks they were having an affair."

"You know, there have been rumors," Liz said.

"About an affair?"

"Not exactly. Just something going on with him. Poor Chief M. To find someone after all these years only to have her die such a violent death like—Oh, sorry."

"That's okay. I've made my peace with what my birth parents did and the chief doesn't seem to blame me anymore."

Although he still had trouble looking at her, Rory thought. Not surprising since she was the spitting image of her birth mother who, along with her birth father, had set the fire that killed the chief's family almost thirty years ago.

"Did Dawn say why the police suspect her?" Liz said.

"First strike against her, she had an argument with Willow during our run-through on Friday."

"And a few hours later, Willow's dead."

"Plus, she was at Willow's house that night. Found the body, but didn't call the police."

Liz whistled. "Way to bury the lead! Do the police know about that?"

"She left a shoe print, and a neighbor saw her pounding on the front door of the house, then go around to the back. That's why they started investigating her in the first place." Rory typed on the keyboard. "Okay, try connecting now."

Moments later, Liz appeared in a window on Rory's display and waved.

"I can see you. Can you see me?"

"Yep. I'm hanging up the phone."

Liz tapped on her own cell phone, then addressed the screen. "What do you want me to do now?"

"Just talk. I want to make sure the recording function is still working properly. Thanks for helping me test this out. I only made a few tweaks so everything should be okay, but I like to make sure. Sometimes little changes can cause big problems."

"Happy to help." Liz leaned forward and frowned. "What's up with your hair? It looks weird."

"I took a cold shower. Wet hair helps keep me cool." Rory studied Liz more closely. "Wait a minute. What about you? Why are you wearing long sleeves? It's in the mid-nineties. Did you get *air conditioning?*"

Liz grinned. "They installed it yesterday while I was working."

Rory could almost feel the cool air washing over her. "After we finish, I'm coming over to your place. I need a break from this heat."

"Let's get back to Dawn. I didn't hear any of the argument on Friday. You were at her place. How much did you hear?"

"Only a few words. 'Never' and 'forgive.' She said something else as she shoved Willow out the door, but I don't remember what it was. Dawn told me Willow was telling her how to teach her painting classes, sending out critical emails to her students, stuff like that, but I can't tell you if that's what the argument was about or not."

Liz pursed her lips in thought. "You recorded Friday's test, right?"

"I see where you're going. I have the file from that session. I'll play it and see if I can get more of their conversation from it."

"You can tell me what you find out when you come over. What else are we going to do on the Dawn front?"

Rory sat back in her desk chair and considered the question. "We need to find out more about Willow. Isn't that what the police would do, find out about the victim? How about I check out her store tomorrow and ask some of her employees?"

"Ooh, that sounds good. And I can ask some of the other business owners in town. See what dirt they have on Wispy Willow. Maybe they know something about those tenant issues." Liz shuddered. "All this murder talk is giving me the jitters. Let's talk about something more pleasant. Have you heard from Tripp?"

"Saw him in church. Dad threatened to have a talk with him."

Liz giggled. "Your dad's funny. Wait, he was kidding, wasn't he?"

"I think so."

Liz closed her eyes and swayed as if in a trance. In a dreamy voice she said, "I predict he'll give you a call soon."

"What, are you psychic now?"

Liz opened her eyes.

"I told you your horoscope said it's a good time to start a romantic relationship. Just in time for your birthday too. We're still going out, right?"

"I'm having lunch with my parents, but other than that, you've got me for the whole day. You never told me what we're going to do. I need to know what to wear."

Liz waggled her finger in an uh-uh-uh gesture. "It's all a surprise. Morning will be casual. Shorts and a tank are fine. You need to dress up for the evening though. What you wore on Saturday will work."

"I'm going to stop the recording now, but we should still stay connected." Rory selected the Stop button on the software and made sure the file was saved. "I'll check the recording out after we finish."

"Do you need me for anything else right now?"

"No, we're done. Do you have a house to show or something? Don't you usually work on Sunday?"

"I showed a couple this morning. I've got the rest of the day off, so I'm hanging out in air-conditioned splendor right now." Liz swept her arms around the living room of her condo in a dramatic gesture.

"I'll check out the recordings. It shouldn't take long. I'll call right before I come over."

"We can have popcorn and watch a rom-com. Maybe *Sleepless in Seattle*, that's a good one. You can tell me more about Tripp. What should I call him? Hunk of Burning Love? Or Tantalizing Tripp?"

Rory rolled her eyes and disconnected the conferencing software. After reviewing the recording of the session she'd just had with Liz, she checked out the file from Friday. But even with the sound as loud as it would go, she couldn't make out any more than she had in person. Audio software that separated the layers of sounds might make things clearer, but she wasn't convinced the effort would give her any useful information in return. The conversation had been far enough away from the microphone, she doubted it had picked up any more than she heard herself.

She was on her way out the door when Tripp called.

"I had fun last night." He cleared his throat. "I was wondering. Do you skate?"

"Inline? I've never tried it, but I'm willing to learn."

"I was wondering if you had time to go skating tomorrow afternoon. It's a rare day off for me. If you're busy, I'll understand."

Rory smiled into the phone. "I'd like that."

"It's a date then."

After setting the time for her to meet Tripp at the skate rental place downtown, Rory headed out the door, grinning from ear to ear. She couldn't wait to tell Liz her prediction had come true.

The next morning, when Rory entered Beach Healing and Acupuncture, the store Willow owned down the block from Arika's Scrap 'n Paint, she found a cluster of customers gathered around the only employee on the floor. The woman, who looked to be about college age, said to the group, "I'm sorry, but Ms. Bingen is no longer with us. You can make an appointment with our acupuncturist, who is also skilled in herbal healing." Most of the customers turned away with disappointed looks on their faces, but two stayed behind to make new appointments.

While Rory waited for the employee to become free, she perused the shelves of vitamins, herbs and books on wellness and natural healing. She was flipping through a paperback on sugar and its detrimental effects on the body when the last customer left the store.

Rory put the book back on the shelf and walked over to the counter. "I wasn't sure you would be open after Willow's passing."

The employee threw her hands up in the air and draped herself over the countertop. "Thank God. Someone I don't have to dance around the issue with." She straightened up and gave Rory a sad smile.

"Been quite a morning, huh?"

"You have no idea. This is the first day we've been open since she was found. I had to call people to reschedule their appointments. I didn't mention what happened to her, of course. Bad for business. But word's gotten around and we've had our fair share of lookie-loos." She peered more closely at Rory. "Wait, I know you. Rory, right? You're that neighbor of Ms. Bingen's, the one who found her, aren't you? You poor thing. You must be so frazzled. That's why you came in, isn't it? I have just the thing to calm you down."

"But I didn't..."

She ignored Rory and walked over to a shelf, returning with a box of tea that she placed on the counter. "This is lemon balm. It'll calm those jangled nerves and help with your digestion. I always have tummy problems when I'm stressed out. The tea helps me when I have a big exam."

"I'm not sure I need..."

She placed the box in a paper bag and shoved it across the counter.

"Take it, on the house. You deserve it after what you've been through."

Rory smiled. "Thanks. How did you know I found Willow?"

"The press was waiting for me when I opened. That reporter with the nose ring, sort of punk looking. You know the one."

Veronica, Rory thought to herself, and nodded.

"Anyway, she gave me the scoop and asked a bunch of questions."

"What kind of questions?"

"Mostly stuff about Ms. Bingen's personal life, but I didn't say anything. Didn't like her attitude."

"What did Willow do here? I know she was into herbal healing, but I don't know much beyond that."

"At Beach Healing and Acupuncture we're interested in the natural way to heal your body. Besides what you see here," she swept her arm around the store, "we also do alternative treatments for all kinds of diseases. Migraines, bacterial infections, heart disease and, of course, the big C."

"Cancer?"

"That's right."

"Do you know anyone who'd want to harm Willow?"

The employee squealed in delight. "I knew it! You're investigating, aren't you? Just like you did a couple months ago, that murder at the hotel. What can I do to help? I'm Asia, by the way." She extended her hand and Rory shook it.

"Did she have a run-in with any customers lately? Were there any problems with the store?"

"No more than usual. You might ask Dr. W. He's with a patient right now, but he should be available soon."

"Has he worked for Willow since the store opened? That was six months ago, right?"

"He's not an employee, he is—was—her partner. Owns half the business. She ran the herbal healing part of the store, made sure the shelves were stocked, suggested courses of treatment to customers, that sort of thing. He takes care of the acupuncture and acupressure patients. He studied in China and everything. He's very good."

"Did they get along?"

Asia lowered her voice and leaned across the counter until her face was so close Rory could smell her minty breath. "Honestly, I think he's a little relieved. Ms. Bingen didn't know a thing about acupuncture or acupressure, but she was constantly telling him about some new study or how he should be doing this or that. Got a little old after a while, if you know what I mean. Heck, even I felt like killing her once or twice." She straightened up and covered her mouth with her hand. "Oh, that's probably not a wise thing to say, is it?"

They heard the sound of a door closing in the back of the store. Asia glanced over her shoulder. "I think Dr. W is available now. Let me go see." She went through the doorway into the treatment area and returned moments later. "I'm sorry. He's not talking to anyone right now. The police were here earlier asking all kinds of questions. Disturbed his chi or something. Maybe if you have an acupuncture treatment..." She selected a brochure from a display on the counter. "Here are our prices. The first treatment is at a deep discount, a real bargain. Almost free, really. We had a cancellation so he can see you right away."

Rory glanced at the brochure and studied the prices. Asia's idea of almost free and hers were vastly different, but this might be the only way to get Willow's partner to talk. Still, the idea of being a human pincushion scared her a little.

"I don't know..."

"It'll do wonders for you. Shall I tell him you're here? It's the best chance you have to ask him questions."

Rory reluctantly nodded her approval. Asia led her into the back area of the store and pointed at a shoe rack on the floor. "Put your shoes here and put these on." She handed Rory a pair of slippers. As soon as Rory exchanged her footwear, Asia led her down the short hallway past a partially open door into a softly lit room. Soft music came from inside the other treatment room as they passed by.

Asia took a gown out of a small cupboard and handed it to Rory. "Put this on and lie down on your back on the table. You can leave your underwear on. The doctor will be with you shortly."

Rory changed, lay down on the table and stared at the ceiling tiles, wondering what she'd gotten herself into. Less than five minutes later, a short man wearing scrubs and exuding a calm air entered and introduced himself. After taking her blood pressure and conducting a short interview and examination, the doctor declared himself ready to begin.

She braced herself for pricks of pain, but to her surprise, she felt nothing as he placed the needles. "I'm sorry about Willow."

Dr. Wagner turned his back on her briefly and returned with more needles. "I understand you found her."

"That's right. Did you know each other long?"

His lips tightened. "Long enough."

Rory searched her mind for some way to get him to say more. "She seemed concerned about people. She came over to my mom's store the other day with some tea, worried about how my parents were."

"She was always concerned about her patients." He stepped back and surveyed his work. "That's it. Didn't hurt at all, did it? Just relax and let the needles do their work. Someone will be back in twenty minutes to take them out. You can close your eyes and take a nap, but stay in the position you're in right now."

Before Rory could ask any more questions, he turned the music up and shut the door. She closed her eyes and tried to let the soothing sounds lessen her anxiety, but the music failed to drown out the creaks and groans of the building. When she heard footsteps on the floor above her, all she could think about was what would happen if the ceiling caved in and fell on top of her, driving every one of the tiny needles into her body. She tried to push the thought out of her mind, but she kept on visualizing her body crushed under ceiling tiles, needles embedded in places they were never meant to be.

An agonizing twenty minutes later, Asia opened the door slowly. "How are you doing?" she said in a soft voice. "I'll be taking out the needles now."

As the woman worked, Rory said, "The doctor wasn't very talkative."

"He gets that way sometimes. You know who you might try, Teresa Mut. She and Ms. Bingen were really tight. She used to come in here all the time. Now that I think about it, I haven't seen her in a while. Anyway, I've got her phone number somewhere if you want it."

"That's okay. I know her. We've taken painting classes together."

Asia worked in silence, carefully pulling out each needle. She ran her hand lightly over Rory's body, checking to make sure she'd found all of them. "You're all done. You can sit up now, not too fast. I'll leave you to get dressed. No rush."

When Rory was in the store paying her bill a few minutes later, Asia said, "I hope you find out who killed Ms. Bingen. She might have been annoying, but she didn't deserve to die like that. Let me know if I can be of any help."

"Thanks for everything." Rory exited the store onto a street busier than usual for this time of day. Curious, she joined the stream of people heading down Main Street in the direction of City Hall.

Chapter 9

Rory slipped into the back of the crowd gathered in the plaza in front of City Hall. Reporters clustered around a podium set up near the entrance while residents stood behind them in groups, chatting among themselves.

"What's going on?" she asked the man standing beside her.

"The mayor's giving a press conference about city safety."

Liz slipped in beside Rory. "Did I miss anything?"

Rory shook her head. "Hasn't started yet. How did you hear about this?"

"Another realtor in the office told me. Did you go by Willow's store?"

"It was an interesting visit. I'll tell you about it after this is over."

Veronica elbowed her way through the crowd to claim a place directly in front of the podium. She'd barely settled into her spot when the mayor of Vista Beach stepped up to the microphone and raised her hand. Behind her stood the city's chief of police, members of the city council and Detective Green.

The crowd quieted down and focused their attention on the city official.

"Thank you for coming. I know a lot of you are concerned about the spate of home invasions and burglaries that have occurred in neighboring cities. We're here to assure the citizens of the great city of Vista Beach that we're on top of this matter. Now,

Police Chief Marshall will say a few words, then we'll take some questions. Chief."

Chief Redmond Marshall replaced the mayor at the podium. Almost as wide as he was tall, Rory noticed a pallor on his face she'd never seen there before. The chief's gaze swept the sea of faces, resting for a fraction of a second on each one before moving on.

"Thank you for coming," he said, his voice booming over the crowd with no need for the microphone in front of him. "First let me say, this is a safe city and we intend to keep it that way. But there are only so many of us. We need your help. We can't be everywhere at once. Residents and neighbors play a key role in the prevention of crime and the apprehension of criminals when crime does occur. If anyone sees suspicious activity or something out of the ordinary, call it in, no matter how insignificant you think it is. Let us check it out. And make sure your outside lights are on at night, and close those windows. You don't want to make it easy for someone to break in. Now, I'll take some questions."

"What do you consider suspicious activity?" a reporter said.

"Seeing someone you don't know in a house when you know the owners are gone. Someone ringing doorbells and walking away quickly or someone walking down the street, trying door handles or looking into windows of parked cars. Transactions taking place out of a car window or trunk. Or even a stranger loitering in a residential area for an extended period of time."

"Should residents call 911 under all those circumstances?"

"People need to use their best judgment. 911 is for emergencies, such as a crime in progress, life-threatening issues, anything that requires an emergency response. For non-emergencies call the police department number. Everyone should have that by their home phone or on their cell. Next question."

"What, specifically, is the city doing to ensure residents' safety?" one of the reporters said.

"We're adding extra patrols, especially at night. We've contacted all of the Neighborhood Watch block captains to make sure they get the word out to everyone in their areas. So far we've had no incidents in the city. We want to keep it that way."

"What about the murder on Seagull Lane?" Veronica said. "Wasn't that a home invasion?"

"While it had several of the earmarks of acts that have occurred in neighboring towns, we're not prepared to discount other possibilities. We have our best detective on the case. Be assured, we're prepared to protect every citizen, and we will catch the person or persons responsible."

"Could it be one of the homeless? They're everywhere these days," a woman near the front of the crowd asked.

"We're looking at all possibilities," the chief repeated.

"What about *you* personally, Chief Marshall?" a belligerent voice near the back of the crowd shouted.

Everyone turned their heads to look at the speaker, a young man in shorts and a tank top so tight that the contours of his abdominal muscles showed through it.

"You were there, in my girlfriend's house, the night she died. You can't deny it. A neighbor saw you," Lance continued. "You're supposed to protect this city. What did you do to protect *her*?"

Everyone swiveled their heads back toward the podium and silently waited for the police officer's response. For the first time in Rory's memory, Chief Marshall didn't seem to know what to say.

"Is that true, Chief?" Veronica shouted. "Were you there? Why were you there? Did you see anything?"

"He was having an affair with her, that's what he was doing there. He's been sneaking around. Every time I go out of town, he's there," Lance cried out.

The crowd erupted, everyone talking at once.

Reporters continued to shout questions, not giving Chief Marshall the chance to respond.

"How long has the affair been going on?"

"Did you see anything?"

"Are you a suspect?"

The mayor stepped up to the podium and raised her hands to

silence the crowd. "The Chief is not a suspect. This is all idle speculation. There's no need to sully a good man's name. That's all for now. You can direct any further questions to the city's public relations department."

A stony look on his face, Chief Marshall headed toward the entrance to city hall with the mayor by his side. Council members and Detective Green followed closely behind. As soon as they all disappeared inside, the rest of the crowd dispersed and reporters surrounded Lance, peppering him with questions.

Veronica made her way to the back where Rory and Liz stood by themselves. "Did you see the chief? Were you the neighbor?" she said to Rory.

Rory frowned. "Leave it alone."

"But you know who it was who saw him, don't you?" Veronica studied her for a moment, then light dawned in her eyes. "Of course, Mrs. Griswold. She's the Neighborhood Watch block captain on your street and lives right next door to the victim. Thanks for the tip." She waved her hand and joined the group around Lance.

Once Willow's boyfriend had answered all the questions and everyone had their quotes, the reporters headed toward their cars, leaving the man standing by himself. His gaze zeroed in on Rory and he headed in her direction.

"You don't really think the Chief's responsible for Willow's death, do you?" she asked as soon as he was within earshot. "He couldn't have known what would happen."

"He could have insisted she close her windows. I'll always blame him for that. Have you seen Sekhmet around yet? I'm worried about her."

Rory shook her head. "Sorry. No one on the block has mentioned seeing her to me either."

"It's so frustrating." Lance kicked a pebble, sending it skittering across the nearly empty plaza. "There's still police tape around the house. They won't let me in to look for the cat or get any of my things."

"I'll talk to Detective Green and see if we can get access to the house. Maybe he'll let us in if we promise he can come along," Rory said.

Lance frowned. "I guess that'll have to do. I'd better get going."

Liz watched the muscular man walk down the street away from City Hall. "Why would Willow have an affair with the chief when she could have *that*?"

"We don't know they were having an affair. What did you find out?"

Liz turned her attention back to Rory. "Willow wasn't winning friends and influencing people in the business community, that's for sure. Everyone I talked to said she was constantly giving them unsolicited advice, telling them how to run their businesses."

"Same with her partner at the store. What about her tenants?"

"I talked to the woman who owns the clothing store next to your mother's building. The owner wasn't happy about the lease change, but she didn't seem overly concerned. Guess business is good. I'm not so sure about the gift shop on the other side of Beach Healing."

"Monica's Treasures?"

"That's the one. They were closed so I didn't get a chance to talk with Monica herself, but there was an 'Everything Must Go' sign in the window."

"I knew she was having a hard time, but I didn't realize business was that bad."

"Sounds like Willow's intended change to the lease agreement was pricing Monica out of business, or at least out of the downtown area." Liz peered up at Rory's ear. "What's that?" She stood on tiptoe, removed something and held out her hand. In its palm lay a tiny acupuncture needle. "Getting a little natural healing done of your own?"

Rory sighed.

"It was the only way I could talk to Willow's partner, Dr. Wagner. Not that it got me anywhere. He didn't tell me a thing. The clerk at the store thought we should try Teresa, said they spent a lot of time together. I knew they were friends, but I didn't realize they were that close."

"I should have thought of her myself. Give her a call now. See if she's available."

Rory dialed the woman's home number, but the person who answered wasn't Teresa but a woman with an accent who repeated "No English, no English" several times before hanging up.

Rory stared at her phone. "That was odd. Did Teresa and her husband hire a housekeeper? I thought they took care of the house and the kids themselves."

"Maybe her wedding-planning business is taking off and she needed the extra help."

"Let me try her cell. She might be working. I can set up a time to talk with her." Teresa answered on the first ring. Rory heard voices and cars in the background.

"I'm waiting for a client, but I have a few minutes. What's up?" Teresa said.

"We had some questions about Willow."

"That's a longer conversation than I have time for right now. I have an idea. I have a cake tasting at that new bakery in town Tuesday afternoon. Ingersoll's. I usually do it with the bride, but she lives up north and is leaving the decision to me. I could use a second opinion. Why don't you join me?"

Rory agreed to help, ending the call after they set up the time and place to meet the next day. "That's a good start, asking Teresa, but I feel like we need to explore other avenues. I'm going by my mother's store later. I'll talk to Dawn and see what else she can tell me."

"I'll see what else I can find out about the building Willow bought." Liz glanced at her watch. "I've got to get back to work. Call me if you find out anything."

Chapter 10

That afternoon, Rory sat down in a chair next to Kit's hospital bed, clasped his hand in hers and bowed her head in prayer.

"Rory?" a weak voice said. "Is that you?"

She looked up and smiled. "Hi, Kit," she said softly. "How are you feeling?"

He looked around, confusion written all over his face. "Where am I?"

"You're back in the hospital. How are you?"

He closed his eyes. "Tired." A moment later, they opened again. "There's something...I can't remember..."

"Is there something you want to tell me? Do you remember who hit you?"

"Not that...I saw...something." He frowned as if finding the right words was difficult.

"What did you see?"

"Willow...Friday."

"Were you at Willow's house the night she died? Did you see someone?"

"So tired..." Kit said before falling asleep.

Rory waited ten long minutes to see if he would wake up again and tell her more, but he was still sleeping when she left to meet her date.

* * *

"I have to warn you, I'm not very coordinated," Rory said to Tripp as they exited the skate rental store.

"Don't worry, I'm a good teacher."

Skates, pads and helmets in their hands, the two headed down the hill toward the pier. Sitting on a bench facing the ocean, they laced up their inline skates, strapped pads to their knees and elbows and put on their helmets.

Rory rose to her feet, holding the back of the bench until her legs stopped wobbling. Knees locked in typical new skater's stance, she took a deep breath, let go of the bench and moved tentatively forward. When she was more than an arm's length away from any support, her legs separated. Feeling as if her feet would come out from under her, she flailed her arms, groping for something to steady herself against, finding Tripp's arm moments before she fell.

"Relax, you're doing fine. Don't lock your knees. Bend them a little," he said as she regained her balance.

She let go of his arm and slid forward. Two glides later she smiled and said, "I did it." She turned to share her moment of victory with her date, lost her balance and fell forward onto her hands and knees.

"You're doing fine," he assured her. "Everyone falls at first. Up you go."

He helped her to her feet. This time she made it twice as far before sitting down hard on the pavement.

"You're doing good. You're almost there."

Before long she was able to skate in a straight line and stop without falling down. "I did it!"

"Great job. You're almost ready for the path."

She practiced stopping and starting before they stepped onto the path reserved for bikers and skaters and began skating side by side going north. Before long, she felt more confident and was even beginning to enjoy herself.

"You're doing great for a first-timer," Tripp said.

"Tell that to my muscles."

Three young kids whipped around them on skates, causing Rory to wobble. Tripp reached out for her hand to steady her. She smiled and, hand in hand, they continued down the path.

"Have the police discovered anything new about who hit Kit?" Tripp asked.

"I haven't heard anything."

"With all those people on the beach, you would think someone would have seen a fight."

"Maybe they don't want to get involved." Rory hazarded a look at her date, but soon regretted it when she momentarily lost her balance. She gripped his hand tighter and steadied herself. "He said something to me today that makes me think he may have been at Willow's house the night she died."

"Are you sure? Is he in danger?"

"I hadn't thought about that. I'm sure the police will protect him. You're really concerned about him, aren't you?"

"I know what it's like to be in his position."

Rory remained silent, waiting to see if he would tell her more.

"My family was homeless for a while when I was a kid," he continued. "We lived in our parents' car. It was a scary time. Sometimes my sister and I were so frightened, we stayed up all night."

"I'm sorry, I didn't realize." Rory's thighs ached from the unaccustomed exercise. "Can we turn around? My legs are getting tired."

Tripp helped her make a U-turn on the path. He asked questions about decorative painting the rest of the way back. When they stopped at the base of the pier and stepped off the path onto the parking lot beside it, someone yelled, "Watch out!"

They both turned toward the sound to see a skater hurtling down the hill, her arms waving wildly as she headed straight for them. Rory froze. At the last second, Tripp grabbed her and pulled her toward him, avoiding a collision with the out-of-control skater. The two landed in a heap on the pavement with Rory on top. The skater sailed past them, grabbed a concrete pylon and skidded to a halt.

Her own face inches from Tripp's, she stared down at the attractive man's face and blushed.

They disentangled themselves and sat up.

"You okay?" he said.

"I think so." She wiggled her feet and arms. "Everything feels okay."

He checked her ankles and legs for injuries before helping her up. "I can give you a more thorough examination at the clinic, if you like, but I think you're fine."

Rory skated over to a nearby bench and sat down to take off her skates. "That's not necessary. What about you? You took the brunt of it."

Tripp moved his shoulders and swiveled his wrists. "Don't worry, I'm good." He offered her his hand. "Let's return the skates then get some ice cream. My treat."

Hand in hand, the two of them headed up the hill.

The bell over the front door tinkled when Rory entered Arika's Scrap 'n Paint. She paused at the entrance, basking in the cool air before stepping all the way inside. She sat on a stool behind the counter and waited for her mother to finish ringing up a customer's purchases.

"Aren't you working today?" Arika closed the cash register drawer and stared over at her daughter. "Or is your place too hot?"

"I went skating."

Arika raised an eyebrow. "Date?"

"With Tripp, the guy dad threatened to have a talk with on Sunday." Rory looked around the store. "Are you alone today?"

"Dawn's in the back getting some wood pieces for the new display." Her mother gestured toward a nearby shelf half-filled with merchandise. "She seems a little down. Not her usual cheery self. Do you know what's going on?"

"She hasn't told you?"

Before Arika could respond, Dawn walked onto the sales floor from the back of the store, carrying an armload of unfinished wood. Her face brightened when she saw Rory. "Any news?"

Arika looked from one to the other. "News about what?"

Rory filled her mother in on the police's suspicions about Willow's murder and Dawn's request that she help.

Arika frowned. "I'm not sure looking into Willow's death is such a good thing for you to do."

"I'm being careful and I'll let Martin—Detective Green—know whatever I find out. Promise." Rory shifted her weight on the stool. "What do you two know about Willow? I stopped by her store earlier, but no one could tell me much."

Dawn stacked the wood pieces on the shelf next to a finished version of the project. "We didn't spend much time together. She took a couple classes from me here at the store and we went out to dinner once or twice. She grew up in New Mexico, if that helps. What kind of information are you looking for?"

"I'm not really sure. Her birth date would be helpful. There are places I can check online if I have it."

"That I can't help you with. Have you asked Teresa? The two of them hung out a lot." Dawn frowned and stared at the shelf she was straightening. "Though I haven't seen them together lately. Something was going on between the two of them. I'm not sure what."

Rory tucked the information away in the back of her brain.

"I know her birthday," Arika said. "Don't you remember, Dawn? She had that dinner month before last, right before I got sick. Her fifty...sixth if I'm not mistaken. That's what she said, anyway."

Rory jotted down the date her mother mentioned using the memo feature on her phone and quickly calculated in her head the year Willow had been born. "That's helpful." She hopped off the stool and shoved her phone in the pocket of her shorts. "I need to get back to work. I'll let you know if I find out anything."

"I can't thank you enough." Dawn gave Rory a quick hug before heading over to help a customer.

Arika looked with concern at her daughter. "You don't have to solve everyone's problems, you know. It's not your responsibility."

"I can't let her down after what she did for you."

Arika patted her on the arm. "You have a good heart. Be careful."

"You don't have to worry about me."

"I'm a mother. It's part of my job description."

Rory hugged her and headed out the door, armed with the new information.

Later that afternoon on a break from work, Rory walked into her kitchen for a diet Coke to cool herself down. As she took a sip of the cold beverage, she glimpsed movement out of the corner of her eye. She glanced outside and saw a streak of brown run across the lawn and disappear into the bushes along the side of her house.

Rory set her bottle of soda on the counter, opened the back door and softly called out Sekhmet's name. A plaintive meow answered her call. She parted the leaves of the bush nearest the back door to find the chocolate Abyssinian staring up at her. Sekhmet cautiously sniffed the finger Rory held out, then gave an inquiring meow.

"I bet you're hungry, aren't you? Why don't you come inside? I'll try to find something for you to eat." Rory walked to the door and held it open. The cat studied her for a moment before walking, tail high, into the kitchen, stopping when she was inside the door to survey her surroundings.

As soon as Rory stepped inside, the cat wandered across the tile floor and sat down next to the refrigerator as if waiting for food. Rory filled a cereal bowl with water and laid it on the floor. While the cat lapped it up, she searched her cupboards and refrigerator for something to feed her, unearthing slices of leftover turkey and a sample of dry cat food she'd received in the mail. She put the food on a plate and set it on the floor next to the water dish. Without hesitation, Sekhmet dug in, wolfing it down as if she hadn't eaten in days. For a cat who usually spent her evenings tucked safely inside a house, the Abyssinian seemed none the worse for the nights she must have spent outdoors.

After she downed every morsel, the cat wandered into the living room, sniffing what seemed like every inch of the wood floor before gracefully jumping onto the sofa and curling up against a pillow. Rory smiled and left her new friend to nap in peace. She phoned Lance's number to let him know she found Willow's cat, but when the call went straight to voicemail, she hung up and texted him that she would keep Sekhmet safe inside until she heard from him.

Hoping the cat wouldn't need to potty until after she got back, Rory drove to the grocery store and picked up cat food, litter and a litterbox. When she turned onto her block on the way home, she saw someone slipping through the side gate of Willow's house.

She pulled into her driveway and, leaving her purchases in her car, walked down the sidewalk, ducked under the yellow police tape and traced the same path she'd seen the intruder take. She cautiously peeked around the corner of the Tudor-style home. The French doors leading into the kitchen were partially open, and she heard the sound of a chair scraping against the wood floor. As quietly as possible, she tiptoed up the steps and peeked inside.

Lance stood on a chair, rummaging around on the top shelf of a bookcase in the living area next to the kitchen.

Rory knocked on the door. "Lance, what are you doing here?"

The man jumped at the sound of her voice. He steadied a hand on the bookcase to regain his balance before turning around to face her. "Hi, Rory, what are you doing here?" He quickly hopped down from the chair and met her at the doorway.

"I saw someone going through the gate, didn't realize it was you. Did the police finally release the house?"

Lance's face reddened. "No, but I couldn't wait any longer. I wanted to see if Sekhmet had come home."

Rory glanced toward the bookcase, wondering what it had to do with the cat.

He followed her gaze. "Willow stashed a catnip toy behind the books after Sekhmet got a little too wild with it. It's her favorite. I thought it might lure her out of hiding."

"Didn't you get my text? I found her an hour ago in my backyard. She's inside my house right now sleeping."

Lance ran a hand through his hair. "Sorry, I didn't see it. That's a relief."

They stood awkwardly staring at each other. Rory sensed he wanted her to leave, but she didn't think it right to let him stay inside the house without the police department's knowledge.

"So, did you want to take care of Sekhmet?" she finally asked.

"I wish I could, but animals aren't allowed in my apartment. Could you keep her at your place until I can make other arrangements?"

"Sure. It'll be nice to have company. I bought cat food and a litterbox. Does she need anything else?"

Glad her view of the area where she'd found Willow's body was blocked by the kitchen island, Rory helped the man gather some of the Abyssinian's favorite items to help the cat adjust to her new surroundings.

They were heading out the back door when Rory said, "What about the toy?"

"Huh?"

"The one you were looking for when I came in. If it's her favorite, we should get it. It'll help her feel more at home."

"Oh, right. I couldn't find it. Willow must have hidden it somewhere else."

Lance handed her the bag of items for the cat and locked the back door behind them. As she watched him drive away, she wondered what he'd really been looking for in the bookcase. She doubted it was a catnip toy. Whatever it was, she intended to find out.

Chapter 11

"Recognize anything?" Detective Green said.

Rory's gaze swept the glass case filled with jewelry. A burly man waited nearby to see which ring, necklace or bracelet she would point out. She momentarily salivated over a diamond and sapphire ring before shaking her head. "There are one or two things I wouldn't mind having myself, but nothing that looks familiar."

The detective nodded at the pawn shop owner. "Thanks for your time."

They left the shop and returned to his car. While she settled into the passenger seat, Detective Green sat behind the wheel and crossed off an item in his notebook. "One more to go."

The two had spent the better part of Tuesday morning driving to pawn shops within a ten-mile radius of Vista Beach, looking for the jewelry stolen from Willow the night she was killed.

"What happens if we don't find anything?" Rory said.

The detective put the car into gear and eased out of the parking space onto the busy street. "The pawn shops in the area have a description of what we're looking for. The thief or thieves might be waiting for things to cool down before pawning the items. If they do, we'll catch them."

"Have you thought about online auction sites?"

"Someone's looking at those right now, using the descriptions you gave me."

"If you want, I can look at some of them myself. I'll have a better chance of recognizing the jewelry than anyone at the police department will."

He glanced over at her. "You sure you have the time?"

"I'll make the time."

He nodded and continued driving to their next destination. When they entered the last pawn shop on the list, the man behind the counter held his arms out wide and boomed a welcome.

"We're looking for jewelry," Rory said.

He cocked his head, studied the two of them and broke into a smile. "Ah, young love. I can spot it a mile away. You're looking for an engagement ring, aren't you? I have just the thing for you." He selected a diamond ring with a stone of at least two carats and held it out. "This will look beautiful on your hand. Try it."

Rory shook her head and avoided looking at the detective. "We're not together. Okay, we're together, but we're not a couple."

Detective Green looked uncomfortable as he held up his badge. "Police business. We're looking for stolen jewelry."

The pawn shop owner replaced the ring and swept his hand around the store. "I can assure you everything's on the up and up here. No shady business whatsoever. Please, look around all you want."

Rory stared at the jewelry case filled with rings, watches, necklaces and bracelets. An amber ring attracted her attention, but when she looked at it more closely, she realized it wasn't the one they were looking for.

"Sorry. None of it looks familiar."

The detective thanked the man for his cooperation. As they were leaving, the pawn shop owner called after them, "Keep us in mind for those special occasions."

Rory followed the detective out the door and to the car, not daring to look at his face. An awkward silence settled over them as he drove Rory home. Halfway there, he finally broke the silence. "How's your friend? The one who's in the hospital?"

"Kit? No change when I checked on him today. It's touch and go, but I'm hopeful. Any leads on who hit him?"

"Nothing new. Unless he can tell us who attacked him, I doubt we'll ever know. Has he said anything to you?"

"He rambled on about something odd. I'm not sure what to make of it." She told him what Kit had said when she visited him the previous day.

"Could be something. Could be nothing. He sounds delirious."

"I know, but I can't help wondering if he saw something that night. He *was* out of the hospital the night Willow died."

"None of your neighbors mentioned seeing him anywhere near the house on Friday when we questioned them."

"Doesn't mean he wasn't there."

"True."

Rory's phone quacked. She glanced down at its display and grinned when she read the text.

"What's made you so happy?"

"Just a text from a friend."

"A friend. I see." He pulled up in front of Rory's house and stopped. "Thanks for your help today. Let me know if you see anything on those auction sites."

Rory nodded and got out of the car. As he drove away, her cell phone rang.

"What's with you and Dashing D going to pawn shops?" Liz said without bothering to say hello.

"How did you know about that? I just barely got home." Rory tucked her phone in the crook of her neck so she could unlock her front door.

"My spies are everywhere."

Rory snorted. "He called me last night and asked if I would help him. We were looking to see if any of Willow's jewelry had been pawned. He brought me along to see if I recognized anything."

"Did you?"

"No. I'm going to check out some online auction sites next." When Rory sank down onto the couch, Sekhmet hopped up on her lap and demanded her attention. She tickled the cat under the chin. "I got a text from Tripp when I was in the car with Martin."

"Awwwwkward. What did it say?"

"Just thanked me for the date. What did you find out about the building Willow owns?"

"She bought it six months ago when she moved to town. Got a good deal on it, but it was still expensive. She put down a super hefty down payment."

"I wonder where she got the money."

"Maybe she inherited it."

"Do you know what happens to the building now?"

"Not sure," Liz said.

"Monica might know. I'll stop by and ask her."

"Was that a cat meowing?"

"Didn't I tell you? Sekhmet's my guest at the moment."

"Willow's cat? I thought Luscious Lance was going to take care of her."

"His apartment doesn't allow pets."

"What are you going to do?"

Rory planted a kiss on top of the cat's head. "I'll take care of her for now. Maybe she'll like it here and adopt me." She frowned. "Lance was acting a little odd yesterday."

"How so?"

"I found him going through a bookcase in Willow's house." The cat curled up on Rory's lap and started purring as she stroked her fur.

"So? He did live there."

"He said he was looking for one of Sekhmet's toys to lure her out of hiding, but I'd already told him I found her."

"In person or did you leave a message?" Liz asked.

"I texted him, but he said he never got it. Something about his behavior was very odd. What do you know about him?"

"He works as a personal trainer at the gym I belong to. That's about it."

"Why was he wearing a suit when I saw him get out of the taxi the day I found Willow, then? Doesn't sound like something a personal trainer would wear."

"Don't know. You did say he was in San Diego on business. Probably had something to do with that. I swear some women at the gym have memberships just so they can watch him work."

Rory wrinkled her forehead in thought. "With so many people watching him, maybe one of them can tell us something useful. When was the last time you went to the gym?"

Chapter 12

Rory left early for her appointment at the bakery that afternoon, giving herself time to stop by Monica's Treasures. Before going inside, she studied the window display of the gift store. The Everything Must Go sign Liz had mentioned was nowhere to be seen.

She entered the store and made her way through the maze of shelves holding every kind of gift imaginable toward the sales counter where Monica herself was wrapping up a wooden Noah's ark set for a customer.

"...perfect piece for your new grandson's bedroom." Monica placed the painted animals into a wood box shaped like an ark. "You're lucky to get this. Dawn Ogden's work is very popular. She's local, you know..." The store owner looked up and smiled. "I'll be with you in a moment, Rory."

Rory nodded and studied the jewelry in the glass case next to the ancient cash register while she waited.

Monica wrote out a paper receipt and stuffed a copy in the bag along with the purchase. "Let me know how your daughter likes the ark, Kate. Have fun at the baby shower." As the customer headed toward the front door, Monica turned toward Rory, a big smile on her face. "What can I do for you? Your mother tells me your birthday's coming up. No better time to treat yourself." She reached into the glass case and produced a tear-shaped necklace on a silver chain. "It's said that whoever owns turquoise will never be without friends. Go on, try it on."

Rory put on the necklace and stared at herself in the small mirror on the counter. "It's beautiful. I'll take it."

While Monica wrapped up the jewelry, Rory pointed at the going-out-of-business sign propped against a nearby wall. "Are you closing the store?"

"Not anymore. I thought I'd have to for a while, but the good Lord answered my prayers."

"What changed?"

"My rent was going to go up, but that's not going to happen anymore."

"Because of Willow's death?"

Monica handed Rory's credit card back to her. "You know about the lease?"

"The whole city does. There was an article on Vista Beach Confidential about Willow and the changes she was planning to make. Didn't Veronica interview you for it?"

"Oh, that blog thing. Computers. Don't have one, don't want one."

"Don't you need one to run your business?"

"I've been running it the same way for thirty years. No reason to change now. Of course, that didn't meet with everyone's approval."

"Willow?"

The store owner reached under the counter and brought out a gift box. "Why would you say that?"

"She was your landlord, and she did love to tell people what to do."

"That she did. She told me I needed to enter the twenty-first century." Monica held up the bag with the necklace in it. "I added the matching earrings as a birthday gift."

"Thank you, but you didn't have to do that."

"My pleasure." She waved her hand as if it were nothing.

"What's going to happen with the building now?"

"Dr. Wagner's inheriting it, and he's promised he won't change the lease terms. Of course, that's what Willow said six months ago, but he actually keeps his promises."

"Any idea where she got the money to buy the building?"

"I got the impression she had some money socked away, but I never heard where it came from." The store owner waved at a customer who was browsing in a nearby aisle. She leaned forward and lowered her voice. "What do you know about Willow's death? Do the police have any leads?"

"I don't know much, but I'm sure they'll find out who did it."

"You wait, it'll turn out to be a home invasion. Probably the same people who have been causing all the trouble in those other cities."

"Were the police here?" Rory said. "They must have questioned you since you're one of her tenants."

"They had the gall to ask me where I was when she died. I told them to mind their own business."

"Bet they didn't like that."

"Not one bit. I've never even been to Willow's house. Didn't know where she lived until your mother told me. Of course, I could have just admitted I was here by myself, working in the back, but they annoyed me with their questions."

"I'm glad things turned around for you."

As Rory headed out the door, she wondered if the threat of losing her store could have made Monica angry enough to kill.

A short time later, she walked into Ingersoll's Bakery, pausing in the doorway as the heavenly scent of freshly baked bread wafted toward her. Her mouth drooled at the display cases filled with loaves of bread, muffins, cupcakes, cookies, tarts and other baked goods. Half a dozen people milled around the sales floor, waiting for their numbers to be called for service.

"Rory?" Teresa waved at her from the far corner of the store. "We're set up over here."

The wedding planner motioned toward a table situated in an alcove, out of the traffic area of the store. "Thanks for doing this. I have a good idea what my client wants, but it's nice to have a second opinion."

Rory sat down in one of the three chairs placed around the table.

"I'm happy to help. Tell me about the bride."

"She's in the technology field like you are. Lives up north. VP of some tech company. As you might imagine, she's very busy, so she delegated the cake selection to me."

"She's missing all the fun. She's getting married here in Vista Beach? Why not up north?"

"She grew up here. Her parents still live in her childhood home. You're doing me a huge favor. This is a new bakery for me. She's insisting I use it." Teresa leaned forward and said in a conspiratorial whisper, "I think the owners are friends of the family."

A woman wearing an apron emblazoned with Ingersoll's logo walked over bearing a platter filled with small plates of various flavors of cake. "Sorry to keep you ladies waiting." After introducing herself as one of the owners, the woman sat down and began going over the various options of cake flavors, fillings and icing. After she explained everything to them, she stood up. "Remember, we can make each layer of the cake a different flavor. I'll leave you to it. Let me know if you need anything or have any questions."

"This place is busy." Rory eyed the constant stream of customers coming in and going out the door as she took a bite of the cake nearest her.

"People were lined up down the block the day they opened their doors and it hasn't stopped since."

"I can see why. If the cakes are any indication, this place is incredible." Rory took a bite of a lemon cake with lemon filling. "This one's really good. My favorite so far." Her next bite was of a white cake with raspberry filling. "It's sad about Willow, isn't it? Asia, over at her store, said you two were close. How long did you know her?"

"We met when she moved here. I went into her store to check

it out and we hit it off instantly. Those were good days," Teresa said a bit wistfully.

"Do you know anything about her family? I heard she moved here from New Mexico."

Teresa laid down her fork. "She mentioned that to me too, but she never really said anything else about her past. For some reason I got the impression she was married once, but I didn't get any details."

"Did she have any conflicts with anyone that you can think of?"

"She was complaining the other day that she lost her sunglasses. They're expensive. So expensive she had her name and phone number stamped on the eyeglass case."

"No one called to say they found them?"

"Not that I heard of. She thought one of the homeless people near the pier stole them."

"Why would she think that?"

"I have no idea. Doesn't make sense to me either." Teresa pointed to the plate nearest her. "What do you think of the chocolate? It's good with the raspberry filling."

Rory took a bite and sighed. "I love it. Do people have chocolate cake at weddings?"

"Pretty much anything's done now. Some people don't even bother with a cake, others have cupcakes. This bride's a bit of a traditionalist. Wants the bride and groom on top of a tiered cake and everything."

Rory was trying a bite of orange cake when she felt someone watching her. She glanced up to see Detective Green standing to one side, a curious expression on his face. She raised her fork in greeting, then turned to answer a question Teresa had asked. When Rory looked up again, the detective was going out the door with a bag in his hand.

Before Rory could ask any more questions about Willow, Teresa's phone rang. When she looked at the cell's display, a concerned look came across her face. "Sorry, I have to take this. I'll be right back." As Teresa headed toward the door, Rory heard the words "you can't!" and "lawyer." When Teresa returned to the table ten minutes later, her face was pale and there were traces of mascara under her eyes. Avoiding Rory's gaze, she picked up her pen and consulted her notes, her hand trembling as she wrote something down.

Rory set down her fork and looked with concern at the woman. "Is everything all right? Was it bad news?"

"It wasn't good news, that's for sure."

"Is it your kids? Are they okay?"

"I wouldn't know."

Rory had never seen a more devoted mother than Teresa. She volunteered at the school her children attended, helped them with their homework and never missed a recital, play or sporting event her three kids were involved with. She couldn't imagine the woman not knowing where her children were every minute of the day.

"What are you talking about?"

Teresa directed her words at the table and said in a hushed voice, "Trent kicked me out last week. He changed the locks on the house and barely lets me see the kids. Now he's talking about getting lawyers involved. He's threatening to sue for full custody and move away. I can't live without my monkeys." A tear trickled down her face. She reached into her purse for a tissue, took off her glasses and dabbed at her eyes.

"He can't do that, can he? You're their mother."

"He knows important people, big-time lawyers and judges. He's already been spreading it around that I have psychological problems."

"Why would he do that?" Rory said, her voice subdued.

Teresa looked around to make sure no one was within earshot, then lowered her voice and continued, "Because I had an affair. Well, you can't even call it that. It was only one night. Trent's been so busy with work. It was nice to have someone pay attention to me, to think I'm sexy. I got carried away. I regretted it the next day. It's not like he hasn't done the same thing. I forgave him, but he thinks because I'm a woman it's different. I felt so guilty about it I had to tell someone. This mess is all *her* fault! I'm glad she's dead."

"Who? Willow?"

"That's right. I told her about my...mistake in confidence. She wasn't supposed to repeat it to anyone. I guess I should have seen it coming. She kept on harping about how important it was to be honest in a relationship. It never occurred to me she would actually tell him."

"She told your husband?"

Teresa blew her nose. "She decided it was the best thing for us. She always thought she knew what was best for everyone, no matter the consequences. Damn her!" She slammed her pen down on the table so hard the plates rattled. "I don't know why I'm telling you all this. You won't tell anyone, will you?"

Rory made a zipper motion across her lips. "You can trust me. Do you need any help?"

"Thanks, but I'm okay for now. I've been staying at the Akaw for the last week since Trent kicked me out."

"That must be costing you a bundle."

"Not a cent. I know one of the owners. He's letting me stay for free until I work things out with my husband."

Rory thought back to last Friday when they were testing out the conferencing software.

"Last week. You weren't just borrowing that room for a few hours."

"That's right." Teresa blew her nose again and picked up her pen. "Let's get back to work. I can't do anything about my situation right now, but I can do my job. It's all I have at the moment. You've tasted them all. Give me your top three."

As they went over the cake flavors, half of Rory's mind was on Teresa and how she blamed Willow for her marital problems. Given her devotion to her children, the idea she might not be able to see them could have pushed Teresa over the edge. She could have fought with Willow and, in the heat of the moment, grabbed the knife and plunged it into her chest. Once she realized what she'd done, she could have tried to make it look like a burglar entered the house.

As they finished up, Rory wondered how she could find out where Teresa was Friday night after the software test. She went through her mental Rolodex to see who might be able to give her the answer.

"Are you sure this is going to work?" Liz stared at the laptop screen as Rory typed. The two sat side by side at a table in Liz's condo that evening, air conditioner humming in the background, keeping them cool.

"You can find loads of information on anyone if you know their birth date and name. And if you know their place of birth, it's even better."

Liz shuddered. "That's scary."

"Welcome to the twenty-first century." Rory directed the browser toward a website that specialized in finding people. "One of my clients told me about this one. She found an old school friend through it." She keyed in the information they had on Willow and clicked the Search button. Before long, they had a list of records, but only one with the exact birth date. She selected the one she wanted, plugged in her credit card number and moments later, they were staring at the information.

Liz leaned forward and peered at the display. "Is it the right person?"

"Move your head, I can't see." Rory scrolled through the record until she came across a list of last known addresses. "That's Willow's place here in Vista Beach. We hit the jackpot."

"The next address is one in New Mexico. You said that's where she was born, right?"

"That's what Dawn said."

"I have an idea. Let me take it from here."

Rory printed out the report on Willow before the two women swapped places.

"I'm thinking one of her old neighbors in New Mexico can tell us something." Liz directed the browser to the appropriate county assessor's office and searched for addresses on the street where Willow had lived before moving to Vista Beach. "Bingo! One of these should do the trick."

They stared at a list of properties that included the names of the current owners.

"Let's try these two." Liz pointed at two lines on the screen. "They're the houses on either side of the one she lived in. We need to find their phone numbers."

"That's easy. Reverse phone lookup."

Minutes later, they had the information.

The first number Liz tried, the person on the other end of the line hung up when she mentioned Willow's name. They had better luck with the second. A quivery voice came over the cell phone's speaker. Liz introduced herself to the woman on the other end of the line.

"Did I hear right? You're a real estate agent in California?" the woman said.

"That's right, ma'am. I have a client who's thinking of renting a house to a Willow Bingen. She gave your name and number as a reference."

Rory crossed her fingers and listened on in silence.

"Glad to hear she's not homeless anymore."

Rory and Liz exchanged puzzled glances.

"Did you say she was homeless?" Liz asked.

"I'm not surprised she didn't tell you that. Not something she was proud of. Got evicted from the place next door." She talked a mile a minute all about her former neighbor without Liz having to ask a single question.

When the woman stopped talking, Liz said, "Just to be sure we're talking about the same person, could I text you a photo?"

"Sorry, love, I don't have a cell phone. No need, I'm home all day. But I do have email. You can send it there."

Liz wrote down the email address, then thanked her and hung

up. A short time later they sent her a photo they found of Willow taken at an event at Arika's Scrap 'n Paint.

Half an hour later, they received a reply saying, "That's not the Willow who lived next door to me," followed by a photo of a stranger.

"Who the heck is Wispy Willow, then?" Liz said, voicing Rory's own question. "Do you think the police know?"

"I haven't heard anything. Maybe they're keeping it quiet."

"Or they don't know. You'd better call Dashing D and tell him, just in case."

A few minutes later, Rory was on the phone with the detective.

"News about the jewelry already?" he said in his deep voice.

"No, this is about Willow herself."

He sighed and mumbled to himself. "What about her?"

She quickly told him what they'd learned, leaving out the part where she'd paid for some of the information.

"How did you find this out? Wait, don't tell me. I don't want to know. We'll verify it."

"How come she hasn't been caught using a false name?"

"She probably bought a birth certificate and social security number from the homeless woman in New Mexico. As long as they're about the same age and race, it's not that hard to get away with, especially since the woman lived in another state."

"What about the real Willow's family?"

"She probably doesn't have any. Thanks for the information. We'll look into it. Do me a favor though, will you? Stop investigating."

Chapter 13

Wednesday morning, Rory stood in a hallway at the gym, staring at yoga-pant-clad bodies contorting themselves into positions she could only imagine trying. Her muscles ached just watching the women. "I'm not doing that. I wouldn't be able to move for a week."

Yoga mat under one arm, Liz waited with her friend outside the exercise room with a half dozen other students for the current class to finish and another to begin. "It's not that hard. You wouldn't be doing those moves anyway. That's an advanced class."

"It doesn't make sense for us to be in the same place. We'll have better luck splitting up. You can do your yoga thing while I check out other parts of the gym. Someone must know something about Lance. Meet you here after class." Rory headed down the hall toward the area reserved for cardio equipment while Liz joined the group entering the exercise room for the yoga class.

Rory looked over the sea of equipment before heading toward a row of treadmills. She stepped onto one and studied the console. Unsure what program to select, she chose one at random, following the start-up instructions on the machine's display. Holding lightly onto the handrails until she became accustomed to the motion, she kept up the pace until the treadmill accelerated and she found herself huffing and puffing. She stabbed at the buttons until it slowed down to a walking pace and at an incline she felt she could handle.

A middle-aged woman dropped a towel over the machine next

to Rory's and put a water bottle in a holder. She pressed buttons on its display and, once the treadmill started moving, put her feet on the belt and started walking. She glanced over at Rory curiously. "You're new here."

"Guest pass. A friend thinks I should join." Rory winced and rubbed the front of her right leg, which was beginning to throb.

"Not used to exercising, are you? You shouldn't overdo it on the first day. You could injure yourself. I'm Marcia, by the way."

"I'm Rory. It's not the treadmill that's the problem. I went skating the other day for the first time."

Marcia cast a sympathetic glance in Rory's direction. "That's hard on your legs. Don't worry, keep on exercising and your quads and hamstrings will toughen up in no time. Have you gotten the official tour yet?"

"Tour?"

"Everyone who comes in on a guest pass gets a tour. They let you explore a while on your own, then snag you before you leave. One of the PTs will show you around."

"PT?"

"Personal trainer."

"Someone mentioned one to me who's supposed to be really good." Rory tilted her head to one side as if she couldn't quite remember what her fictitious friend had said. "Vance. No, that's not it."

"Lance?"

"That's right. Lance. Do you know him?"

The woman's face took on a dreamy quality. A smile played about her lips as she stared into the distance.

"Marcia?"

She brought herself out of her reverie. "Sorry. I'm afraid you're out of luck. He only takes male clients these days. Something about a jealous girlfriend."

"Really?"

Before Rory could ask any more questions, a woman walked by and cocked her head toward the next room.

Marcia's eyes lit up. She pushed a button on her treadmill. It had barely decelerated to a stop when she grabbed her towel and water bottle. "Excuse me. I need to go. Enjoy your workout."

Marcia and half a dozen other women headed toward the exit. Curious, Rory followed them into the weight room next door where the clang of weights and murmur of voices filled the room. As if they'd done it dozens of times before, the women scattered around the large space filled with weight machines, positioning themselves next to various pieces of equipment already occupied. They pretended to wait their turns, but all their attention was focused on two men in the middle of the room. Lance was spotting a gray-haired man doing bench presses with a barbell that held an amount of weight Rory couldn't imagine lifting in a million years.

Audible sighs could be heard around the room as the women watched Lance work, sighs the personal trainer either didn't hear or had learned to ignore.

"That's him, that's Lance," Marcia said as Rory joined her by a rack of free weights. "The one standing. He's always here during the week about this time. Except last Friday when he was away on business. Disappointing day for everyone here."

"Business?"

"He's trying to get funding for an exercise product he invented. Not sure what it is, but I bet it's awesome." She picked up a pair of five-pound weights and began a set of bicep curls, her gaze fixed on the two men as they worked. Rory picked up a set of two-pound weights and mimicked the other woman's actions.

Lance glanced in their direction and a slight frown came over his face.

Rory turned her back to him and focused her attention on Marcia, who was showing her how to do a triceps kickback even as she kept an eye on the personal trainer.

His fans seemed to have Lance under constant surveillance while he was at work. Rory sucked in her breath as a thought struck her. Maybe one of his admirers had gone beyond looking. Her gaze flitted from one woman to the next, all middle-aged, all gaga over the trainer. Could one of them have killed Willow in a jealous rage?

"Lucky woman, that girlfriend of his. Do you know anything about her?" Rory said in a quiet voice.

"Some stick of a grandma. She must have money. Don't know what else he sees in her."

"You've met her? Does she belong to the gym?"

"I've seen her once or twice. She stops by occasionally. Don't think she's strong enough to exercise. Haven't seen her recently. Evelyn, over there," Marcia nodded toward a woman using the leg curl machine, "even talked to her once."

From the things she said, she didn't seem to know Willow was dead. Or maybe she only wanted it to appear that way.

Marcia gave a nervous laugh. "That sounded a bit stalkerish, didn't it? Don't worry. We're not like that. We just appreciate a handsome man. Look, don't touch, that's what my mama always told me." She looked over Rory's shoulder. Her eyes widened and she hastily replaced the weights on the rack. "Nice talking with you. Hope you join," she said before beating a hasty retreat.

"Rory?" a male voice said from behind her.

As she turned to face Lance, he stuck out his hand as if meeting her for the first time. "I'm Lance. One of the trainers here. Are you ready for your personal tour?"

Rory could almost feel the jealousy radiating from the other women as he took her elbow and led her around the weight room, pointing out various pieces of equipment. As soon as they exited the room and were alone in the hallway, looking through a window at a Zumba class in progress, he leaned toward her and said in a low voice, "I know why you're here."

Rory's heart beat faster and her eyes opened wide. "You do?"

"Look, I loved Willow. She wasn't some fling to me. I know some men are capable of it, but I can't think about dating anyone right now. You understand?" He placed a hand on her arm.

"But I'm not—"

He held up his hand to stop her. "You don't have to say anything. You're attractive. I'm sure you won't have any problem finding someone else. I just wanted to be upfront, make sure you understood the situation." He glanced at a clock on the wall. "I'll let you look around the rest of the gym by yourself. I've got another client to take care of." He waved and left her standing in the hallway staring in disbelief at his retreating figure.

Moments later, Liz found her still shaking her head over the incident. "You look odd. Everything okay? You didn't hurt yourself, did you?"

"You wouldn't believe it." Rory sketched out Lance's belief she was interested in him to her friend.

"Some men are impossible. Be nice and they think you have the hots for them." She lowered her voice and leaned in. "Doug was in my yoga class. We're meeting him in the juice bar. He's got the skinny on Luscious Lance. Come on."

The two headed toward the front entrance to the gym where the juice bar was located and settled into seats at a table where Liz's date from Saturday night was sipping a smoothie.

"Go on. Tell her what you told me." Liz nudged him with her shoulder.

Doug looked around as if to make sure no one was listening and lowered his voice. "Lance has issues."

"What kind of issues?" Rory said.

"Two, no, three weeks ago, he got into it with another personal trainer."

"Do you know what it was about?"

"Jealousy. Lance thought the other trainer was having an affair with his girlfriend."

"You mean Willow?"

He nodded. "Happened right here in this gym. In the weight room. The other trainer was with a client and Lance walked up to him, shouted something about staying away from his girl and shoved him. It was completely unprovoked. He said he knew the other guy was secretly seeing her and he wouldn't stand for it."

"Are you sure?"

"Saw it myself."

"What happened then?"

"The other trainer—Big Jim—denied it, said he was seeing Willow on a professional level. He has some health issue he wouldn't talk about. Lance didn't believe him. A member had to pull them apart. Lance almost lost his job because of the incident."

"I wonder why he thought they were having an affair. She has a natural healing business downtown. A lot of her clients must be men."

"Maybe he's just the jealous type. You remember him at the press conference. He accused the chief of having an affair with Willow," Liz said.

"Big Jim told me later that he'd been seeing Willow at her house instead of the store," Doug said. "Lance found out about it and got the wrong idea."

"Any idea why he didn't go to the store?"

"He didn't want anyone at the gym to know about his health issues."

"Did Jim have any problems here at work after the incident?" Rory asked.

"None that I know of. He's still a personal trainer here. Hasn't lost any clients either."

"This Jim guy wouldn't have a reason to kill Willow, anyway. He'd have gone after Lance if he'd gotten fired or something," Liz said.

"We should still talk to him," Rory said.

"I thought you might say that." Doug shoved a business card across the table. "Here's his number. If there's nothing else, I need to get to work."

"Thanks," Rory and Liz said in unison.

After the man left, Rory said to her friend, "Jealousy could be a motive for Willow's death. Lance accused at least two people of having an affair with her. Who knows how many others there are that we don't know about."

"There must be some reason he thought she was being unfaithful. Maybe he confronted her and, when she admitted it, he killed her in a rage." Liz plunged an imaginary knife into her own chest.

"Lance wasn't the only one who's jealous. He's got quite the following here at the gym." Rory told her about the women watching him work in the weight room. "Some of them have met Willow and even talked to her."

Liz's face lit up with excitement. "One of his groupies could have followed her home and killed her." She made another stabbing motion.

"Stop stabbing yourself in the chest. It's unnerving. If Lance killed her, I doubt he would state so publicly his thoughts about her cheating."

"He might if he thought he had an alibi. Wasn't he out of town?"

Rory nodded. "In San Diego. He flew down there, but it's only a two or three-hour drive, depending on traffic. He could have borrowed a car, driven back up here hoping to find her shacked up with someone. Maybe he saw the chief leave her place, assumed the worst and confronted her, killing her in a rage."

"It could have happened that way."

"He's not the only possibility. There's Teresa." Rory told her what the woman had said during the cake tasting the previous day. "She's been staying at the Akaw for a week now."

"Not being able to see your kids, that's rough. She loves being a mom. What do we do now?"

"We need to check out both of their alibis."

"How are we going to do that?"

"I'm not sure about Lance—yet—but I have an idea how we can check on Teresa."

Chapter 14

The automatic doors whooshed open for Rory and Liz as they walked into the Akaw hotel in downtown Vista Beach a short time later. Guests milled around the lobby of the beach-themed hotel situated on a hill overlooking the ocean. A woman in a Hawaiian print dress with a badge pinned to her chest looked up from the concierge's desk and smiled.

"Welcome back to the Akaw. I haven't seen you two since you attended that painting convention in June. What brings you here?" Nell Fremont said.

"We're visiting a friend, Teresa Mut," Liz said.

The hotel manager's smile faded.

"Is there a problem?" Rory asked. "She's okay, isn't she?"

"No, no problem." Nell sighed. "I love managing this hotel, but sometimes I wish I did something else. Mrs. Mut has, shall we say, overstayed her welcome."

"What do you mean?"

"One of the owners has been allowing her to stay at the hotel free of charge during her recent...troubles. Weddings are now a big percentage of our banqueting business, largely thanks to her. But this is a busy time of year for us and we need that room. Plus her room service charges have been huge. Now the owner wants me to throw her out. As far as I can tell, she has nowhere to go. I hate the idea of tossing her out on the street. Maybe you two can help me."

"You want us to tell her to leave?" Rory asked, a shocked tone in her voice.

"No, no, but you could help her find a place to stay until she gets back on her feet. Maybe with one of you?" Rory looked at Liz, who frowned and gave an almost imperceptible shake of her head.

"She could stay at my place," Rory said. "But only if she's willing. I'm not kicking her out for you, but I'll make the offer."

Nell breathed a sigh of relief and the smile returned to her face. "I understand. You're doing me a huge favor. I don't know how I can ever thank you." She furrowed her brow in thought, then her face brightened as if she'd come up with an idea. "Would you like a complimentary meal at the hotel restaurant?" She held out a coupon she picked up from a drawer in the desk.

Rory waved away the piece of paper. "No thanks. We would like some information though. Do you happen to know if Teresa left the hotel Friday after about nine?"

"Let me check." They followed the hotel manager over to the front desk where she typed on a keyboard and studied the results on the display. "She had room service delivered at 7:35 that night. Nothing else after that."

"What about phone calls? Extra towels? Turn down service?"

"I don't see anything here. She probably used her own cell phone. Most people do. She has a car parked in hotel parking, but I can't tell you if she took it out that night or not. We don't keep track of entries and exits."

"What about security cameras? Is there one near the parking garage elevator or on any of the entrances to the hotel?"

"Sorry, can't give you access to those. We erase the footage every three days anyway. If there's nothing else, let me call Teresa and let her know you're here." Nell picked up the phone and dialed. After a brief conversation, she hung up and gave them the room number.

As soon as the elevator doors closed, Liz turned to Rory. "What are you thinking? Letting her stay with you? She could be a murderer."

"If she is, it must have been a spur-of-the-moment thing. She didn't bring the murder weapon with her, it was on the kitchen counter. I don't think she's a threat to either one of us."

"I suppose." Liz frowned.

"She needs friends right now. We don't know what her financial situation is. I don't like the idea of her being homeless with no place to go, especially if I can do something about it."

"Maybe she'll let something slip when she's staying with you. Ooh, ooh." Liz punched Rory on the arm. "We can get one of those nanny cams, something cute like a teddy bear. Put it on the dresser in her room. She'll never know it's there."

Rory rubbed her arm. "We can't do that."

"Right. No video in the bedroom. Audio then. Voice-activated digital recorder hidden in a plant. I know where I can get one."

"I'm not doing that."

Liz gave her friend an exasperated look. "Some detective you are," she mumbled as the elevator doors opened onto the second floor.

By the time they knocked on a door halfway down the hall, Liz was back to her usual chipper self.

Teresa answered, a smile on her face. "How nice of you both to visit. Come in, come in." She pulled two chairs from around a table, placed them at the end of the bed and sat down facing them. "I was surprised when I heard you were downstairs. What brings you here?"

Rory and Liz settled down in the chairs. Liz raised an eyebrow and nodded, indicating Rory should start the conversation.

"We're worried about you. I was wondering if you would like to stay with me until things get resolved. I've got a guest bedroom."

"You want to know if I'd like to stay with *you*?" Teresa's face registered surprise.

"Just until you get back on your feet. It must be lonely staying in a hotel," Liz said.

Rory could almost hear the wheels turning in the woman's brain as she considered the offer.

"The hotel wants me out, don't they?"

"I would have asked anyway," Rory said. "Come stay with me."

"Really? You would do that for me?" Teresa took off her glasses and wiped a tear from the corner of her eye. "Can I use your kitchen?" A wistful expression appeared on her face. "I miss baking for my monkeys."

"My kitchen is yours." Rory frowned as a sudden thought struck her. "You're not allergic to cats, are you? I'm taking care of Willow's cat right now."

"Sekhmet? She's a doll. We get along great. Cats aren't an issue for me at all." Teresa pushed her glasses up her nose and sat up straighter. "I know you work at home so I'll be as quiet as a mouse. I'll only stay a few days until I can make other arrangements. I'll earn my keep. Cook, clean, do laundry, whatever you need me to do."

"That's not necessary."

"I insist."

Before they left, Rory arranged for Teresa to move in the next morning, giving Rory the rest of the day to make sure her place was ready for company.

"You can't back out now even if you want to," Liz said as the hotel room door closed behind them.

When they exited the hotel and parted ways, Rory felt as if someone were watching her. As casually as possible, she looked behind her at the Akaw's entrance but saw no one acting suspiciously. She dismissed the thought and headed to her car. On the drive home, she glanced in the rearview mirror. Several times, she spotted a silver SUV two car lengths behind her, mirroring every one of her movements, changing lanes when she did and turning onto the same streets after her. The SUV stayed far enough behind her she couldn't see who was driving or read the license plate. She wasn't even sure if the driver was a man or a woman.

Instead of taking her usual route home, Rory drove in the opposite direction, turning onto several streets she usually didn't go down, checking her mirrors after each turn. The suspicious vehicle followed her at a distance for a while, then sped down Main Street past Rory, its driver not even glancing at her as the car passed by.

Rory's shoulders relaxed. Either she'd been mistaken or the culprit had realized she knew someone was tailing her and had stopped the pursuit.

As she turned onto Seagull Lane, she saw the gate into Willow's backyard swing shut as if someone had walked through it seconds before. Curious. The last time she drove past the house, the gate had been latched. Crime scene tape still encircled the property, but the police hadn't left anyone on guard.

Figuring Lance had been given the go ahead to pick up his things, Rory parked her car in her own driveway and headed to Willow's house to talk with him. She ducked under the yellow tape and went through the gate into the backyard, her footsteps muffled by the grass.

She had one foot on the bottom step of the deck when she spotted two figures through the open French doors, neither of them the man she expected to see. Dressed all in black, they walked toward the bookcase in the living room next to the kitchen. The hoods of their sweatshirts covered their heads, obscuring their faces. Their backs to her, the taller of the two reached for something on the top shelf.

Rory backed away as silently as possible, crouched down by a plant and dialed 911 on her cell phone. In a whisper, she explained the situation to the operator. After she hung up, she thought about leaving the way she came, but she was afraid she would make too much noise and alert the intruders to her presence. She quietly crept forward as close to the bush as possible so they wouldn't know she was there. When her foot hit one of the rocks that formed the border of the flower bed, an involuntary cry sprang from her lips.

"What was that?" The taller intruder looked toward the back door.

Rory crouched down by the shrub and stayed as quiet as possible, her gaze fixed on the living room.

The intruder listened for a moment, then dropped what he was holding and said, "I don't like this. Let's get out of here."

Their heads bent down, the two scurried out the French doors and raced down the side of the house toward Seagull Lane. Keeping a safe distance behind them, Rory followed, but by the time she reached the street, they were long gone.

Seconds later, a patrol car drove up and slid into a parking spot in front of the house. A uniformed officer stepped out and walked toward her. After she explained the situation to him, he went through the gate into the backyard to make sure no one else was in the house. By the time he returned, Detective Green had arrived in his own car. The two conferred, then the uniformed officer left.

The detective walked over to Rory. "You okay?"

"I'm fine. Sorry I didn't see where they went."

"That's not your job. It's ours. I wish you would stop interfering in police business."

"I didn't know someone had broken into the house. I wouldn't have gone in the backyard if I had."

"Tell me what happened."

After she explained her reason for being there, he said, "There were two of them?"

"That's right. One taller than the other. Teenagers, I think. At least the one voice I heard sounded like a male about that age. They had on black hoodies that hid their faces. Sleeves rolled up to the elbow. I remember thinking it odd, it's hot and they're in long-sleeve sweatshirts and long pants."

"Anything else you remember? Any distinguishing marks?"

Something niggled at the back of her brain, but no matter how hard Rory tried she couldn't figure out what it was. Finally, she gave up and said, "Not that I can think of. Only one of them talked. I can't even be sure they were both male."

He wrote down the information in his notepad. "Did they have anything in their hands?"

"Not when they left. One of them dropped something next to

the bookcase. That's where they were when I saw them, in the living room at the back of the house next to the kitchen."

Out of the corner of her eye, Rory saw a police car pull up and park in the driveway. A rotund man in a uniform climbed out of the car and walked toward them.

She sucked in her breath. She leaned down and said in a whisper, "What's the chief doing here?"

He continued writing without looking up. "He owns the place."

Rory stepped back. "Really?"

He glanced up and nodded. "Really."

Chief Marshall nodded at her then addressed the detective. "What have we got?"

As Detective Green explained what he knew so far, Rory studied the chief of police. When she saw him at the press conference the other day, she hadn't noticed how tired and worn out he looked. The weight of the world appeared to be pressing down on his broad shoulders, or at least the weight of keeping the residents of Vista Beach safe.

The chief turned to her. "Show me where you were standing when you saw them and where they were." He led the way down the side of the house into the backyard, the other two trailing behind him. She pointed to the spot at the bottom of the steps where she'd been standing when she first spotted the intruders.

"Why were you in the backyard in the first place?" Chief Marshall asked. "Do you make a habit of snooping in your neighbor's yards?"

"I was driving by and saw someone going through the side gate. I figured it was Lance so I followed. I wanted to talk to him about Sekhmet, Willow's cat. I'm taking care of her right now."

Detective Green examined the lock on the French doors. "No signs of a break-in. Whoever was here had a key. Or it was unlocked. What were they doing when you saw them?"

"They were over by the bookcase." She pointed toward the sitting area of the large room. "One of them took something off the top shelf. Dropped it as soon as they heard me and took off."

Detective Green motioned for her to stay on the deck while he and Chief Marshall entered the house through the French doors, careful to touch as little as possible with their gloved hands. When they reached the bookcase, the detective bent down to study something on the oak floor.

Chief Marshall stared down at the item, a puzzled look on his face. Rory craned her neck trying to see what they'd found, but a sofa obstructed her view.

"What's that? A wood box?" the chief finally said.

The detective picked up the painted box and held it in front of him. "From the right angle, it looks like a bunch of books."

"That's one of Willow's trompley projects then," the chief said.

Rory puzzled over his words until she realized what he meant. "Loy. It's pronounced tromp-loy," she said under her breath from her position near the back door. "It means trick the eye," she said in a louder voice so they could hear.

Chief Marshall waved a hand as if the information was unimportant.

"There's a small hole in the front and a camera inside it," Detective Green said. "The SD card's missing." He looked at the bookcase. "We'll look at the crime scene photos to confirm, but I think it was right there." He pointed to an empty spot on the top shelf and looked to Rory for confirmation. After she nodded her agreement, he stood next to the bookcase and looked in the direction the books would have been facing. "Looks like the camera had a view of the kitchen."

"So it could have recorded Willow's murder." Chief Marshall frowned. "You're better than this, Green. Why didn't you find this earlier?"

The detective's face closed down.

"Lance was looking at that spot when I found him in here the other day," Rory said. "He must have known the camera was there."

"Why didn't you tell me this before?" Detective Green asked through tight lips.

"He lives here."

"Not officially," Chief Marshall said. "We'll look into it." He turned to the detective. "Get everyone out here again and do a sweep for more cameras. The entire house. Now."

While Detective Green pulled out his phone, the chief looked at Rory and said, "You can go home now. Don't say a word about this to anyone."

Rory nodded and retraced her steps to the front yard where she found Veronica leaning against the police car. Notebook in hand, the reporter headed toward Rory who prepared to say "No comment" to anything she asked. But Veronica brushed past her as if she weren't there and accosted the chief of police as he came through the gate. "You own this house, don't you, Chief? Is that why you were here the night your tenant died? Collecting rent? Or was it more personal?"

His face turned red. He opened his mouth to say something, then clamped it shut and brushed past her.

"How about a security system? The house doesn't have one, does it? You're the chief of police—why not? Is it because you don't want the city's residents to think it's not safe here?" Veronica continued to pepper him with questions about the safety of his property and the city all the way back to his car, not stopping until he drove away.

As soon as he was gone, the reporter zeroed in on Rory. "Did you know the chief owned the house? What were you both doing in the backyard? Did something else happen?"

Rory held up her hand and uttered a "No comment" to every question the reporter asked. Once she realized Rory wasn't going to say anything else, Veronica turned away and headed back toward Willow's house where she ducked under the police tape and disappeared into the backyard.

Breathing a sigh of relief, Rory walked toward her house. She was almost at her own driveway when she encountered Mrs. Quakenbush, the neighbor on the other side of Willow's property, walking toward her with her toy poodle in her arms.

The woman stopped and nodded at the crime scene personnel

who had arrived. "What's going on? What's with the police tape around Willow's house?"

"You haven't heard?"

"We were out of town for a few days at our property in Big Bear. Trying to stay cool, you know. Everything was fine when we left, and we came back to this." She gestured toward the yellow tape around Willow's house.

"I'm afraid Willow's dead. She was murdered."

Mrs. Quakenbush's eyes widened. "In her house?"

"Afraid so. I found her last Saturday. The police think she was killed Friday evening."

The woman sucked in her breath and tightened the hold on her dog. "We left on our trip Saturday morning. You mean she was killed while we were home? Have the police caught him yet?"

"Him?"

"There was this man hanging around. I saw him in Willow's backyard peeking into her window Friday night."

"Did you call the police?"

"I was going to, but he must have seen me because he hightailed it out of there. I figured there was nothing the police could do. I saw him head down our street and watched to make sure he didn't return. I didn't see him the rest of the night."

"What did he look like?"

"About your height, maybe a little shorter. Thirtyish. Beard. Wore shorts and a t-shirt."

Rory pulled up the picture of Kit and Buddy on her phone. "Is this the man you saw?"

Mrs. Quakenbush stared at the photo. "Yep, that's him."

"What about today? Did you see anyone over at Willow's house?"

"Was there another break-in? What's going on in this city? It used to be such a safe place. Do you think the two things are related?"

"Maybe. Did you notice anything?"

She shook her head. "I was walking Toodles here." She glanced down at the dog in her arms. "I suppose walking is a bit of a stretch. She's getting older so it's more of a half-walk, half-carry. She enjoys the fresh air."

"The police are looking into it now. They'll probably be by to talk with you soon."

"If I remember anything, I'll be sure to tell them."

Rory walked toward her front door, then changed her mind and headed back to Willow's house to tell Detective Green what Mrs. Quakenbush had said about Kit. She thought about what the woman had told her. As Rory had suspected, Kit was at Willow's the night she was killed. He must have seen something that scared him. If only he could tell them what it was, they might know who had killed her neighbor.

Later that afternoon, Rory made her way down the hospital hallway. As she drew near to her destination, she heard a voice coming from Kit's room. Hoping that meant he was awake and feeling better, she increased her pace. She stopped in the doorway and looked inside the room to find Tripp sitting in a chair beside the unconscious man's bedside, reading from a book.

Rory leaned against the doorframe and watched as he read from a well-worn copy of *Treasure Island*. She smiled to herself as she listened to his gentle voice relate the tale of the adventures of Jim Hawkins.

He must have sensed her presence because he stopped at the end of a sentence and turned his head in her direction. A smile lit up his face when he saw her.

"I didn't mean to interrupt," Rory said.

Tripp closed the book and placed it on the bedside table. "You're not. I just finished the chapter. My voice was getting tired anyway."

She stepped into the room and stood at the end of the bed. She nodded toward Kit. "How's he doing?"

Tripp sighed and sat back in his chair. "The head wound's not an issue anymore, but he still has an infection. No change there. He's on some pretty heavy antibiotics. I won't lie to you, I'm a little worried."

"It's nice of you to stop by."

"I didn't want him to be alone. I wanted to make sure he knew someone cared."

Rory's heart melted. Not many people would take the time to visit someone they barely knew in the hospital, let alone read to him.

She nodded toward the book he'd been reading from. "Why *Treasure Island*?"

"It's his favorite."

Her brow furrowed in puzzlement. "How do you know that?"

"He mentioned it one time at the church."

"I thought everyone picked up their lunches and left."

"Sometimes I put a few chairs out in the lot and sit down with some of our guests. I talk to them while they eat. I've had some interesting conversations. Kit and I talked for quite a while about the books we enjoyed reading as kids."

"What's your favorite book?" she said curiously.

He nodded toward the table. "*Treasure Island*. That's my copy. I've had it ever since I was a child. It was one of the few books we owned. My sister and I both read it over and over again." He smiled to himself. "The adventure of it all seemed so wonderful. Maybe that's why I do so much traveling now. How about you?"

"I'm not sure I have a favorite. I liked a lot of things. The Mrs. Piggle-Wiggle books were fun and Encyclopedia Brown, *The Mouse and the Motorcycle*..."

"Sounds like you were quite the reader." Tripp stood up, stuffed the book in his backpack and slung it over his shoulder. "Well, I need to get going."

As he passed by her, she reached out to touch his arm. She looked into his eyes and said, "You're a good man."

He blushed and shook his head slightly.

Chapter 15

Later that night, Rory settled down in front of her computer and tried to work, but her mind kept going back to the thieves who had entered Willow's house. She wondered if the intruders were responsible for the earlier break-in or the spate of burglaries that had been plaguing neighboring cities. They hadn't disturbed much, but Rory didn't know if that was because she'd interrupted them or because they'd gotten what they came for—the SD card from the hidden camera.

She leaned back in her desk chair and swiveled it back and forth. If the teens had gone there to steal the card, someone must have told them exactly where to find the camera. It wouldn't be obvious to the casual observer. Lance could have hired them. He was jealous enough he might have planted the camera himself to check up on Willow when he wasn't around. He could have been trying to get rid of it when she saw him the other day. He had been looking at the shelf where it was found.

Rory stopped swiveling and sat up straight in her chair when she thought of another possibility. Willow could have put the camera there herself, but Rory didn't understand why she would do something like that. Unless she was using the recordings to blackmail people. She had seen at least one client in the privacy of her home, maybe there had been others. Anyone who didn't want to be seen going to her shop might be willing to pay to keep their secret. Which meant one of her victims could have hired the teens to get the evidence back. The average person probably wouldn't consent to being blackmailed though. It would have to be someone who was famous or who would lose their job if the truth came out. She made a mental note to ask Liz if she knew of anyone in the city who matched that description.

She shook her head. Both of the theories were a possibility, but she had no idea how to figure out if either one was true. One thing she could do was look for the jewelry stolen when Willow was killed. She'd promised Detective Green she would look through some online auction sites on the off chance she would find one of the items.

Rory scooted her chair closer to her desk and began searching sites, scrolling through pages of amber watches and rings, trying to find one that looked familiar. She tried site after site until her eyes were so tired she found it difficult to focus. One more, she told herself, and she would call it quits.

When another page appeared on her display, Rory blinked several times, leaned closer to the screen and stared at an amber ring. The stone was typical of many other pieces of jewelry she'd seen in her search, but the setting was unusual. She studied the pictures of the item showing its various sides until she was sure it was the ring she'd seen on Willow's finger. She checked the user who was auctioning off the item to see what else they were selling. A photo of an amber bracelet watch appeared on the screen, one that Rory was positive she'd last seen on Willow's wrist. The information on both pieces indicated they'd been put up for auction three days after her neighbor's death.

Rory copied the name of the seller and auction site data into a file and sent it to Detective Green's email address. Once the information had been sent, she set to work preparing the house for her guest. As she cleaned and tidied, she wondered if she was making a mistake letting Teresa stay with her. Even though Willow had been her friend, Teresa had a motive to kill her. Willow's decision to reveal the other woman's one night stand had changed her life forever. Rory went to bed that night wondering if she'd invited a murderer into her home.

* * *

Thursday morning, the heat wave finally broke, dropping the temperature to a more tolerable level. A breeze once again flowed inland off the ocean, cooling down the city's residents.

A row of faces stared down at Rory from the second floor of the steel and glass structure that housed the Vista Beach library. The chairs facing the windows were filled with patrons reading or working on laptops. They only had to look up to take in a breathtaking view of the ocean and pier.

When she visited Kit earlier that morning his condition had alarmed her enough that she dropped everything and headed to the library where the homeless man spent a considerable amount of time to see if anyone had information that could help her find his family.

Rory entered the building and wended her way through the tables filled with library patrons toward the information desk. In a quiet voice, she showed Kit's photo to the librarian seated behind the desk and asked her if she knew him.

"Kit's something special. We've had a lot of interesting conversations. On my lunch break, we often sit outside and talk." The woman tucked her long hair behind her ears and nodded toward the courtyard that surrounded two sides of the building. "He comes inside too, of course—everyone's welcome here—but he doesn't stay long. Doesn't want to leave Buddy by himself too much. I always make sure the dog has water and something to eat when Kit's inside." The woman frowned. "I haven't seen either of them in a while."

"Kit's in the hospital," Rory said.

"Sorry to hear that. Nothing serious, I hope."

"We're not sure. I'm trying to find out his last name so we can contact his relatives."

"Must be serious if you're looking for family. I'm afraid I can't help you though. We never talked about his past." The librarian glanced over at a table where a homeless man was sitting, arms draped over the backpack on the table in front of him, head resting on top of the rough canvas. "Excuse me a minute." She walked over to the table and gently touched the dozing man on the shoulder. "Marco, it's time to take a walk, okay? No sleeping in the library."

He shook himself awake, picked up his backpack and headed toward the exit.

"Where were we?" the librarian said when she returned to her desk. "You were asking about Kit." She drummed her fingers on the counter in front of her. "There's someone who might be able to tell you more." She stood up and surveyed the room, her gaze zeroing in on a table where a grizzly of a man sat, in the corner next to shelves filled with the latest issues of local and national newspapers. "See the man in the far corner, reading the *LA Times*? I've seen the two of them together a lot. He might be able to tell you something about Kit's family."

Rory thanked the librarian and headed across the room. She picked up last week's issue of the *Vista Beach View* and sat down at the table beside the man. She pretended to read as she studied him surreptitiously from behind the newspaper.

He was older, in his sixties was Rory's best guess, though she supposed life on the streets could age someone prematurely. His beard and hair were unkempt and his clothes appeared more ragged than the ones Kit wore.

She sat there for a good five minutes trying to figure out how to start a conversation before the man said without looking up from his paper, "Staring's going to cost you. Dime a minute. Goes up to a quarter if you want to ask questions." He turned the page and kept on reading.

Rory looked around, but didn't see anyone else nearby. "Are you talking to me?"

"See anyone else staring?" he said in a gruff voice.

She folded the newspaper, put it down on the table and stuck out her hand. "I'm Rory."

The man tapped the table with his index finger.

She stared at his finger for a moment, puzzled, until she

realized what he meant. She fished a dollar bill out of the pocket of her jeans and placed it on the table.

He put his hands over the money and drew it toward him in a protective gesture. "That gives you four minutes. Ask your questions."

"What's your name?"

"Ben. Skip to the chase. Times a wastin'." He made a *tick tick tick* sound with his mouth.

Rory brought up Kit's picture on her phone's display and showed it to him. "I was wondering if you know him. His name's Kit."

Surprise flitted across his face shortly replaced by suspicion. "Why?"

"He's in the hospital. I'm trying to find relatives, but I don't know his last name."

Ben settled back into his chair and studied her. "He gonna die?"

"I don't know. Can you tell me anything that will help me contact his family to let them know about his situation?"

"Not sure he wants them to know." He studied her as if looking for something in her eyes. He must have found whatever he was looking for because he said, "Don't know much about him. Last names don't matter to me. I don't tell anyone mine and don't ask for theirs. But he talked about a girl once or twice. The name was something short."

"Zoe?"

"That's it. Don't know a last name to go with it though, or where you might find her. What's wrong with him?"

"He has a head wound and an infection."

Ben raised an eyebrow. "Someone hit him?"

"We think so. Last Friday around lunchtime. Do you know if he had an argument with anyone around that time?"

"Don't know nothing about that." He pushed the money across the table. "Here. You can have it back. Anything to help Kit. He's been good to me."

Rory pushed the money toward him and added a larger bill. "Keep it. Thanks for your help. Stay safe."

He put a hand to his head as if tipping an imaginary hat to her. "Same to you."

Rory returned the paper to its place, waved at the librarian as she passed by her desk and headed outside. In the courtyard Veronica and the man the librarian had told to leave sat side by side on a stone bench. The reporter handed him a flip phone similar to the one Rory had seen Kit use. He nodded and stood up, tucking the phone and a charger in his backpack.

As soon as he left, Rory sat down on the bench next to Veronica. "Did you just give that man a cell phone?" She gestured toward Marco, who was on his way back into the library.

"What of it?" The reporter pressed the notebook she'd been writing in against her chest so Rory couldn't see what was on the page.

"Do you do that a lot? Pass out cell phones to random people?" Rory asked.

Veronica looked around as if to make sure no one was within earshot, then lowered her voice. "You're not in the business so I can tell you. That was me adding another recruit to my army."

"Army?"

"My army of informants. I can't be everywhere at once. They're my eyes and ears around town."

"These...informants, they tell you when something newsworthy happens?"

"That's right. In exchange for the use of the phone they tell me if they see anything they think I should know about."

That must have been how she heard about the police activity at Willow's house, Rory thought. "How many of these informants do you have?"

Veronica tilted her head toward the library. "He's number ten on my list."

"Have you gotten enough information from them to make the cost worthwhile?"

"It's not that expensive. The burners are pay-as-you-gos. I buy the cheapest ones possible. I only add money to one if the informant tells me something useful. Even with no money added they can still be used to dial 911, so it's a win-win for both of us."

"What's in the book?" Rory nodded toward the notebook, now closed on Veronica's lap.

"I keep track of when I give out a phone, who I give it to and what they've told me."

"What if they won't tell you their name?"

"I write down a description, something like male, beard, brown hair, that kind of thing. Anything that will jog my memory and remind me who I gave the phone to. I call all of them once a week and check in."

Rory showed Kit's photo to her. "Did you give one to him? His name's Kit. He had a phone that looked like the one you gave Marco."

"He looks familiar. Let me check." Veronica thumbed through her notebook until she found the right page. "Here it is." She looked up from her notes. "Before I show this to you, tell me why you want to know."

"He's in the hospital. I'm trying to locate relatives. I'm hoping you can tell me something that will help me find them."

"I don't keep track of personal information. I don't ask and they don't volunteer."

"Can I see what you have?"

Veronica handed over the book, open to the page on Kit. Rory stared at the information in disappointment. Other than the man's name, a date and a phone number, nothing else was written on it.

"You gave him the phone two weeks ago. He didn't give you any tips in that time?"

"Nothing yet. I guess I'll have to write him off. If he's in the hospital, he won't be giving me anything anytime soon."

"You won't hear from him even when he gets out of the hospital. His phone's missing."

Veronica frowned.

"Why didn't you tell me that in the first place? You're sure it's missing?"

"We didn't find it anywhere on him or in his things. He was hit on the head. Maybe he became disoriented, dropped it and someone found it."

"Only one way to find out." Veronica dialed the number of the phone she'd given Kit, hit the speaker button and waited. Three rings later a young male voice answered.

"Who is this?" Veronica asked.

"Who are you?" the voice said.

"Veronica Justice, reporter for the *Vista Beach View*. That's my phone you're using. I'd like it back."

A pause where Rory imagined the person on the other end of the call was deciding what to say. "Is there a reward?" he finally said.

Rory held up her hands and flashed ten fingers twice.

Veronica nodded and said into the phone, "Twenty bucks."

"Forty."

"Thirty, but you have to give it to me right now."

"Okay. I'll meet you at the pier by the snack shop."

Veronica hung up and the two women walked the short distance to the Vista Beach pier. Near the hut that served snacks a teenager in well-worn jeans and a t-shirt paced back and forth. When they approached him, he said, "One of you Veronica?"

The reporter stepped forward. "That's me. Do you have my phone?"

"Where's the money?"

Veronica snapped her fingers.

Rory dug two bills out of her jeans and handed them to the woman, who waved them in the air. "Before I give this to you, tell us where you found it."

The teen eyed the money hungrily and pointed in the general direction of the street. "Go right at the top of the hill. I found it on the sidewalk in front of the alley two blocks down."

"When?" Rory asked.

"Last Friday around lunchtime. I don't remember the exact time."

"Did you see anyone around?"

He shook his head. "Can I have my money now?" He held the phone out to Veronica, who took it and turned it on. As the screen lit up, Rory said, "You've had it for almost a week. How did you keep it charged?"

He nodded toward the man working in the snack shop. "He charged it for me. Where's the money?"

Veronica looked up from the phone. "I'm not giving it to you until I verify it's mine." She compared the number in the phone's information section with the one listed in her book. "It's the right one." She handed the money to the teen, who grabbed it and left, almost running as he headed up the hill.

"We have a good idea where Kit was attacked now," Rory said. "Let's see who he called."

She looked over Veronica's shoulder as she examined the call list. Ignoring any calls made after the teen had found the cell phone, only one number was on it, called multiple times, the last time the morning Kit had lost the phone.

"Do you recognize it?" Veronica said.

After Rory shook her head, the reporter dialed the number and put it on speaker. Five rings later, the call went to voicemail and a female voice asked them to leave their name and number after the beep.

Veronica looked at Rory. "Is that who I think it is?"

Rory nodded and wondered why Kit had Willow's phone number in his cell, and what they'd talked about the day she died.

Chapter 16

"What could the two of them have to talk about?" Veronica said. "From what I've heard about Willow, she didn't think very highly of the homeless."

"Maybe she was more tolerant than everyone gave her credit for," Rory said.

"Scuttlebutt has it she was starting a petition for the city to change its laws and oust them from our streets. She wanted Vista Beach to outlaw giving out food too, like your church does every Friday. Thought it only brought more of them into the city. That doesn't sound very tolerant to me."

"She lost some very expensive sunglasses recently and blamed a homeless person for stealing them. Maybe that's why she started the petition." Rory thought back to the conversation she had with Teresa two days before. "Her eyeglass case had her phone number on it. Maybe Kit was calling to say he found them. Sounds like something he would do, but I'm not sure that explains the multiple calls. Unless she wasn't answering the phone and he didn't want to leave a message."

"Did you see him with her glasses?"

Rory visualized looking through Kit's belongings. She hadn't seen glasses among his things, but she could have missed them. "No, but that doesn't mean he didn't know where they were. He was at Willow's Friday night. Maybe they had an appointment for him to return them. That could be why he left the hospital." She made a mental note to ask Detective Green if the police had found Willow's sunglasses in her house.

"How do you know Kit was at Willow's? Did he say something to you?"

Rory shook her head. "A neighbor saw him. She said he was in her backyard, then suddenly left. He must have seen something that frightened him off. If only we knew what."

"I don't think Willow and Kit talked at all. The calls didn't last long." Veronica scrolled through the list of incoming calls. "Whatever was going on between the two of them, it was one-sided. No phone calls from her to him."

"What about from other people?"

"Just me. If he didn't get her number from the eyeglass case, I wonder where he got it."

"Let me check something." Rory looked through her wallet until she found a business card Willow had given her when she first opened her store. She compared the phone number on the card to the number in the cell phone. "It's the same number. Kit probably picked up one of her business cards. She gave them to pretty much everyone she saw."

"We've learned all we can from this." Veronica stuffed the phone in her tote bag. "You said someone hit Kit, right? Maybe they were fighting over those expensive sunglasses you're talking about."

"Why?"

"Someone could have thought there would be a big reward and wanted it for themselves. If you stamp your name on an eyeglass case, you really want it back."

"I doubt anyone thought the reward would be large enough to warrant a fight. Let's go to the place where the phone was found and see if we can find anything there."

Minutes later, the two stood at the entrance of the alleyway the teen had pointed out and stared into the dimness. Even though they were close to the pier, the area was quiet. No pedestrians strode by on the sidewalk and few cars passed by on the street behind them.

Rory stepped inside and turned around to face the entrance. The pier and ocean were visible from the mouth of the alley, but take two or three steps inside and you could have a private conversation no one would overhear or notice from the street. "This could be where Kit was hit. Let's say he had an argument with someone, got hit, stumbled out of the alley and dropped his phone on the sidewalk, not realizing he did it. He could have wheeled his bike down to the beach and ended up under the pier where I found him."

Veronica glanced over at the pier. "That's not very far. He could have had a delayed reaction from being hit and not collapsed until later." She pulled a small flashlight out of her tote bag and shown it around the alley. "Is that blood?" She pointed the beam at a spot on the concrete.

Rory bent down to examine it. "Could be. Hard to tell." She stood up and peered into the gloom. "There's something leaning against that wall. Point the light over there."

Veronica directed the flashlight to the place Rory had indicated, its beam highlighting a plank of wood.

"That could have been used to hit him. Did any of your informants report hearing an argument or seeing anything suspicious around here last Friday?"

"No, I would have looked into it if they had. But that doesn't mean no one saw anything. I'll contact everyone in my crew and see if they know anything that might be of help. I'll even post about it on Vista Beach Confidential. Someone with information might come forward." Veronica took photos of the wood and the alley. "I'll let you know if I find out anything," she said before she left.

After calling Detective Green to tell him about their find, Rory checked out the rest of the alley while she waited for the police. Nothing else jumped out at her as being important.

Once the detective and his crew arrived, she pointed out the piece of wood to him. As they collected evidence, he said, "We found the person who was selling that jewelry online. I'd like you to come down to the station and see if you can identify her." He gave instructions to the others before he and Rory headed to the police station.

Inside the station, Rory followed him to an area where a black and white monitor sat on a desk, showing the Vista Beach police department's interrogation room. She shuddered when she remembered her own experience in the claustrophobic room five months before.

She shook off the bad memory and stared at the monitor, studying the girl sitting alone in a chair next to a table shoved up against the wall. Dressed in a tank top, the girl looked squeaky clean, an all-American type, not the kind of person Rory expected to be burglarizing homes or killing unsuspecting residents. "She looks young. How old is she?" she said to the detective, who stood beside her.

"Eighteen. Do you recognize her? Could she have been one of the people you saw at Ms. Bingen's house?"

Rory folded her arms in front of her and leaned forward at the waist, studying the girl, who was twirling her long straight hair around her index finger over and over again. She stood up straight and shook her head. "She could be, but I'm not sure. Sorry, I wish I could say yes, she's the one or no, she's not, but I really can't be sure. Do you think she's part of this burglary ring? She doesn't look the type."

"Appearances can be deceptive. I'm not ready to say yea or nay yet."

"She had Willow's jewelry?"

"She was selling the ring and watch you noticed on the auction site online. We found them when we searched her parents' house."

"Are they here?" Rory looked out the door of the room into the station. She didn't remember seeing anyone she would have pegged for concerned parents when she came in.

"Neither one was home when we served the warrant. Their housekeeper didn't know where they were, just that they're out of town today." He nodded toward the screen. "She's an adult now. We don't need their permission to question her."

"Have you asked her where she got them yet?"

"I'm going in right now. Watch her as I talk to her. Maybe something about her mannerisms will seem familiar." He picked up a folder and two plastic bags from a nearby table and headed toward the door into the interrogation room.

Rory watched the screen as Detective Green entered the room. He pulled up a chair so he was facing the girl, placed the folder on top of the plastic bags on the table and leaned back as if getting ready for a chat with an old friend.

Before he could say a word, the girl stopped twirling her hair, jutted her chin out defiantly and said, "You're in big trouble. My dad knows people. Important people. He'll have your job for this."

"We're just having a conversation," he said in his most soothing tone. "Tell me about your family, Emily. I can call you Emily, can't I?"

The girl looked taken aback, as if she hadn't expected the policeman to be so friendly. "Sure," she said a bit uncertainly.

"Your family?" the detective gently prompted.

"My dad's a manager for Vista Beach Bank, the branch on Main. My mom's a doctor, dermatologist. Are they here? Can I talk to them?" She looked toward the door as if expecting her parents to walk in at any moment.

"Brothers, sisters?" he continued.

Emily returned her attention to him and shook her head.

"Only child." He nodded, as if her answer had confirmed his assessment of her. "I know how that goes. I was one myself. Busy parents, time-consuming jobs. No time for you, I bet." He nodded his head sympathetically, the last sentence coming out more as a statement than a question. "Makes you independent, strong."

Her shoulders relaxed, and she smiled for the first time. "Exactly."

"Now, Emily." He moved his chair closer, leaned his elbows on his knees and looked up into her eyes. "There's something I don't understand, something I'm hoping you can help me with. Maybe you can explain it to me. You've never been in trouble with the police. You come from a good family. How does an upstanding citizen like yourself end up with stolen goods?" He unearthed the plastic bags from under the folder and pushed them toward her.

When she saw the ring and watch inside the bags, her eyes lit up in recognition. "Where did you get those? They're mine. I didn't steal them."

He shook his head in disbelief and a sad expression came over his face. "Then why do they match the description of jewelry taken from a homicide victim?"

Emily stared at him in horror. "You mean, like, murder?"

The detective opened up the folder and showed her a photograph. Rory couldn't tell what it was of, but from the appalled look on the girl's face, she suspected it showed Willow's body.

Emily shoved the picture across the table and averted her gaze, looking like she was about to throw up. "Take that away. I don't know anything about that. The jewelry's mine. I didn't steal it."

He put the photo back in the folder and closed it. "Your parents have money. They must give you whatever you want. Why sell it?"

She snorted. "My allowance barely covers a movie once a week. My parents want me to earn money. They're even threatening to charge me rent. They think because I'm eighteen now and out of high school I should be more responsible." She air quoted the last word. "That's what I'm doing, being responsible."

"How does selling your jewelry do that, exactly?"

"Me and my friend, we find stuff in dumpsters people have thrown away, clean it up and sell everything at swap meets or online. It's completely legal. Anything anyone throws away is fair game."

"Is that where you found these?" He tapped his finger on the plastic bags. "In a dumpster?"

She nodded. "You should see all the stuff we find. You wouldn't believe what people throw away. Perfectly good clothes, DVDs, furniture. There's even a market for VHS tapes if you look hard enough. We found a stash of records once. You know, those vinyl discs people used to listen to all the time." She leaned forward. "That one was funny. Some guy came looking for them. His girlfriend got mad at him and threw all his stuff out. He didn't care about most of it, but those LPs he wanted real bad. We got to them first. Made him pay top dollar to get them back." She raised her head in pride.

"Where did you find the jewelry?"

She screwed up her face in concentration. "On Seashell Lane. A few blocks from that church. Don't remember the name. Good something or other. You know the one."

"Didn't it strike you as odd such expensive-looking jewelry was in the dumpster?"

"People throw away good stuff all the time. Saturday evening. That's when we found them. Tim and I go dumpster diving every Friday and Saturday after dark. We used to do it during the day, but some people don't like us rooting around in their trash. They call us names. Someone even chased us away with a broom once. Ask Tim, he'll tell you we found the watch and ring there."

"What about Friday evening?"

"Like I said, we were looking through dumpsters then too. Ask Tim."

Detective Green wrote down her friend's contact information on a notepad, picked up the evidence bags and stood up. "Wait here. I'll be back."

His image disappeared from the screen. Rory looked across the room to see him close the interrogation room door behind him.

He walked over to her. "Anything?"

She shook her head. "I don't think she's one of the teens who broke in."

He nodded and went over to a phone. He glanced at his notes and dialed. Rory strained to hear what he was saying, but couldn't make out any of the words. After a short conversation, he returned to the interview room. "Tim confirms your statement, Emily. He told me how you found the jewelry on Saturday and that you two were also together Friday evening."

A look of relief came over the young girl's face. "I can go now? That's all you wanted to know?"

"For now. We may need to talk to you again."

She stood up and held out her hand. "Jewelry please."

"It stays here."

"Why? The watch and ring are mine."

"They're stolen property and evidence in a murder investigation."

Detective Green escorted the girl out the door. After handing her over to a uniformed officer, he walked over to Rory.

"She and her friend could be in it together," she said to him. "They could have robbed Willow on Friday."

"There's no evidence she's involved in any of the other burglaries. I think she's telling the truth."

Rory looked curiously at him. "Were *you* telling the truth in there? Are you an only child?"

"You get them to talk any way you can," was all he said.

"There's still the charm bracelet. They might not have noticed it in the dumpster. It could still be there."

"I'll send someone to check it out, but chances are the dumpster's already been emptied."

"We may never find it then," Rory said softly. She pictured the bracelet disappearing into a landfill, never to be seen again.

The inviting smell of freshly baked cookies greeted Rory as she opened the back door to her house. When she stepped inside the kitchen, she found Liz sitting at the table with an almost-empty plate of chocolate chip cookies in front of her and Teresa standing in front of the open oven door.

Liz reached for a cookie, withdrawing her hand as soon as she saw her friend. "Don't look at me like that. I didn't eat all of them. I saved a couple for you."

"Don't worry, there's more." Teresa picked up the plate and added the batch she'd taken out of the oven moments before to it.

Rory sat down at the table and picked up a cookie. "I thought you weren't eating dessert these days."

Liz munched on another cookie. All Rory heard was a muffled *wa-wa-wa-wa* similar to the way adults spoke in the Peanuts cartoons. She swallowed. "Sorry. I said, 'These are too good to pass up.'"

"They are good. You didn't have to do this, Teresa."

The woman blushed at the praise. "Consider it a thank you for letting me stay here." She placed an envelope and a newspaper on the table in front of Rory. "These came for you while you were out."

Rory put the half-eaten cookie down on a napkin and picked up the envelope. Her name and address were written on the front in block lettering. No return address, no stamp, no indication it had ever been sent through the mail. She opened the unsealed envelope and drew out a piece of plain white paper. Written on it in the same block lettering was "Stop it or else." She turned the paper over, but nothing was written on the back. Rory stared at the note in disbelief. "Where did you get this?"

"It was in the mailbox when I got back from the grocery store."

"Did you see anyone on the street?"

"A few of your neighbors. At least I assume that's who they were. No one was acting suspiciously, if that's what you mean. Why? What does it say?"

Rory placed the note down on the table so the other two could read it.

"What are you supposed to stop doing?" Teresa asked.

"Beats me."

Liz put her hand over her mouth as if stifling a yawn.

"Not a very effective threat. Hashtag boring. What is this, the third anonymous note you've gotten since you started solving crimes?"

"Something like that." Rory examined the envelope. Nothing on it gave her any indication who could have sent it.

"It's handwritten," Liz said. "Very old-fashioned. Odd since everyone has computers these days."

"Do you think they're talking about you investigating Willow's murder?" Teresa asked.

"Could be, but like Liz said, it's not very effective. Tell me about the people you saw on the street when you got home."

Teresa puckered her face in concentration. "I didn't really notice much. Let's see. There was a man across the street looking in his mailbox. That's why I checked yours. I figured the mail had come, but all I found was the note. There was a woman walking a dog and another jogging. Oh, and a couple cars were driving down the street."

Rory put the note back in its envelope and put it on the table.

"You're ignoring it, then?" Teresa said. "Shouldn't you call the police?"

Rory wondered for a split second if her guest was the person who had written the note, though she didn't know what it would gain her.

"I don't think I'll bother. Seems pretty lame to me."

She picked up the copy of the *Vista Beach View* and studied the front page. Beneath a photo of Willow and Dr. Wagner at the grand opening of Beach Healing and Acupuncture taken six months before was an article on the herbal healer's untimely death. A bare-bones description of the crime, it included the usual quotes from the police about how they were doing everything possible to identify and apprehend the culprit and that they were pursuing some promising leads.

Below the fold was an update on the rash of burglaries plaguing neighboring cities with a grainy photo of the two suspects taken from a home security camera. Rory peered closely at the photo. Neither of them looked anything like the two people she saw at Willow's the previous day or the girl selling the jewelry.

Teresa was reading the article when a cell phone lying on the table rang. She glanced down at its display and pressed a button to silence it.

"Don't worry about us. You can answer it if you want to," Rory said.

"It's just Trent. I told him where I'm staying. If he wants to talk with me he can come here in person."

"What if it's about your kids?" Liz asked.

"I checked in on them a little while ago. My mother took them to the zoo. Last big outing before they go back to school. She'll call me if there's anything I need to know." Teresa filled the tea kettle with water and put it on the stove. "I'm making tea. Do either of you want some?"

Rory and Liz shook their heads. Teresa pulled up a chair and sat down at the table while she waited for the water to boil.

Sekhmet wandered into the kitchen from the front of the house, sat down on the floor and yawned. Teresa looked down at the Abyssinian and smiled. "Sleepyhead's up, I see. You hungry?"

The cat meowed as if she understood every word. Rory started to get up to feed her, but Liz placed a restraining hand on her friend's arm. She leaned over and said in a whisper, "Let her. She needs someone to mother right now."

Rory nodded and sat back in her seat while Teresa opened a packet of cat food into a bowl and set it on the floor. The cat delicately picked up each morsel, munching contentedly on the food.

"She seems to have adjusted to her new surroundings," Liz said.

"I wonder if she realizes Willow is gone for good," Rory said. "Speaking of Willow, Teresa, you spent a lot of time with her. What do you know about Lance?"

Teresa prepared her tea and sat down again. "They met when he came into her store looking for some help with migraines he was having and they hit it off. He's a real fitness freak. Have you seen his body? It's pretty amazing. She liked tight bodies. Plus Willow preferred younger men."

"Any recent problems between the two of them?"

"He has a fitness product he's been trying to get funding for, a new kind of portable gym. He asked her to help, but she wouldn't give him any money."

"She had money?"

Teresa bobbed her tea bag up and down in the cup. "Lots of it, from what she told me."

"Any idea who it goes to?"

"She never mentioned anything to me. As far as I know she doesn't have any relatives. Maybe the acupuncturist she owns the store with, Dr. Wagner, gets it."

"I heard he gets the building—maybe he gets everything. Lance seems to think she was having an affair with someone. Do you know anything about that?" Rory said.

"Willow? An affair?" Teresa snorted into her cup. "Wouldn't that just be peachy? Her having an affair after talking to me about how important it was to be honest in a relationship."

"You don't think she was then?"

The woman put her cup on the table. "Not that I saw. She seemed pretty devoted to her project, as she liked to call Lance."

"Project?"

"The way he eats is pretty healthy, but he still likes his meat. She was trying to get him to become a vegan like she was, only it was slow going."

"Why would she refer to him as her project? I thought she loved him," Liz said.

Teresa took a sip of tea. "He certainly loved her. Maybe too much, if you know what I mean. Very protective of her. Didn't like any man talking to her. Not even the chief of police. I heard what Lance said at the press conference. He was her landlord. Of course the chief's going to talk to her now and then."

Rory and Liz looked at each other. "So they weren't having a fling?"

"Willow and the chief?" Teresa shook her head. "Not likely. He's still hung up on that wife of his who died in that fire years ago."

Rory looked down at the cookie in her hand, uncomfortable at the turn the conversation had taken.

Liz cleared her throat and said a little too brightly, "Did you get the email from Dawn about Sunday's class? She gave us our first assignment."

"Haven't seen it yet. What does she want us to do?" Teresa said.

"We're supposed to go to the chalk festival on Saturday and check out all of the entries. Apparently a lot of them will be examples of trompe l'oeil."

As part of the annual end of summer festival, the last big event before kids went back to school, the city of Vista Beach was staging its first chalk art festival, where artists would create temporary works of art on the pavement.

"I heard Dawn's participating," Teresa said. "I'm not sure what she's going to be drawing, but she hopes it will bring in interest for her classes."

As the two women continued to talk about the class and the upcoming festival, Rory wondered how much money Willow had and who would inherit it now that she was gone.

Chapter 17

Friday morning, an ocean breeze blew over Vista Beach for the start of the three-day end-of-summer festival, kicking off with the city's annual sidewalk sale. Most businesses downtown participated, displaying their wares on tables and racks in front of their stores. By ten a.m. the sidewalk was crowded with customers enjoying the cooler weather and looking for bargains.

Rory stared down at the display of painting and scrapbooking supplies on the table in front of the entrance to Arika's Scrap 'n Paint and went over her checklist in her mind. Two-ounce bottles of acrylic paint in a rainbow of colors, check. An assortment of brushes, check. Stamps and stickers, check. She got to the end of her list and frowned. Something was missing, but she couldn't remember what it was.

A bell tinkled and Arika stuck her head around the front door of the store. "How's it going?"

"I think I'm missing something, but I'm not sure what."

Arika stepped outside and studied the display. "Gel pens. You're missing the gel pens."

"Of course." Rory followed her mother into the store and returned moments later with boxes of pens in various colors.

A teenage girl in a black hoodie with sleeves rolled up to her elbows, revealing a long scar on her right arm, stood by the table. Almost against her will, Rory's gaze zeroed in on the scar. It seemed oddly familiar, but she couldn't remember where she'd seen it before.

The girl's eyes widened and she pushed her sleeves down. Embarrassed to be caught staring, Rory said, "Let me know if you need any help," and focused her attention on adding the pens to the display.

A sudden gust of wind sent a bottle of varnish rolling onto the sidewalk. The teen chased it and put it back on the table. Rory smiled her thanks. The girl mumbled something Rory couldn't quite hear and returned her attention to the table.

Rory was studying the changes to the display when, out of the corner of her eye, she saw the girl pick up several bottles of paint and examine the labels. After a quick look around, she stuffed the bottles in the pocket of her hoodie and walked away.

"Hey!" Rory said, starting after her.

The girl looked behind her. When she saw she was being followed, she pushed her way through the crowd and sprinted down the street.

Rory shouted "Stop her!" in a loud voice and took off after the fleeing thief. People looked around in confusion, staring at the runners. As they ran by Monica's Treasures, the store owner grabbed at the girl's sweatshirt, but she wriggled out of her grasp. Taller than most people around her, Rory was able to keep her eyes on the teen as she weaved in and out of the crowd.

The girl slowed down when she almost collided with a couple walking side by side down the sidewalk, pushing a double-wide stroller in front of them. Rory was within arm's distance of her prey, reaching out for the sleeve of the thief's sweatshirt, when she darted into the street. A horn honked and a car slammed on its brakes, narrowly missing her. The girl barely acknowledged the near accident and ran down the street around the family that had been blocking her path.

The car started forward again. Rory held up her hand and raced into the street. The sedan stopped once again, its driver shouting obscenities at her as she followed the girl back onto the sidewalk and down the block. Rory dashed around a group standing in front of the Akaw, almost running into a rack of bicycles, one of many sprinkled throughout the city for anyone to borrow free of charge.

At an intersection, the girl sprinted ahead and rounded a corner. Rory thought she'd lost her and had almost given up hope of finding her again when the crowd parted and she spotted her tossing a plastic bag into a trashcan halfway down the hill.

Rory sped after her, but by the time she reached the garbage can, the girl had disappeared into the crowd. Hands on her thighs, Rory bent at the waist to catch her breath. Once she recovered, she pulled the plastic bag out of the trash can and opened it. Inside, instead of the stolen merchandise she thought she would see was an unexpected prize—a Ziploc bag with an SD card inside.

At the sight of the card, something clicked in her mind and images of the two intruders at Willow's house flooded her brain, including one of a black hoodie and the scar on one of their arms that she hadn't remembered seeing until now. This girl was one of the intruders and this was the missing SD card from the camera, she was sure of it.

Rory stared down at the card, puzzled by what she found. If the girl had the card why would she bring attention to herself by stealing paint? And why did she still have it two days after she took it? If she'd been hired to get the SD card by Lance or someone else, wouldn't they have wanted to get it from her as soon as possible?

With the unanswered questions swirling through her mind, she put the card back in the plastic bag, tucked it under her right arm and headed back to her mother's store. Half a block from the Akaw hotel, a knot of people blocked the sidewalk, forcing her to walk out into the street to get around them. She pulled her phone out of her pocket to call Detective Green and report her find. A pedestrian going around the crowd, coming toward her, jostled her arm, causing her to drop her phone. She was bending down to pick it up when someone grabbed the plastic bag out from under her arm.

An involuntary "Hey!" sprang from her lips. Rory spun around to see if she could spot the thief. Someone on a blue bike raced down the street. She grabbed one of the beach cruisers from the rack next to the hotel and chased after the thief.

She kept an eye on the patch of blue now far ahead of her as she pedaled, pumping hard. She maneuvered the bicycle down the street and around the corner. She was narrowing the gap when the other bicyclist raced across the intersection through a red light, narrowly missing being hit by a car. She kept an eye on the spot of blue as it went around a corner. When the light turned green seconds later, she raced after the thief. She'd almost reached the turn when a dog ran into the street in front of her. She steered her bike sharply to the right and braked hard, losing her balance and falling off the bike onto the pavement. By the time she righted herself and she made it around the corner, the blue bike was nowhere in sight.

Chapter 18

Rory kicked the bottom of the front counter in Arika's Scrap 'n Paint in frustration. "I had it in my hands! The video that could tell us who killed Willow was in my hands and I lost it!" she said to Detective Green and her mother, who were standing near her on the sales floor.

"Stop kicking the counter. Sit down and let me take care of that scrape before it gets infected." Arika pointed to the stool next to the cash register. "I'll be right back. I've got some bandages in the office." She headed toward the back room while Rory obeyed her mother's orders and sat down.

The half dozen customers in the store glanced up from their shopping and eyed her curiously.

Detective Green stood calmly to one side and let her fume. Fifteen minutes had passed since Rory had given chase to the thieves. After returning the bicycle she borrowed to the rack near the Akaw, she called the detective and told him what happened before returning to the store.

"You're going to be the death of me, you know," he said. "I don't know what to do with you. You interfere with crime scenes, investigate when you're not supposed to and now chase after thieves. You could have ended up with a worse injury than a scrape."

"I couldn't let either of them get away with it."

"I would have thought your past experiences would have stopped you from acting so foolishly. I have half a mind to ask your parents to knock some sense into you."

Arika returned to the sales floor carrying a first-aid kit. "Don't bother, we've tried. She's a stubborn one." She set the kit on the counter and began cleaning and bandaging the scrape on her daughter's arm.

"You're sure the girl is one of the two you saw at Ms. Bingen's house?" the detective said.

"I'm positive."

"How can you be so sure?"

"The scar." Rory winced as her mother wiped away the dried blood on her arm.

He looked through his notebook and frowned. "Scar? You didn't say anything about a scar before."

"I forgot about it until I saw her today. She had a scar on her right arm from the palm of her hand halfway up her forearm." Rory traced a line on her own forearm indicating the length and position of the scar.

"Would you recognize her again?"

"Definitely. I wish we had that bag or at least one of the bottles of paint she stole. You might have gotten prints off them."

"Did she touch anything else?"

Rory cast her mind back to the period before the teen had stolen the paint, trying to remember her actions. "She grabbed a bottle that fell off the table."

"Show me."

"Not until I finish this," Arika said in a stern voice.

As soon as the bandage was on, Rory led the way outside and pointed to several bottles on the table. "It was one of those."

Detective Green gathered all the bottles of varnish and placed them in evidence bags, being careful to touch only the tops. "It's a long shot, but her prints could be in the system. If she stole the paint, she might have stolen other things. What about the person on the bike? Could it have been her?"

"I don't think so. I didn't get a very good look, but whoever it was was taller. It might have been the other burglar."

"Let me know if you think of anything else."

"Did you ask Lance about the camera? Did he hire this girl?"

"He denied knowing anything about it, then lawyered up."

"What about the bicycle? Do you think you'll find it?" Rory asked.

"Maybe. Whoever it was probably ditched it somewhere. We'll keep an eye out for it. I'll let you know if we find anything." The detective headed down the street, evidence bags in hand.

Rory was on her way back inside when Liz wended her way through the crowd toward the store.

"What was Dashing D doing here?" Liz stared at the bandage on Rory's arm. "What happened to you?"

"Come inside and I'll tell you all about it." She led the way through the sales floor into the empty classroom where they had more privacy.

"Why would the girl throw the card in the trash?" Liz asked after Rory had brought her up to date. "And why did she take it in the first place? She could pawn the camera, sure, but the card? Doesn't make sense." Her eyes opened wide. "Unless they killed Willow and came back for the evidence."

"But how would they even know the camera was there? It was hidden. Only the person who put it there would know about it."

"That must have been Willow. It's her house. Who else would have done it?"

"Three people had keys to the place. Chief Marshall, since he owns it, Willow and Lance. Don't forget he lives there part time. I don't think it's the chief. When they found the camera, he didn't seem to know what it was at first. I don't think he's that good an actor."

"That leaves Wispy Willow and Lance," Liz said. "He thought she was having a secret affair. Maybe he planted it to catch her in the act."

"Lance told the police he didn't know anything about it, but he was looking in that same spot the other day. I'm pretty sure he knew it was there even if he didn't plant it. There's another possibility." Rory spotted a woman hovering around the door to the classroom and lowered her voice so the customer wouldn't hear. "Willow could have planted it herself and used it to blackmail people. Remember that personal trainer, Big Jim? He was seeing her at her home so no one would know he had health problems. Maybe there were others."

"Willow a blackmailer?" Liz considered the possibility. "I suppose it's possible. Teresa said she had money. Maybe that's how she got it and maybe her killer was someone who was tired of paying."

"There's a problem with that theory though. If she was blackmailing people, the only ones who would bother paying would be public figures who would lose something big if anyone found out. Do you know anyone around town that fits that description?"

"Like a celebrity or sports figure? Nobody I can think of. They all seem to prefer living in other cities." Liz stared wistfully off into space as if imagining the money she could make from the sale of homes to athletes and television stars. "I'll ask around, see if anyone has heard any rumors about her blackmailing people. That still doesn't explain how they knew about the camera."

"Willow could have told them there was one. If you were blackmailing someone wouldn't you show them the footage?"

"I doubt the girl you saw was being blackmailed. From what you said, it didn't look like she had any money."

"No, but someone could have hired her to retrieve it. The killer could have guessed where the camera might be and told her to concentrate on the bookshelf. Even though he denies it, my bet's on Lance."

Liz pounded her fist on the table and said excitedly, "And the trashcan was the drop point. Just like in the movies. But what about the bicyclist?"

"Could be the person who was supposed to pick up the bag. Maybe the bike will tell us more. Come on. Let's go find it."

Rory grabbed her phone off the table and headed out the door.

They kept their eyes out for an abandoned blue bike as they walked toward the area where the bicyclist had taken the bag from her. Liz stared at the racks of beach cruisers near the Akaw. "What if the thief returned it here? How would we find it among all of these?"

"Too many people around. I doubt they'd return it, at least not here. But they did have to borrow it in the first place." Rory pointed toward a man in a red vest who was running toward a stand not far from the rack of bikes. "There's the hotel valet. Maybe he remembers someone taking it."

They asked him if he remembered anyone borrowing bikes earlier that day. He couldn't give them a description of anyone who had, but he'd been busy parking cars and wasn't always at his station.

"Whoever it was could have borrowed it another day anyway, or dropped it off at any of the other racks around the city," Liz said. "Where did you go from here?"

They took the same path Rory had taken in her chase, looking in each alley that they passed for the distinctive blue bike. They almost crowed in triumph when they saw one leaning against a wall on the next block, but their hopes were dashed when it didn't have the city's logo on it and the owner turned out to be an older man in his seventies.

Once they reached the point where Rory had last seen the biker, they stopped to consider which direction to take.

"Let's go this way." Rory pointed to an alley that ran behind some houses. "There's not much traffic there. It would be a good place to ditch it."

They headed down the alley that was barely wide enough for one car, Rory looking on the right side, Liz the left, checking every place where a bicycle could be hidden. They'd almost given up hope when they spotted a man staring at something in his garage. Holding a gallon container of bleach in one hand, he scratched his head in puzzlement.

"Is that your bike?" Rory pointed to the blue beach cruiser with the city logo on it.

"No, and I have no idea where it came from. It wasn't there when I went inside a couple hours ago. I got distracted and forgot to close the garage door. When I came outside a little while ago I found it." He reached his free hand toward it.

"Don't touch it," Rory said. "It might have been used in a crime."

"What's that smell?" Liz asked.

Rory sniffed the air. "I think it's bleach." She pointed at the bottle the man held. "Is that empty?"

"It is now, but it wasn't earlier today, and I didn't empty it."

Rory moved closer to the bike and bent down to smell it, being careful not to touch anything. "I think someone doused it in bleach. Probably wiped all the prints off it too. I'd better call the police and let them know we found it. What's the address here?"

The man told her, then shook his head in disbelief.

Rory called Detective Green and gave him the address. She hung up and the three of them waited for the police to arrive.

Chapter 19

"Pavement is their canvas, pastel chalk their medium," a man dressed as Leonardo da Vinci shouted to passersby. Standing at the top of the hill leading down to the Vista Beach pier, he held up a copy of a printed brochure with one hand, high enough so everyone could see it. "Read all about the artists. Only two dollars. Proceeds go toward providing art supplies for kids who can't afford them." He repeated his spiel over and over again, thanking anyone who bought a brochure with a sweeping bow.

On this Saturday, the street from the top of the hill down to the pier was blocked off, giving pedestrians free rein of the road down to the ocean. Classic rock music from a band playing on a temporary stage in the parking lot next to the pier wafted over the area, carried inland on an ocean breeze.

Rory stood in the middle of the street and flipped through her brochure, passing over the biographies of the participating artists and the band schedule until she got to the last two pages. "Here's a map of all the areas where there's artwork."

Liz turned to the same pages in her own brochure. "Looks like it's taken over two parking lots and the entire pier. Where should we go first?"

Rory pointed to one of the spots on the map. "Let's start with the kids' area. It's closest. We can work our way down to the pier."

The two headed down the hill past a group clustered around a juggler teaching the onlookers how to keep three balls in the air and a woman dressed as a belly dancer handing out takeout menus for a local Moroccan restaurant.

"Too bad Kit can't be here," Rory said. "He would like this."

"He was hit near here, wasn't he?" Liz looked at the sea of faces around them. "Do you think whoever did it is here today?"

"Maybe."

They were almost at their destination when Liz nodded toward a muscular man in shorts and a tight tank top, handing out flyers. "I think that's Big Jim. He matches the description Doug gave me. Have you talked to him yet?"

"Not yet. No time like the present."

Big Jim handed both of them flyers. "You two ladies interested in personal training? We have a two-for-one special going on right now. An hour a day, three days a week, I can get you two in shape in no time. I'm Jim."

"I'm Rory, this is Liz." Rory studied the gym flyer while she collected her thoughts. "My friend's already a member, but I'm considering joining. Another trainer, Lance, gave me a tour the other day."

Big Jim scowled. "I'd stay away from him if I were you."

"Why?"

"The guy has anger issues."

"We heard he had a fight with another trainer," Liz said. "Was that you?"

He held up both hands. "Wasn't my fault. I was just defending myself."

"We know." Rory lowered her voice. "Willow was my neighbor. I heard she sometimes saw clients at her house."

"Whoa! You're not trying to pin that on me, are you? I don't know anything about her death."

"We heard she sometimes asked for...donations to keep visits to her quiet," Rory said.

"She wasn't blackmailing me if that's what you're getting at. I like my privacy, but I'm not going to pay someone to keep their mouth shut."

"What about anyone else?"

"Doesn't seem like something she'd do. She was on the up and up. Like I said, I don't know anything about her death. The last time I saw her was the week before. You should talk to the woman who visited her after me. Lots of anger there."

"What happened?"

"I was in the bathroom at Willow's place when I heard yelling. Went out to make sure she was okay and this woman was in the kitchen, waving a piece of paper in Willow's face."

"Can you describe her?"

"Older, past sixty, looked like she hadn't exercised a day in her life. Willow called her some name that starts with an...M, I think. Whoever she was, she said Willow would pay for it."

Monica, Rory mouthed to Liz who nodded her head in agreement.

"Thanks for your time," Rory said.

As the two women walked away, she said to Liz, "Monica lied to me about never having been in Willow's house. She claimed she didn't even know where she lived. She did stand to lose a store she's had for thirty years."

"She does spend most of her time there. It's pretty much the only thing in her life since her husband died. That might have put her over the edge."

In a parking lot overlooking the ocean, chalk designs were splashed over the pavement on four foot by four foot squares scattered throughout the lot with enough space between them for people to walk between the pieces created by the young artists. Proud parents pointed out their children's artwork to everyone who would listen. Rory and Liz strolled through the lot, careful not to step on any of the colorful pictures.

"How do we know the names of the artists? None of the kids are listed in the brochure. The only names in here are the professionals who entered," Liz said.

"Look, each of them signed their work." Rory pointed to the bottom of each piece they passed.

"I like this one. Very realistic." Liz stopped at a drawing of a dolphin leaping out of the ocean.

A boy standing nearby who looked to be about twelve blushed at her praise.

"This yours?" Rory asked. When he nodded, she gave him a thumbs up.

They were leaving the parking lot headed toward the next stop, when a familiar bark reached their ears.

"Is that Buddy?" Rory turned in the direction the sound had come from.

The golden retriever bounded toward them, practically dragging Bethany along with him. She held onto his leash tightly while a boy and a girl ran beside their mother, and their father brought up the rear with the other dog.

"He's happy to see you," Bethany said when she reached them.

Rory and Liz patted the dog on the head. A man walked by, talking on a cell phone, and bumped into another pedestrian. When he got too close to one of the kids, Buddy growled.

Bethany shushed the dog. "Sorry about that. He's very protective of our kids. He growls at anyone he thinks is a threat to them. That man accidentally ran into my youngest earlier."

Rory looked at Liz. "Are you thinking what I'm thinking?"

"I think so." Liz turned to the woman. "Bethany, do you think we could borrow Buddy for a while? Walk around the festival with him?"

"Sure, he would like that." She started to hand over the dog's leash then held it back at the last second. "You're bringing him back though, right? The kids have become attached to him."

Rory suspected the children weren't the only ones who would miss the dog when he left. "Of course. We'll walk around for a bit. Say an hour? We'll meet you back here."

Looking relieved, Bethany handed Liz the leash. She bent down and hugged the dog. "See you later, Buddy. Be a good boy."

Rory and Liz waved as they headed with their canine companion toward the next parking lot. On their way across the street, they walked by two more jugglers passing brightly colored juggling pins between them.

"Do you think this will work?" Liz asked.

"It's worth a shot. If he's protective of kids he hasn't known that long, he's probably even more protective of someone he's with every day. I bet he would growl at the person who hit Kit if he saw them again," Rory said.

"That won't prove for sure that person hurt him though."

"Of course not, but it's a start. If we find someone we can always check them out and see if they could have been anywhere near that alley when Kit was attacked."

The dog seemed to know and like everyone they met. As they passed by Lance, who was handing out brochures for the gym, he bent down to pet the dog who wagged his tail in delight. They thought they found a suspect when Buddy growled at a passerby, but it turned out to be the same man the dog had considered a threat to Bethany's children.

At the entrance to the lot where the adult amateurs' work was on display, they passed a mime pretending to walk a dog.

"None of the pieces we've looked at so far have 3D effects like Dawn wanted us to see. They must be in a different part of the festival," Liz said when they finished admiring the pieces in the lot.

Rory consulted her brochure. "It says here the 3D illusionistic paintings are all on the pier. Those must be the ones she was talking about. Let's head there next."

Buddy strained at the leash as they navigated their way through the crowd to the bottom of the hill, stopping in front of the bandstand, where Tripp was listening to the music.

"Is that Buddy?" He leaned down to pat the dog, who barked his approval. "I didn't know you were taking care of him. I thought you told me he was with a family."

Rory smiled. "He is. We thought we'd give them a break and take him for a walk. We're headed to see the art on the pier. Do you want to come with us?"

Tripp checked the time on his watch. "I wish I could, but I

have to get to work. I looked at the pieces earlier. They're pretty amazing." He nodded toward the bandage on Rory's arm. "Skating injury?"

"Something like that."

"I wish I could stay longer, but I better be off." He patted the dog on the head and headed up the hill.

Rory and Liz made their way along the pier that had been transformed into a colorful pastel pathway filled with eight foot by eight foot sections of sidewalk art. They passed by reproductions of famous paintings, a bunny popping out of a hole and a scene from Disney's *The Lion King* until, halfway down, they reached a reproduction of Leonardo da Vinci's *Mona Lisa* done in black and white chalk. Veronica stood on a bench, snapping photos of the piece from above. She hopped down when she saw the two of them.

"Doing an article for the paper?" Rory asked.

The reporter nodded as she wrote the name of the artist on a notepad. "I got to take pictures of some of the pieces while the artists were creating them. It was eye opening." She looked around as if checking to see who was nearby, then moved closer to them. "No word yet from my army, but they're still asking around."

Liz looked at the other two, a question in her eyes.

"That's what Veronica calls her informants who give her tips on what's going on around town," Rory said. "She asked them to see if anyone saw anything in the area where Kit was attacked."

"Oh," Liz said. "Sort of like what we're doing now with Buddy."

Veronica frowned in puzzlement. "How's Buddy helping you?"

"We figure he was with Kit when he was hit and might react if he sees the person again. Since Kit's still unconscious and can't tell us anything, we thought maybe Buddy could. We're walking around the festival to see if he reacts to anyone. So far no luck."

"Good idea." Veronica repositioned her tote bag on her shoulder. "I'm off. You should check out the rest of the paintings on the pier. You have to view them from the proper angle though. Otherwise, they look distorted. There's one that Dawn Ogden did of a waterfall I particularly like."

While the reporter headed up the street, the other two continued down the pier. Rory jumped when she saw an alligator emerging from the pavement, then laughed at herself when she remembered it was only a picture. At the end, they found Dawn sitting on a bench by the piece she'd drawn.

Rory experienced a slight sense of dizziness when she stood in front of the depiction of a waterfall. Even though she knew the pavement was flat, she felt she was looking into a deep hole and if she took a step forward, she would go over the edge and plunge down the falls. "How long did that take you?"

"I started yesterday and finished at noon today," Dawn said. "Any news?"

"Nothing solid to report," Rory said. "We're doing everything we can."

After Dawn explained some of the techniques she used, Rory and Liz headed back toward their rendezvous point with Bethany and her family.

"I guess whoever hit Kit isn't here today," Liz said as they walked the dog back up the hill.

"Guess not," Rory said. Disappointed their experiment hadn't worked, they handed Buddy over to Bethany and her family and said goodbye. Rory spent the walk home trying to think of some other way to figure out who had attacked Kit.

Chapter 20

"Now that you've seen what's possible, let's get started on our own trompe l'oeil project. Remember, highlights and shadows are both important in creating a believable three-dimensional illusion," Dawn said to the students in her Sunday afternoon class. Five faces stared at the painting teacher from five separate windows on her computer screen.

In addition to Teresa and Liz, three other women watched their first lesson in the online course from the comfort of their own homes. Rory sat beside Dawn ready to help in case there were problems with the software.

"You should have all prepped your surface, traced on the pattern and basecoated the entire design area in white." The teacher put up a photo of a wooden stool on the display. A cherry pie was painted on its seat. "This is what your finished piece will look like at the end of the six-week course. You don't have to paint the pie on a stool, of course. Any round object will do."

A knock sounded on the front door. Dawn looked up briefly, mouthed "ignore it" to Rory and kept on talking. Another knock, louder this time.

Dawn sighed. "Hold on a minute, class." She turned to Rory. "Could you get that for me and tell them to come back later?"

Rory nodded and answered the front door while the painting teacher continued with her class. On the porch she found Detective Green with three uniformed officers standing behind him.

"Rory. Didn't expect to see you here. Is Ms. Ogden home?"

"She's teaching a class right now. Can you come back later?"

"I need to speak with her *now*."

From the serious look on his face, Rory knew better than to argue. "Come in." She led the way into the dining room where Dawn was answering a student's question about shading. She turned in her chair and looked up, an annoyed expression on her face.

"Sorry, he said it was important," Rory said.

"I'm in the middle of class. Can't it wait?"

"Afraid not." He handed her a piece of paper. "This is a search warrant. You'll need to stop what you're doing and wait in the living room while we conduct our search."

Dawn stared at the warrant as if she couldn't believe what she was reading. "But why? I've told you everything I know. There's nothing of interest to you here."

He merely raised an eyebrow and nodded toward the computer screen, where five faces looked on in confusion. "We'll need to look at that computer too."

Dawn nodded, a resigned looked on her face. She turned to her students. "I'm afraid something's come up. I'm going to have to cut this class short."

Five voices talked all at once, asking what was going on. She silenced them with a raised hand. "I'm sorry. It can't be helped. I'll contact you about rescheduling as soon as I can. In the meantime, look over my instructions and practice."

One by one the windows disappeared from the screen until only Liz's worried face was left. "What's going on, Rory?" she said.

"I'm not sure. The police are here. It looks serious." Rory glanced at the detective, who looked on impatiently. "I'd better go. I'll call you later."

Dawn followed an officer into the living room while Rory bent over the keyboard and shut down the program. After she was done, she joined Dawn on the couch where they sat side by side, silently waiting for the detective to return. A uniformed officer stood near the only door out of the room, making sure they stayed put, while others searched the house. When Detective Green walked into the room, Dawn reached out her hand and Rory gave it a reassuring squeeze.

He held up a plastic bag in front of Rory. "Do you recognize this?"

She studied the gold charm bracelet inside the bag. "It looks like Willow's."

"Are you sure?"

"I recognize several of the charms. I'm as sure as I can be that it's the one she always wore." She cast a puzzled glance at the woman who sat beside her on the sofa.

Dawn folded her hands in her lap and stared down at the floor.

The detective turned toward her. "What are you doing with Ms. Bingen's bracelet?"

"It's not Willow's, it's mine," she said to her hands, then looked up and met his questioning gaze. "That's all I'm saying. I'd like a lawyer now."

As the detective led her away, she looked over at Rory. "Your father, could you call him for me?"

Rory nodded, drew her cell phone out of the pocket of her jeans and dialed her parents' number.

Rory sat in the lobby of the Vista Beach police station, flipping through her email on her phone while she waited for her father to finish talking with Dawn. She was so preoccupied with thoughts of the bracelet the police had found, she had to read one message from a client three times before the words finally registered. She'd been waiting an hour when a shadow fell over her. She looked up to find her father standing next to her chair.

"She wants to see you," he said.

Rory nodded and, without saying a word, followed him into an interview room, where Dawn sat with her hands clasped on the table in front of her. Her eyes brightened when they entered the room. Rory sat on the other side of the table next to her father and waited for Dawn to speak.

Dawn looked down at her hands and cleared her throat. "Thank you for coming. I'm sure you have a lot of questions." She looked at Swan. "Can I talk to her alone, please?"

He nodded and closed the door behind them, leaving the two women by themselves in the room.

"I need to tell you something important." Dawn stopped, as if unsure how to put into words what she wanted to say.

Rory placed a hand over Dawn's. "Whatever it is, you can tell me. I won't judge you. I promise."

"Willow was my mother."

Rory drew back her hand and sat back in her chair, digesting the unexpected news. "Your mother? Should you be telling me this? I'm not your lawyer. Nothing you say to me is confidential."

"I'm not telling you anything the police don't already know."

"What if they ask me to testify?"

"It's okay. Don't worry about it."

"You said Willow was your mother?"

"Mother is too strong a word for it. She gave birth to me, then decided she didn't want me or my brother and left us when I was six and he was four. You grow up fast after something like that. Our father raised us by himself. He tried, but he wasn't the best at keeping house. I ended up taking care of everyone." Dawn looked across the table at Rory, bitterness written all over her face.

"You never heard from her after she left?"

"Not once. She completely cut ties with us. No birthday cards, no presents. Nothing. She might as well have been dead. Then she showed up in town six months ago. I didn't even know who she was. Not until she told me two days before she died."

"You didn't recognize her?"

"I was young when she left, and my dad destroyed any pictures of her."

"All of them?"

"Every single one. She was only a vague memory to me. An

unpleasant one. She didn't even have the same name. I guess the name Laura didn't express her inner being or something. I hear she bought her new one from a homeless woman."

"Do the police know her real name now?"

Dawn nodded. "I told them."

"She didn't tell you who she was right away?"

"No. She took a class from me. We even had dinner once or twice. She didn't say anything about being my mother until one day, she confessed. I didn't believe her at first."

"What convinced you?"

"The bracelet."

"The one the police have?"

Dawn nodded. "My mother gave me one just like it. That's the one the police found, not Willow's. I don't know why I kept it all these years." She looked straight ahead as if looking for answers in the marks on the wall. "I guess I wanted to keep some connection to her."

"If it's a duplicate, you can tell the police that."

"I can't prove it. My dad's long gone and my brother was too young at the time to remember it."

Rory cast her mind back to the day she found Willow's body and the charm found on the floor. "The police found a charm beside Willow. It must have come from her bracelet. A sun. If it's not missing from your bracelet, won't that prove it's yours and not hers?"

"That won't help. Hers had a sun, mine a moon. Otherwise, they're identical. The police will say I had a sun on mine too. After all these years, I have no proof the bracelets were different."

"I'm confused. Didn't you notice it on Willow's wrist? Every time I saw her, she had it on."

"She never wore it to my class or any other time I saw her. I guess she was afraid I would recognize it before she was ready to tell me who she was."

"What happened the night she died?" Rory asked.

"We had that argument during the software test. You were

there. She wanted me to forgive her, to come back into my life."

"So what you told me about the argument was a lie then? How do you expect me to help you if you lie?"

"I'm sorry about that. I just couldn't tell you."

"Why after so many years did she want to come back into your life now?"

"I have no idea. But I couldn't, I just couldn't."

Rory nodded in understanding. If her own birth parents were alive, she didn't think she could forgive them after everything they had done.

"She called me and left a message. Said she was going to contact my brother. Offered me money to spend time with her. Bribing me to spend time with her! I was so mad I went to see her later that night. I pounded on the front door, but she didn't answer. There was music playing inside so I knew she was home."

"A neighbor saw you."

"That's right. Then I went around to the back like I told you before and found her like...that." Dawn looked at Rory pleadingly. "I may have hated her, but I didn't kill her. You have to believe me."

"That's why you didn't want to give your DNA to the police."

Dawn nodded. "I was afraid they would find out we were related. I already had so many marks against me."

Rory reviewed them in her mind: the argument earlier in the day, how Dawn had been seen at Willow's house visibly upset and how she'd found the body and not told the police.

"I thought if I didn't give them my DNA, no one would find out she was my mother."

"How did they, then?"

"Her will. She named me and my brother in it, said I was her daughter. I didn't know she had a will or even that she had money for anyone to inherit."

Rory leaned forward and set her arms on the table. "Now the police think you killed her for her money. How much are we talking about?"

"Half a million."

Rory whistled. "That's a lot. Does anyone else inherit?"

"Her business partner gets Beach Healing, plus the building it's in, and her boyfriend, Lance, gets a small bequest, but the bulk goes to me and my brother. I could use the money, believe me, but I didn't kill her for it."

"You've told my dad all this?"

"He knows. I wanted you to know too, so you would understand why I lied to you." Dawn reached out for Rory's hand. "Will you help me prove I didn't do it?"

"My dad's on your case now. He'll do everything he can."

"I'm not sure it'll be enough."

Rory stood up. "I'll think about it."

When she exited the room, she found her father waiting for her.

"Can you get her out on bail?" she said.

"I'll do my best, but chances are they won't let her out."

"We have to help her."

"We? Your mother told me Dawn asked you to investigate. It's not a good idea." Swan looked at his daughter, a stern expression on his face. "I know she helped out when your mother was sick, but it's too dangerous. Let the police do their job."

"I have to."

He studied her. "I know better than to argue with you. Too bad I can't ground you anymore." He looked at Detective Green, who was standing off to one side. "Look out for her."

The detective nodded and didn't speak until Swan had walked away. "He just wants what every father wants, to keep his daughter safe."

"I know."

"Come with me," he said. "I need your help."

Chapter 21

Five girls filed into the room behind the glass, all teens, all wearing similar clothes, all fitting the description Rory had given to the police of the girl she saw running from her mother's store.

"Take your time," Detective Green said to Rory as she studied each one, all of them staring straight ahead with blank, almost bored, expressions on their faces.

Her gaze zeroed in on the one in the center. "Number three," she said.

When the detective asked the girl to step forward, her expression turned from one of boredom to fright.

Rory stepped closer to the glass and studied her. "Could I see her arms?"

At the detective's direction, number three pushed up the sleeves on her hoodie, revealing a long scar on her right forearm.

"Is it her?" he asked.

Rory nodded. "I'm positive. It's number three. She's the one I chased and one of the two I saw at Willow's house."

Detective Green dismissed the rest of the lineup. Rory and her mother, who had walked into the police station moments before, studied the black and white monitor as an officer escorted the girl Rory had identified into the interrogation room. The sweatshirt and jeans the teen was wearing hung loosely on her body. She appeared thin, too thin, almost emaciated.

"She's just a baby," Arika said.

"How old do you think she is?" Rory asked her mother.

"Fourteen, fifteen. I doubt she's any older than that."

They watched as the detective poked his head in the door of the interrogation room. "You hungry?"

The girl looked up and nodded.

A short time later, he returned with a sandwich, a banana and a can of soda. "Sorry, this is all we have. I can get you something else if you want."

The girl's eyes lit up at the sight of the food. "No, this is okay." She eagerly reached for the sandwich and started wolfing it down as if she hadn't eaten for a week.

He waited patiently for her to finish. When she pushed the empty plate across the table and thanked him, he opened a file folder and consulted the papers inside.

"Can you tell me your name?" he asked. "I'd like to know what to call you."

She stared at him for a moment as if deciding whether to trust him. "Lexie," the girl finally said.

"You live around here, Lexie?"

She shrugged, curled one leg under the other and began swinging her free leg back and forth.

"What about your family? They must be looking for you."

Lexie set both legs on the floor, pushed her shoulders back and sat up straight. "I'm eighteen."

"Eighteen?" The doubt was evident in the detective's voice. He tapped his finger on a piece of paper in the folder. "It says here you're fifteen and you have a habit of running away from foster homes."

She crossed her arms and slumped back in her chair. "If you know that, why'd you bother to ask? Is that why I'm here? Because I ran away? They don't want me anymore."

"Did they do that to you?" He gestured toward the mark on her arm.

She pulled her sleeve down until it covered the scar. "I'm not going back."

Detective Green cocked his head and studied her before continuing. "Do you like art? I went to the chalk festival yesterday. It was pretty interesting. Did you get a chance to see it?"

Her eyes lit up for a moment at the mention of the festival. "I wanted to go, but my friend wouldn't let me after—I couldn't go." A dullness crept back into her eyes.

"I have a friend who's an artist. Her mother owns Arika's Scrap 'n Paint on Main Street. Do you know it?"

Lexie turned pale and bowed her head. "I'm sorry. I'll give the paint back. I promise."

"So you admit you took it?" the detective said in his most comforting voice.

She stared down at the floor and began to swing one of her legs back and forth again.

"She's scared," Rory whispered to her mother.

"Wouldn't you be?" Arika whispered back.

"I like to draw and paint. It's my favorite thing to do in the whole world," Lexie finally said.

"I see. So that's why you took the bottles of paint." He nodded his head in understanding. "What about the SD card? The one you took from a house on Seagull Lane."

"Wasn't me." She looked up at him and shook her head vehemently. "I don't know anything about any camera."

"I didn't say what the card was from. How did you know it came from a camera?" He leaned back in his chair.

"I don't know what you're talking about. It wasn't me!"

"I have a witness who identified you as being in the house. You were with someone. Who was it?" the detective continued.

She crossed her arms tighter and slumped farther down in her seat. "I didn't take anything."

"Did you know a woman was killed there? In that house."

Lexie gave him a startled look. "They never said—"

"They? Did someone hire you to steal that card?"

She studied him for a moment, then nodded her head. "Someone hired Pe—my friend to get it. Gave him enough money so we could get a room for the night and promised more. Never said anything about a murder."

"Did they tell you why they wanted the card?"

She shook her head. "Didn't ask. Said the place would be empty. Gave us a key. Told us where to find the camera and to go there at night, but Pe—my friend—didn't want to do it then. So we went earlier. There was someone else there. We heard them, but I didn't get a good look. We got out of there as fast as we could."

"What were you supposed to do with the card?"

"Put it in a plastic bag and drop it in a trashcan not far from that hotel downtown, the fancy new one. I was on my way there when I saw the art supplies."

"You took the card on Wednesday, but didn't drop it off until Friday. That's two days. Why didn't you deliver it earlier?"

"They gave us time in case we couldn't get in the house right away. And they wanted to do the exchange some place where it was crowded. My friend was supposed to handle it, but he wouldn't do it. Got scared when someone saw us at the house, I guess."

"Where is this friend now?"

"Don't know. He took off somewhere this morning and left me behind."

"What about the key?"

"He took it with him. Probably threw it away."

"You keep on saying they. Did more than one person hire you?" Detective Green asked.

"I don't know. I don't know anything about it."

"Then how were you hired?"

"We were near that bar on Main that has karaoke, seeing if someone would give us their change. I was by the front entrance, my friend was near the back. Somebody walks up to my friend and asks if he wants to make some money. I mean, real money. It was more than we'd seen in a long time so Pete went for it. When he told me, I didn't see any harm in it. No one was going to get hurt. It was only a camera card. That's all I know."

He placed a photo on the table.

"Do you remember seeing him there?"

Lexie leaned forward and studied the picture. "I don't know. There were a lot of people." She looked at her hands. "Can I go now?"

"You've been a big help, Lexie, but I'm afraid you'll have to wait here. Someone from Social Services will be in to talk with you soon." He stood up and walked toward the door.

"Do I have to go back to my last home? They're bad people."

His hand on the doorknob, Detective Green turned and looked at her sympathetically. "I can't make any promises, but I'll talk to your case worker."

As he closed the door to the interrogation room, Rory looked at her mother. "Why would she do that, steal the paint when she already had stolen property on her? It just drew attention to herself."

"She's young. Kids her age don't always make the best choices," Arika said.

As soon as the detective joined them, Arika turned to him. "I'm not pressing any charges against her. It was only a few bottles of paint, hardly worth anything."

Rory nodded toward the girl waiting in the interrogation room. "What's going to happen to her?"

"We'll probably let her walk on stealing the card. There's nothing more to be learned there. Social Services will find her a new home, but she's run away so many times, chances are she'll be back on the streets again soon."

"Was that Lance's picture you showed her?"

He nodded. "I'll question him again, but without a witness I probably won't get anywhere."

On her way home, Rory thought about Lexie and what she said about the person who'd hired them. She still thought it was Lance, but without a description, they needed proof. As soon as she pulled into her driveway, Rory phoned Liz. "You up for some karaoke tonight?"

Chapter 22

"I thought you said there was going to be karaoke." A disappointed look on her face, Liz stared at the stage where a local band was setting up. "I was looking forward to showing off our version of 'I Got You Babe' for the guys. I even practiced in the car on the way over."

"I know, I was there. We'll save it for some other time." Rory pointed to a table in the middle of the room. "There they are."

The two wended their way through the tables to where Tripp and Doug sat talking over bottles of beer. Tripp pulled out a chair for Rory. Liz frowned at Doug when she had to pull out her own. While the two men went to the bar to get their drinks, Rory looked around at the Sunday evening crowd celebrating the end of the summer festival.

"They must be band groupies." Liz pointed to a table next to the stage filled with men and women wearing t-shirts with the band's logo on them. "The ones who are setting up, they won the Battle of the Bands today. I only caught the tail end. Wouldn't have been able to do that if class hadn't been shortened. When do you think Dawn's going to reschedule it for?"

"I don't know if she'll be able to reschedule at all. Dad's going to try and get her out on bail, but I don't know if it's possible since they arrested her for murder." Rory nodded toward a group of women on the far side of the bar. "Speaking of fans. Those are some of the women I saw at the gym who were watching Lance. That's

Marcia on the left and Evelyn next to her. If they're here, maybe he frequents the place too."

"They go wherever he goes? That seems a little too stalkerish to me." Liz leaned closer to Rory and spoke in a hushed tone. "Do you think it was Lance who hired that girl to get the SD card?"

"That's what we're here to find out. See if anyone saw him here last Monday."

"Even if those women know something, how are we going to get the information out of them?" Liz's eyes opened wide. "I know! We'll get one of the guys to go over and charm them."

Tripp placed a glass of Pinot Grigio in front of Rory. "What are you two whispering about?"

"Men, of course." Liz smiled as Doug placed an apple martini in front of her.

When Doug sat down, he reached toward the floor and placed a small cardboard box on the table. "Okay, everyone, I'm declaring this a no-cell-phone night. No calls, no texts, no surfing the web while we're here. Put your phone in the box and be sure to turn it off first."

Rory looked at him in surprise. "You two are doctors. Don't you have to be near a phone at all times?"

"Neither of us are on call tonight," Tripp said.

Liz hugged her purse to her chest. "No phone? What if I have a client emergency?"

"You sell real estate. Your clients will survive." Rory turned her phone off and placed it in the box. "Come on, it's just for a few hours. You can handle that."

Liz reluctantly took her phone out of her purse and added it to the others. "If I have withdrawal symptoms it's all your fault."

Once everyone's phone was turned off and in the box, Doug called a waitress over and asked her to put it somewhere for safekeeping. The woman wrote his name on the side and took it away as if she got the request all the time.

"That way no one's tempted," he said to the group.

After they talked for a while, Liz laid a hand on Doug's arm and gave him her brightest smile. "Could you do me a teeny tiny favor? See that group of women over there?" She nodded toward Lance's fans. "Could you go over and see if they've ever seen Lance here?"

He glanced over at the group. "You two still looking into him?"

Tripp frowned. "That's the boyfriend of the woman who died, right? The one who was murdered near Rory's place. Is that why we're here? Are you two still investigating? I thought they arrested someone for that."

"I'm not convinced Dawn did it, and I don't like seeing innocent people being accused of crimes they didn't commit." Rory looked down at her glass of wine. "I know what that feels like." She told the two men about someone hiring a couple homeless teens to get the SD card from the camera in Willow's house.

"You think Lance paid them?" Tripp sipped his beer and studied her for a moment. "What is it you want to know?"

"If Lance ever comes here, and if he does, if he was here last Monday. And if they saw him with anyone."

"And the kids. Did they see the kids outside and did they see him with the boy?" Liz added. "Don't forget that."

"Got it. Here I go into the belly of the beast. Wish me luck." Tripp took a swallow of his beer and headed toward the gaggle of women.

The band started playing, filling the room with music so loud people had to shout in order to be heard above it. Rory watched her date approach the table and buy the four women a round of drinks. Envy clutched at her belly when he leaned close to each of them and talked. She told herself she shouldn't be so possessive. After all, they barely knew each other. They'd been on too few dates for her to be jealous. Besides, she was the one who wanted the information. And the music was so loud he had to lean close to the women in order to be understood. But no matter how she reasoned with herself, she still felt a twinge of jealousy.

A long half hour later, Tripp returned to their table and sat down. "That was interesting and a little frightening."

Liz leaned forward. "What did they say?"

"Amazing what people will tell you when they've had too much to drink. He was here on Monday all right. Drowning his sorrows in whiskey."

"Who did he talk to?" Rory asked.

"They didn't see him with anyone in particular. He sat over in that corner of the bar." Tripp indicated a table in the back near the restrooms. "Guess he was so drunk, he was talking to himself. One of the girls approached him to make sure he was okay, but he waved her away."

"Did she hear anything he said?"

"She said he mumbled 'have to get it before they find it' or something like that. Could have been talking about the camera, I suppose. They also said he went outside for a while, then came back. No one knew what he did out there."

"What about the teens? Did they say anything about them?" Liz asked.

"They remembered seeing a girl outside the front entrance, panhandling when they went inside. She wasn't there when they left."

"Too bad no one followed him outside," Liz said. "Maybe he was in here figuring out what to do about the camera, remembered the kids and hatched his plan."

"Too bad we can't prove it," Rory said. "There might be security cameras in the area. Did any of you notice any when you came in?"

They all shook their heads.

Tripp stood up. "Now I'm curious. I'll go check. Be right back."

He shouldered his way through the crowd to the front entrance, returning less than five minutes later. "Didn't see any, but it was kind of dark."

"Did you check the alley?" Rory asked.

"Nothing at either entrance."

"That's that, then," Doug said.

"Maybe not. There was an article recently on Vista Beach

Confidential about some people downtown complaining about all the private security cameras in the area. A woman said one was even pointed right at her apartment, one of those that's above a business. I don't remember the exact area or the name of the business. Maybe it's around here. We could read the article and find out." Liz reached her hand into her purse, but it came out empty-handed. "Oh, right, no phones."

"It can wait. You can look it up later." Doug patted her hand.

As they listened to the band, all Rory could think about was the article Liz had mentioned. She itched to know the details. When she couldn't take it any longer, she excused herself and made her way through the crowd toward the restroom. She glanced behind her to make sure no one at her table was watching and took a detour to the bar where she found the waitress Doug had given the box to.

"Where did you put the box of phones from our table?" she whispered to the woman.

"I'm not supposed to give you your phone unless you're leaving," she said, an amused expression on her face.

"Please, I just want to check something."

"So you're leaving then?"

Rory bobbed her head up and down. "That's right. I'm leaving."

The waitress walked around the end of the bar and reached under the counter. She held the box out to Rory. "Here you go. If asked, I'll deny everything."

Rory looked inside the box, finding only three cell phones inside, none of them hers. "It's not here." Panic welled up inside her. "Mine's not here. Are you sure this is the right box?"

The waitress looked at the writing on the side. "It's the only one anyone's given me, and it has Doug written on it. That's the name of the guy at your table, right? Maybe your phone fell out when I put the box under the counter."

The bartender placed some drinks on the tray on the bar.

"I'm sorry," she said. "I'm sure it's around somewhere. I'll look for it after I deliver this order." She put the box back under the counter and headed to the other side of the room.

Rory fretted about her missing phone as she stood in line for the restroom. When she passed by the bar on her way back to the table, the waitress stopped her. "I found it. It must have fallen out of the box." She surreptitiously handed Rory the phone. After making sure no one was watching her, Rory stepped to the side and looked up the article on VBC. As soon as she read it, she put her cell back in the box and headed back to her friends.

Rory wrote something on a napkin and handed it to Liz under the table.

"That's disappointing," Liz whispered. "Nowhere near here, huh? You know, the police department has a voluntary program where people register their cameras. You must have heard about it. If a crime happens, the police know where they might get information."

"What about the guy you sold that house to in the department? Can he tell you anything?"

"Maybe. I'll ask him about the cameras tomorrow. There might be some around here."

Rory took the napkin from Liz and crumpled it up. She hoped they would find a camera nearby that could show them for sure who had hired the two kids. That might bring them a little closer to discovering Willow's murderer and clearing Dawn's name.

Chapter 23

A brown blur raced out the front door onto the lawn, then made a sudden left and disappeared into the bushes next door.

"Sekhmet!" Rory called after the escaping cat, hoping for an answering meow, but all she heard was the twittering of a bird in a nearby tree.

"Teach me to leave the door open," she mumbled to herself as she stepped out onto the front porch, being sure to close the door behind her. The Monday morning sun shone down on her as she walked toward the cat's former home. She called out the Abyssinian's name and looked under every bush she passed by.

Rory had barely reached the edge of Willow's property when a police car pulled into the driveway. Chief Marshall emerged from the driver's side, looking as tired and worn out as she had ever seen him. He hitched his pants over his noticeably smaller paunch and began taking down the yellow crime scene tape.

He was halfway across the lawn when he faltered and put a hand to his head. He recovered and took a step forward, then the tape slipped out of his hands and he crumpled to the ground.

Rory raced forward and knelt down on the grass beside him. "Chief, are you okay?"

He opened his eyes and stared at her, confusion written all over his face. "What happened? Where am I?"

"You fainted. You're on the lawn in front of Willow's house—your house. Are you okay?"

"I think so." He struggled and finally managed to sit up. As if suddenly aware of his surroundings, he said, "Help me up. I don't want anyone to see me this way."

Rory helped him to his feet. When he was standing once again, he shook off her hand. "Thank you."

She stood uncertainly by his side. He looked so pale she was afraid he was going to faint again. "I think I should call someone." She pulled her cell phone out of the pocket of her jeans.

"No!" the chief bellowed, then seemed to realize how loud his voice had become. "Sorry, didn't mean to shout. Go home. I'll be fine."

"I don't like the idea of you being by yourself right now."

"I said I'll be fine!" When he bent down to pick up the end of the crime scene tape, he staggered as if dizzy.

Rory crossed her arms in front of her chest. "No, you're not. You need to rest. Let me help you into the house."

"Okay, if it'll make you go away." The chief leaned on her as they walked up the path to the front door. When he fumbled with the keys, she took them out of his hands and unlocked the door. As soon as he was resting on the sofa, she walked to the kitchen in the back of the house to get him some water. The place smelled clean. She glanced down at the wood floor, happy to see blood no longer decorated its surface. She dialed Detective Green's number and explained the situation to him.

After getting an "I'll be right there" from him, she returned to the living room.

"Here. Drink this."

Rory handed the chief a glass of water and sat down on a chair facing him.

He took a sip and eyed her. "What were you doing here anyway?"

"Looking for Sekhmet. She raced out the door of my house. I figured she came back here. What about you? Can't one of your officers take down the tape? Doesn't seem like a job for the chief of police."

"I'm going to put Willow's things in storage. I wanted to get an idea of how much there was."

"I thought you came over all the time," Rory blurted out. "At least that's what I heard."

"From who? That busybody next door?" He jerked his head toward Mrs. Griswold's house. "Does everyone think I was in a romantic relationship with Willow?"

"Wouldn't blame you if you were."

A knock on the front door cut off any further conversation. Rory answered it and let Detective Green inside. "I'll let you two talk."

She went into the adjoining room, shutting the door behind her, and leaned against the door and listened.

"What's going on, Chief?"

"I told her not to call anyone. I should have known I couldn't trust her."

"You collapsed outside. Of course she's going to call someone. Any decent person would. You need to take some time off." The exasperation was evident in the detective's voice.

"Martin, I'm the chief of police. I can't be seen as weak."

"It's cancer, for God's sake. People will understand if you take some time off."

"I told you before, I don't want anyone to know. Especially the citizens of this city. They need to believe their police chief is able to protect them."

"At least take better care of yourself. Slow down a little."

"I'm doing everything my doctor says. That herbal remedy Willow gave me has helped a lot. It's looking much better for me. I'm just a little tired right now."

So that's why the chief came over to the house so often, Rory thought. Willow was seeing him there so no one would know he was sick.

As she listened to the rest of the conversation, her gaze rested on a stack of opened mail on a nearby table. She rifled through it, pausing when she came to an envelope from a local bank. She dropped the rest of the mail back on the table, then glanced toward the closed door before opening the envelope and looking over the bank statement. The checking account had a large balance, but none of the deposits listed were big enough to suggest blackmail payments.

The door between the living room and dining room swung open, almost hitting her in the face.

Rory put her hand behind her back so Detective Green couldn't see the letter she was holding.

He raised an eyebrow at her. "I've got it from here. You can go home now."

She nodded and, as soon as his back was turned, dropped the envelope back on the top of the stack of mail.

When Rory got back to her house, she spotted an unfamiliar man dressed in a suit coming down her front steps. As soon as he saw her, he stopped at the bottom and waited.

"Can I help you?" she said as she walked across the grass toward him.

"Is Teresa here?" he asked. "I'm Trent, her husband."

"She's with a client, but I expect she'll be back soon. Would you like to come inside and wait for her?" Rory opened the door and pointed him toward the couch in the living room. After getting a glass of water for her guest, she sat down in the chair facing him.

Trent took a sip and set the glass down on the coffee table. "Thank you for letting my wife stay here."

Rory nodded and waited for him to continue.

"I don't know how much she's told you about our...disagreement, but I want her to come back home. The kids miss her. I miss her." He fiddled with his glass, turning it around on the coaster.

"She'll be glad to hear that."

He looked up at Rory, relief in his eyes. "Will she?"

"Have you talked to her recently?"

"A few phone calls, none of them pleasant. She's been stopping by the house every night, parking on the street and sitting in her car. I thought she would come in, but she never made a move to walk up the path or knock on the door. I was so mad at her I let her sit there."

"You're sure it was her?"

"Positive."

"And she's been doing this for how long?"

"Every night for the past two weeks. Comes by around nine thirty, leaves at midnight when the lights go out."

Rory made some mental calculations. That meant Teresa had a potential alibi for the night Willow died. "That includes the Friday before last, right? You're sure?"

"That's right. Why are you interested in that day?"

"No particular reason."

Trent eyed her curiously, then glanced at his watch. "I can't wait any longer. Would you let her know I stopped by? Maybe I could leave a note?"

After he'd written the note, Rory placed it on the bed in the guest bedroom where Teresa would be sure to see it.

With Liz by her side, Rory jogged north along the path reserved for walkers and joggers that paralleled the ocean, taking one step for every two the much shorter woman took. On the bike path below them, a pack of helmeted bikers raced by going in the opposite direction.

Liz led the way around a mother pushing a stroller, returning to the right side of the cement path before they encountered a group of midday joggers coming toward them. "So Lance was wrong. Chief M wasn't having an affair with Willow after all."

"Doesn't look like it. Lance had nothing to worry about, at least from the chief."

"Do you think he's going to be okay? I can't imagine the city without him."

"The chief? I don't know. He says he feels better after the treatments Willow was giving him, but he hasn't given up on chemo. Who knows which is helping more." Rory stopped on the right side of the path, bent at the waist and put her hands on her knees. "I'm tired. Why are you making me do this again?"

Liz jogged in place next to her friend. "I've been eating too many of Teresa's goodies. I'm getting fluffy. Got to get rid of a little weight. At least it's not hot anymore."

Rory straightened up and started walking. "And you're dragging me along because...?"

"You've been eating them too."

"We could just stop eating the cookies. Seems like a much easier solution."

"Like that's going to happen. They're too good."

"We may not have to worry about them for too much longer. Trent stopped by the house. He wants to see if he can work things out with Teresa. He told me she was sitting in her car outside their house at the time Willow was killed."

"You actually asked him for her alibi?" Liz stared open-mouthed at her friend.

"Nothing as direct as that. I didn't tell him I was asking for an alibi. He volunteered that she's been sitting outside their house every evening for the past two weeks. I made sure he confirmed that included the night Willow died."

"I'm glad to hear she has an alibi. I really love those cookies. When's she moving back home?"

"She's not...yet. She's letting him stew a while. At least that's what she told me."

"I hope they work it out. Race you to the McMansion at the next street. Loser buys lunch." The words were barely out of her mouth before Liz took off down the path. When she crossed the imaginary finish line, she raised her arms above her head in triumph. She walked back and forth to cool down until Rory reached her.

"Okay, Flash, you win. Where are we going to eat?"

Liz pointed to a cafe at the top of the hill.

Rory sniffed her t-shirt.

"Do you think we're presentable enough for a sit-down restaurant?"

"A lot of bikers stop there. They have to smell worse than we do. The place has an outdoor seating area." Liz shielded her eyes from the summer sun and looked up at the restaurant. "I see a couple of them on the patio right now. Come on!" She sprinted up the hill as if she had just started exercising.

Holding her side, Rory followed at a walking pace. By the time she got to the cafe, Liz was sitting at a table on the patio studying a menu.

"Took you long enough. I'm having the roasted veggie quesadilla. After all that exercise, I'm starving."

Rory plopped down in the chair opposite her friend and studied the chalkboard that listed the lunch specials. "It's the avocado burger for me."

After they ordered, Liz said, "I checked with my contact at the police station. No cameras near the bar. At least none registered with the city. I guess we'll never have confirmation Lance was the one who hired those two kids to get the camera card. Of course, the murder and the camera don't have to be related."

Rory took a sip of her diet Coke. "What do you mean?"

"Lance could have planted the camera to try to catch Wispy Willow having an affair and not wanted the police to find it. It would make him look guilty. You said you saw him looking at that shelf right after Willow died. He was probably looking for it then and you interrupted him."

"He did have a lame excuse about looking for one of Sekhmet's toys, which he still hasn't given to me, by the way." Rory waited while the waiter set down their plates before continuing. "On the other hand, Lance could be the murderer and he was covering his tracks. Maybe Dawn arrived before he had a chance to take it away with him."

"We don't know if he has an alibi yet. I'll see what I can find out." Liz took a sip of her iced tea. "Did you ever find Sekhmet?"

"She was at the back door waiting for me when I got home."

"Besides Luscious Lance, what other suspects do we have?"

"Let's see." Rory broke open a packet of crayons that was on the table and began writing names and motives on the back side of her paper placemat. "There's Monica. Willow's death means she won't lose her store. Marcia and Lance's other fans. That's jealousy. Her partner, Dr. Wagner. Then there's the possibility we're wrong about the camera and Willow was blackmailing someone. I saw a bank statement at her house. The balance in the account was huge, but there were no large deposits."

"Doesn't prove anything. She could have another account somewhere. I asked around, but no one's heard any rumors about blackmail."

"I can't think of anything else, can you?"

"You can't forget Dawn. There's a lot of evidence against her. Is she still in jail?" Liz asked.

"Dad couldn't get her out on bail. I visited her this morning. She's beginning to lose hope."

"You're doing everything you can."

For the rest of the lunch, they talked about the trompe l'oeil project they were both working on. When Rory glanced at her cell phone to check the time, the screen indicated she had a new message. "Looks like I have voicemail. Guess I missed a call."

"Voicemail? I don't know why anyone bothers with it anymore. No one checks it. Texting's the thing." Liz put her napkin on her empty plate and sat back in her chair.

"I do. Or at least I usually do. I've been so busy I forgot to check to see if I missed any calls." Rory listened to the message. "Kit's awake and wants to talk with me. His nurse left the message when we were at the bar last night, and I didn't have my phone by me. Visiting hours are still going on."

Liz motioned toward the patio exit. "Go. See what he wants to talk to you about. I'll take care of the check."

"But you won fair and square. It was supposed to be my treat."

"Next time."

Walking as fast as her tired muscles would let her, Rory

headed toward her house to shower and pick up her car for the drive to the hospital. A short time later, she hurried down the hallway toward Kit's room, only to find the bed empty, appearing as if no one had ever occupied it. Fear gnawing at her stomach, she walked toward the nurses' station and asked about him. One look at the nurse's face and Rory knew the worst had happened. Whatever Kit had wanted to tell her had died with him.

Chapter 24

Rory took a tissue out of the Kleenex box on her coffee table and blew her nose. "I didn't know Kit that long, but I'm still going to miss him. I didn't even get the chance to finish telling him my story about solving the murder at the painting convention."

Liz placed a comforting hand on her friend's arm. "I'm sure he appreciated the time you spent with him."

The two sat on the couch in Rory's living room Monday evening, a Canadian bacon and pineapple pizza lying uneaten on the coffee table in front of them.

"You'll feel better if you eat something." Liz put a slice of pizza on a plate and pushed it across the table.

Rory waved it away. "I can't think about food right now."

"It's your favorite. I even got pepper flakes." She dangled the packet of spicy peppers in front of her friend's face. "You can use as much as you like. I promise not to say a word about how you're ruining the pizza."

Rory gave her a sad smile and took the packet, sprinkling a quarter of it all over the slice on her plate.

Liz scrunched up her nose in disapproval. "I don't know how you can eat that."

"I thought you weren't going to complain."

"It wasn't a complaint, it was an observation."

They ate in silence, each thinking about the day's tragic turn of events. When Rory finished, she put her empty plate down on the coffee table. "That was good. Thanks for bringing it over."

Liz peeked inside the pizza box. "You've got a couple slices left for breakfast." She closed it up and sat back on the sofa. "Do you have any idea what Kit wanted to talk to you about?"

Rory shook her head. "We'll probably never know."

"Where's he now?"

"The nurse said they took him to the hospital morgue, waiting for the coroner's office to pick him up." She glanced at the time on her cell phone. "They should have him by now."

"How long do you think the autopsy will take?"

Rory considered the question. "I'm not sure there's going to be one. I'm not familiar with the rules, but I don't think there's anything suspicious about his death. It wasn't completely unexpected. He was under a doctor's care and had a bad infection." She wiped her fingers on a napkin and crumpled it up on her plate. "We need to find out his full name so we can get a hold of his relatives. Someone could be searching for him. I would want to know if someone in my family died."

"What about fingerprints? The police might be able to identify him that way. Maybe they already took them. Dashing D might know. Call him."

Rory grabbed her phone and placed the call. She listened carefully as the detective explained the situation to her.

When she hung up, Liz said, "What did he say?"

"The coroner's office will be taking his fingerprints to see if they can identify him. He promised to check with them and let us know what he finds out, but the search could take a while and there's no guarantee his prints will even be in any database."

"Don't worry, we'll cross that bridge when we come to it." Liz glanced at her watch. "Where's Teresa? Did she move back home?"

"She's at a client's house right now, going over wedding plans. She'll be back later."

"She's been a busy beaver lately."

"Keeps her mind off her troubles." Rory went into the kitchen for some aluminum foil. She was wrapping up the extra slices when her phone crowed.

"Who was that?" Liz said after Rory hung up.

"One of the nurses from the hospital. She has a bag of stuff Kit wanted me to have. She's there now. Says it's a good time for me to pick it up."

"Why didn't she give it to you when you were there earlier?"

"This is a different nurse. She just came on duty and learned about Kit. Apparently, he gave her instructions to give the bag to me if he didn't make it."

Liz grabbed her purse and headed for the door. "Let's go then. Maybe something in his things will give us a lead."

Rory drove the two of them to the hospital where they made their way to the floor where Kit's room had been. When they neared the nurses' station, a woman in navy blue scrubs brought a plastic bag with Kit's name on it out from behind the counter and handed it to Rory.

"So sorry for your loss. Kit seemed very nice. He wanted you to have this. He said you would know what to do with it."

Rory took the clear plastic bag, glancing at its contents. "Thanks. We're looking for his relatives. Did he ever talk about family or tell you his full name?"

The nurse shook her head. "We didn't have much time to talk. He was in and out of consciousness a lot. He didn't have a wallet on him when he came in, but you probably know that already."

"You have no idea what he wanted to talk to me about?"

"I asked, but he wouldn't tell me. It was important to him though."

Rory thanked the nurse again. She suppressed her curiosity about the contents of the bag until they got back to the car, where she opened it and looked inside. "The only thing in here is clothes."

"There might be something tucked in between that you can't see."

Rory took out each item and inspected it before handing it to her passenger.

Liz looked at the pile on her lap. "Sandals, t-shirt. There isn't much here. I wonder why he wanted you to have this stuff."

"Maybe he wanted me to give them to a shelter. He might have thought the hospital would throw his clothes away." Rory was about to hand over the last item in the bag, a pair of cargo shorts, when she felt something hard in one of the pockets. She pulled out a small key and held it up to the overhead light. "Maybe this is why. What do you make of it?"

Liz took the key and turned it over in her hands. "There's a number written on it in black Sharpie. A little worn off, but I think it says 253."

"Looks like a padlock key. What would he need to padlock? I don't remember seeing anything that needed one in the bags he had on his bike."

"Unless it's for the bike itself. Did he have a lock for it?"

"Not that I remember. I think I would have noticed one. They're usually on the end of a chain, aren't they?"

"Maybe you missed something else. Did you look through all of the bags?"

"Mom and I looked through everything. I suppose we could have missed something. His stuff is still at the store. Let's head over there now. She's open late tonight."

"To Arika's Scrap 'n Paint, it is then. Onward, James! And step on it."

Fifteen minutes later they were on the sales floor of the craft store, explaining to Rory's mother what they planned on doing.

Arika led the way into the back room. "Not much space to spread things out in here." Her gaze strayed to the adjoining classroom. "I don't have any classes scheduled until tomorrow. You can use the tables in there as long as you promise to clear it all out by the time you leave."

"Thanks, Mom. We'll be sure to do that."

Rory and Liz untied plastic bag after plastic bag from the bicycle and deposited them on one of the two eight-foot tables in the classroom. Once they had everything off the bike, they opened each bag and laid the contents out on the other table, sorting them as they went. Before long, they had a pile of clothes, a pile of books—mostly paperback, but a few hardbacks—and a pile of odds and ends, but nothing that had a padlock attached to it.

"Looks like another dead end," Liz said.

Rory flipped through the books, then turned them upside down to see if anything fell out. A business card and an envelope fluttered to the floor. Rory glanced at the card before handing it over. "Willow's business card. At least now we know for sure where he got her phone number."

"What's that say?" Liz nodded at the piece of paper Rory drew out of the envelope.

"Not much. Just a four-digit number. Not long enough for a phone number. Could be an address, but there's no street name."

"Let's see what Google says." Liz keyed in the digits and "Vista Beach" into the browser on her phone. "There's a bank at that address on Dewey. I'm not sure what it would have to do with the key though. Banks don't use padlocks. Keys for safe deposit boxes look completely different." She handed it back to Rory, who sat down on a nearby chair and twisted it around in her hands, trying to see if she had missed any distinguishing marks.

Arika poked her head around the corner. "How's everything going in here? Find anything useful?"

"Afraid not," Rory said. "We still don't know what this opens." She handed the key to her mother, who examined it.

"Reminds me of the key to our storage locker," Arika said as she handed it back.

"Of course," Rory said. "Why didn't I think of that?"

"Do you think he had enough money to rent one?" Liz said. "He was living on the streets."

"Just because he couldn't afford an apartment doesn't mean he couldn't afford the rent on a storage locker," Arika said. "The amount of money needed to move into an apartment is a lot more than the cost to rent a unit. You can get a small one at some of the newer places for a dollar a month for the first six months."

"It's worth looking into," Rory said. "Can we use your computer, Mom?"

Arika waved her hand in agreement and went back to help a customer on the sales floor.

Rory and Liz packed the clothes and books into a box to take to a local charity. They put the bag of odds and ends to one side to decide what to do with later before settling down in front of the computer in the back room. A search of all the storage facilities in the area brought up page after page of results.

"There are a lot of them," Rory said. "I didn't realize there was that much of a call for extra storage."

"I see it over and over again. A lot of my clients use them when switching between houses or when they move into a smaller place. They say it's temporary, but..."

"Kit would want to have easy access to the storage place. He could take public transportation and go almost anywhere."

"Except there's Buddy to consider. Do they allow dogs on the bus?"

"Good point. Let's assume he biked or walked there and got something closer. We'll eliminate any places that use those pods that are delivered to you. He would want access to his stuff." Several taps on the keyboard, and before long, they had a printout of self-storage places within five miles of Vista Beach. "We'll start with these. We can expand the search if we need to. It's too late to look at any of them tonight. We'll start first thing tomorrow."

"How are we going to find the right place? We don't know his full name."

Rory waved her phone. "I've got a photo of Kit and Buddy I took a couple weeks ago. We can show it around."

Before leaving, they printed out a list of their destinations, ready for the next day's storage locker hunt.

Chapter 25

First thing Tuesday morning, Rory and Liz consulted their list of self-storage facilities and headed to the nearest one.

"What did Dashing D say when he called you this morning?" Liz said as she pulled her car out onto the street.

Rory entered their destination into the navigation app on her phone. "No luck on the fingerprints. The coroner's office will put Kit's description on their website. They're hoping someone will come forward and identify him."

"What if no one does?"

"In a month, they'll cremate him, but they'll keep his ashes for two or three years in case they find relatives."

"No funeral? Everyone should have a funeral," Liz said.

"Don't worry, we'll make sure he gets one. If we can't find his family soon, I'll claim the body and cover the funeral costs."

"You won't have to do it alone. I'll get people to chip in. As soon as we're done here, I'll start working on getting donations." Liz stopped at a light and looked over at her friend curiously. "What happens to his ashes after two or three years?"

"They'll be scattered at a service held once a year for unclaimed remains." Rory consulted her phone. "Turn right at the next light. It'll be on the left halfway down the block."

A short time later, Liz pulled into the parking lot next to the storage facility's office. They checked with the employees inside, but no one recognized Kit's photo. They were on their fourth place when they struck pay dirt.

The scarecrow of a man behind the counter at Beach Storage squinted at the photo on Rory's phone as she held it up for him to see.

"He seems familiar to me. Yeah, he rented a unit a few months back. Why do you want to know?" he said, a suspicious look in his eyes. "One of you an ex-wife or something?"

"Do you know the number of the unit?" Rory crossed her fingers, hoping it would be the same as the number written in black Sharpie on the key they found.

"Got a name?" the man said.

She gave Kit as the first name and mumbled gibberish for the last, hoping the man would supply it himself.

"Kit what? Speak louder. I can't understand you."

Rory mumbled it again.

"Sorry, can't help you. No name, no info."

"Can't you just look and see if you have a unit rented out to someone named Kit?" Liz said.

"We have a hundred and fifty units here. That's a lot of looking."

Rory placed a twenty on the counter and pushed it toward him. "You would be doing us a big favor."

He stared at the bill, a glint of interest in his eyes. He was reaching for the twenty when a customer walked into the office. Instead of picking up the money, he shoved it back across the counter. "Sorry, no can do." He waved them away and turned his attention to the new arrival.

Disappointed, Rory and Liz left the office and stood by the main gate into the storage facility. Behind it, they could see row after row of storage units with gray metal doors.

"We have the unit number. We can go see if the key fits," Liz said.

"How do we get in?" Rory eyed the metal gate. "I'm not climbing that."

They were turning away in disappointment when a car drove up. The driver stopped in front of the gate and typed something into a keypad.

"Of course." Rory pulled a piece of paper out of the pocket of her jeans and stared down at the four-digit number on it. "I bet this is the access code."

Liz looked toward the office and grabbed Rory's arm. "Scarecrow's staring at us. Let's see if we can find a different entrance to try it out on. Somewhere he can't see us."

They walked across the parking lot and around the corner until they found another entrance on a side street.

"What about the security cameras?" Rory nodded toward one pointed toward the metal gate.

"Scarecrow was busy watching something on his phone when we walked in. I bet he doesn't even glance at them. If we look like we belong here, he won't even notice."

Rory typed the code in the keypad and the gate slid open. They quickly slipped through, walking as fast as they could to the nearest row of units, and followed the signs until they were standing in front of a two-story building.

Liz pointed at the range of unit numbers painted on its side. "Looks like it's on the second floor."

They walked up the stairs and searched each hallway, checking the number written on the wall above each unit until they found the correct one.

"Here goes." Rory slipped the key in the padlock and twisted it open. She handed the lock to Liz and pulled up on the metal roll-up door.

They studied the five foot by five foot space, about the size of a small walk-in closet, three-quarters full of cardboard boxes, piled two high in some places. Rory tilted her head to read the writing on the sides of each neatly labeled box: kitchen, bedroom, living room, books.

"He must have put everything in storage when he no longer had a place to live," Liz said.

Rory spotted an antique table leaning against the back wall. "Not much furniture. Probably sold as much as he could. We're looking for paper, photo albums, anything that might tell us his name or lead us to a relative. You take the right side. I'll take the left."

Dividing the space down the middle, the two set to work. They started with the boxes on top. When they didn't find anything of interest, they put them out in the hallway to get to the ones underneath.

"I've got pictures and some photo albums," Liz said.

Rory abandoned the box she had just opened and went over to stand by her friend.

"Here's a wedding album." Liz took a white eleven-by-fourteen album out of the box and held it in her hands so Rory could look at it with her. Embossed on the front was a date and the names Zoe and Christopher.

Rory pointed to the names. "Zoe. That's the name on the photo Kit had."

"And Kit could be short for Christopher. No last name though."

They flipped through the album, looking at photo after photo of the smiling couple. Formal shots were mixed with more candid ones of guests at the reception.

"Looks like a nice wedding," Liz said. "I don't recognize anyone. Do you?"

"Not a single person. And the reception could be at any ballroom in any hotel anywhere."

"They look so happy. I wonder what happened to her," Liz said as she put away the album.

"Maybe one of these other boxes will give us some answers."

After going through every box, they still hadn't found any papers or items that might give them a last name. They were returning the ones they'd put out in the hallway to the storage unit when Rory's foot bumped into the table. It tilted forward, revealing a small box behind it.

"Eureka!" she said when she opened it. "We've found the mother lode. File folders filled with papers." She was about to open a promising folder labeled "Insurance" when they heard voices.

"That sounds like Scarecrow," Liz said. "I think he's coming this way."

"Help me get the rest of these boxes inside. We can take this with us and look through it later."

They shoved the boxes that were out in the hallway inside the unit and rolled down the door. Rory was reattaching the padlock when they heard footsteps coming toward them.

They ran on tiptoe to the end of the hallway and peeked around the corner. Scarecrow led another man down an adjoining hallway. As soon as the two men had their backs toward them, Rory and Liz ran as quietly as possible toward the exit, racing down the stairs and across the pavement to the metal gate where Rory entered the exit code and impatiently waited for the gate to slide open. Walking as fast as they could, the two headed up the street toward the safety of their car.

"Whew!" Rory said when they were pulling out of the lot. "Let's head to my place and go through the box there."

The smell of baking cookies greeted them when they got back to the house. Rory took the contents of the box and spread it out on the coffee table in the living room, dividing the folders into three neat piles.

When Teresa brought in a plate of chocolate chip cookies, Liz crossed her index fingers, creating an X, and held them out in front of her. "No more cookies. I'll have to jog from here to Malibu and back to get the extra weight off."

Rory picked one up and waved it in front of her friend. "Such chocolaty goodness. How can you refuse? Me want cookie! Me want cookie!"

"That is the worst Cookie Monster imitation I've ever heard. It's not fair. You're a lot taller than I am. You get to eat more." After a moment of indecision, Liz gave up, grabbed a cookie and munched on it as Rory assigned each of them a stack.

"What are we looking for?" Teresa picked up her pile of folders.

"Anything that will give us Kit's last name or that talks about relatives. He mentioned someone named Zoe once. We now know that's his wife, so look out for anything to do with her."

They munched on cookies as they worked, opening folder after folder.

In the last folder in her pile, Rory found a single piece of paper. "I know what happened to Zoe," she said. "She died. I've got her death certificate here."

Liz looked up from her work. "Really? That's sad."

"At least we know Kit's full name now. He's listed as next of kin on the death certificate. Christopher Laughlin."

"What did she die of?" Teresa asked.

"Cancer. A year ago."

"That seems to go with these bills I found from a hospital in Santa Barbara." Liz passed a piece of paper over to Rory. "Looks like they went to collections."

She looked at the dollar amount on the bill. "Wow. That's a lot of money. I wonder if that's why he's homeless."

"I've heard of people losing everything after a major medical issue. That would fit," Teresa said.

"Well, we know we can't find Zoe. I haven't found anyone else who might be a relative. What about either of you?"

Teresa held up a greeting card. "Here's a name. Angel Portrero. Probably a relative or a friend."

"Portrero's a Hispanic name, isn't it? Might be a man. Angel's a pretty common male name in Spanish-speaking countries," Liz said.

"Man, woman. Whichever they are, maybe they'll know of some relatives. It's an unusual enough name. Let's see what we can find out."

Rory headed to her work area where she typed "Angel Portrero" and "Santa Barbara" into a browser. She thought she had struck pay dirt when she found a phone number online, but when she called it a gruff-voiced man answered and denied knowing anyone by that name before hanging up.

"You would think this Angel would have left more of a digital footprint," Rory said. "I've tried various social media sites and Google, but haven't found anything."

"We don't know how old he or she is. Could be older and not really into going online," Liz said.

"I'm sure if I had access to other databases I could find something."

"You know who might be able to help—Candy."

"Of course," Rory said.

"Who's that?" Teresa asked.

"She's a private investigator we met a while ago. She was working for this other PI while she was studying for her own license," Rory said.

"She probably has access to all sorts of information. She has her own license now. I've sent lots of work her way. She owes me a favor," Liz said.

"Call her," Rory said. "See if she's willing to help."

Liz dug around in her purse and pulled out her cell phone. After she hung up with Candy, she said, "She's on a case, but she'll talk to us. Let's go."

Teresa looked at the other two women. "What should I do?"

"Look through everything again and see if we missed anything." Rory grabbed the death certificate and followed Liz out the door.

Chapter 26

Rory and Liz approached the black SUV parked on a street across from the Akaw hotel. A woman with lavender hair styled in a bubble cut sat behind the wheel, a camera with a zoom lens in her hand, her gaze fixed on the hotel entrance. Liz knocked on the passenger window. Candy glanced over and motioned to indicate they should get in the backseat before returning to her surveillance.

Liz had barely closed the door when the private investigator said, "Got you, you pig." She raised her camera and took several shots of a man and a woman kissing in front of the hotel.

"Duck!" Candy motioned with her hand for them to scrunch down in the backseat. They made themselves as small as possible, only sitting up again when the PI declared the coast to be clear.

The woman put the camera on the seat beside her and turned to face them. "Divorce case. Or it will be soon anyway. What can I do for you ladies?"

"We're looking for some information on these two people." Rory handed over a printout of the photo she had on her phone. "Their names are Zoe and Christopher Laughlin."

Candy studied the photo. "Cute couple. What have you got on them so far?"

Rory handed over Zoe's death certificate and a piece of paper with everything they had learned about the two of them. "Christopher had been homeless for a while. Everyone called him Kit. He passed away recently, and we're trying to find his next of kin. We haven't had much luck so far so we were hoping you could help."

"Happy to do what I can. People should know when loved ones die. What else?"

"We think someone named Angel Portrero might be able to help. He, or she, knows them, but we're not sure if they're related or just a friend," Liz said. "We don't even know if Angel is a man's or a woman's name."

Candy nodded. "Angel Portrero. Got it. I'll see what I can do."

"You can call either one of us when you find something," Liz said.

When they returned to the house, they found Teresa still in the living room sifting through the folders. She looked up from the stack she had on her lap. "I've looked through most of these again, but haven't found anything new. What about you two? What did the PI say?"

"Candy's looking into that Angel person and searching for next of kin. She'll let us know if she finds anything," Liz said.

"Now that we have Kit's full name, we should call the coroner's office and tell them what we know. They might be able to find his relatives." Rory sat down in front of her computer and pointed her browser at the county website. A few keystrokes later, she found Kit's case in the unidentified persons section. "I'll call them right now."

"We'll start getting donations for a funeral in case we can't find any relatives." Liz settled down onto the sofa in the adjoining living room to make her own calls while Teresa went into the kitchen to make tea.

After giving the woman on the other end of the phone line the case number, Rory waited while the coroner's office representative checked the records.

A few *tap tap tap*s of the keyboard later, the woman repeated the string of digits Rory had given her. "That's the case number you're interested in, right?"

"That's right."

"We have his name on file already. Haven't had a chance to update the website yet. The body's been released to the next of kin."

"Who?"

"His brother-in-law."

Brother-in-law? Rory sat up straighter in her desk chair. "Do you have a name?"

"Let's see." A few more taps on the keyboard and the woman had the answer. "Interesting name. Tripp. Tripp Keating."

Rory stared at her phone in disbelief. "Did you say Tripp Keating? You're sure?"

"That's what it says here. He made the arrangements earlier today, and the mortuary already picked up the body. Is there a problem?"

"No, no," Rory said. "I'm just surprised. I didn't realize he was taking care of it. Thanks for your time."

Puzzled by what she'd learned, Rory hung up the phone and stared off into space for a moment before she walked into the living room where Liz and Teresa sat side by side on the sofa, sipping tea and talking about starting a GoFundMe page. The two looked up from their notes.

"What's wrong?" Liz said.

Rory settled down into the chair next to the sofa. "We may not need to raise any money after all. Someone already claimed the body."

"Who?" Teresa asked.

"Tripp."

"*Our* Tripp? Why would he do that?" Liz said.

"Apparently, they're related. He's Kit's brother-in-law."

"And he never told you?" Liz stared in bewilderment at her friend.

"He never said a word to me. He insisted he barely knew him." Rory thought back to the time in the hospital when she had found Tripp reading to the unconscious man. "I did get the feeling he cared about him though, more than you would expect from an acquaintance. I wonder why he lied to me."

"Maybe he didn't," Liz said.

Rory stared at her friend. "What do you mean?"

"Maybe he lied to the coroner's office, said he was Kit's bro-in-law. He wasn't in any of the wedding pictures we saw. Wouldn't he have been if Zoe was his sister?"

"But why would he lie to them?"

"He might have been afraid they wouldn't release the body to him otherwise."

"That would explain it," Teresa said.

"I'm not buying it. I think they require proof of the relationship before releasing the body."

"You're not going to find out the truth talking to us." Liz pointed toward the front door. "Go, talk to him. Ask him about it. There'll be a nice dinner waiting for you when you get back."

Rory thought about calling Tripp but decided this was a discussion they should have in person. She wanted to see his face when she asked him why he'd lied. She headed to the church where he was currently living to see if he was there. She found him in the sanctuary with Reverend Paulson. As she walked toward them, she heard the words "service" and "eulogy."

"We were just talking about you," the minister said when she was within earshot.

"Oh?"

"We're planning Kit's funeral. We were wondering if you would say a few words," Tripp said.

"I'll speak if you want. What about relatives?" she asked, giving him a chance to come clean.

"I wish we had better news. We haven't found anyone yet," Reverend Paulson said.

Curious. Tripp hadn't even told the minister about his relationship with Kit.

"Why don't the two of you discuss the details? I'll be in my office if you need me."

As soon as the minister left, Tripp turned to her. "What's wrong? You seem a little on edge."

"You tell me."

"I have no idea what you mean."

"I called the coroner's office to see about Kit's burial."

A mixture of concern and confusion shown in his eyes. "But I already made the arrangements."

"I didn't know that then. They told me his brother-in-law had claimed the body."

"Oh." Tripp sat down heavily onto a wooden pew and placed the pad of paper he was holding on the seat beside him. Rory sank down on the pew behind him.

"Why didn't you tell me you two were related? You acted like you barely knew him," she said in a soft voice. "Or did you just make that up so they would release the body to you?"

He stared down at his hands before twisting around in his seat to look at her. He put his arm on the back of the pew and looked her squarely in the face. "When I saw Kit, I didn't realize it was him until he told me. He'd grown a beard and lost some weight. We only met a few times."

"But he was married to your sister."

"Zoe and I lost touch years ago. I got a little overprotective, thought she was too young to get married. When I told her that, she told me to mind my own business. After that, she didn't want anything to do with me. Wouldn't answer my letters or take my calls. I was out of the country when they got married. She never told me. I had to hear about it from a friend."

That explained why he wasn't in any of the wedding photos, Rory thought. "That must have been hard."

"It was. We'd been so close growing up. I left her alone, hoping she would come around some day, but she never did. Not until it was too late, anyway. Zoe...passed away a while back. Cancer."

"I'm sorry," she said softly, not wanting to tell him she already knew.

"I was her big brother. I was supposed to take care of her."

Rory briefly laid a hand on his arm. "It's not your fault she got cancer."

"I know, but I didn't even know she was sick. I was out of the country, working with Doctors Without Borders. By the time I returned to the States and found out, she was...gone."

"How did you find out?"

"She wrote me a letter. Sent it to the last address she had for me. It eventually made its way to a friend who gave it to me when I got back in the country. She wanted to mend fences, but by the time I got the letter, it was too late. I looked for Kit, but he'd moved away. I figured I would never find him. I had no idea he was in Vista Beach when I came here."

"When you realized who Kit was, why did you leave him on the streets?"

"I offered to help him find a place to live and pay for it, but he wasn't interested. He felt like living on the streets was his penance for not taking care of his wife. He felt he'd failed her. They had to sell pretty much everything they owned to pay her medical bills. It still wasn't enough. That's why he was homeless."

"I still don't understand why you didn't tell me you knew him. When he first went into the hospital, I asked you about him. You could have at least told me his name."

"He asked me not to tell anyone we knew each other or anything about his past. If I told you, you would ask about his background, and he didn't want to talk about that."

"Why didn't you tell me when he died?"

"Honestly? I was embarrassed." Rory waited as Tripp gathered his thoughts and struggled for the right words. Finally, he continued, "I'd already lied to you. I didn't think you would believe my explanation. You haven't known me very long."

"I would have understood."

"I'm sorry I didn't tell you. Can we put it behind us?" Tripp looked at her, an earnest expression on his face.

"Don't lie to me again though, okay?"

He nodded.

"What about Kit's things? His bike and clothes are at my mother's store."

"Why don't you go ahead and take care of them. Give everything away to charity. Something that helps the homeless. That seems right."

"There's a storage locker too, but I forgot the key. Some of your sister's things might be in there. You should look through everything. You might want some of it. I'll bring the key to you later."

"Sounds good." Tripp picked up a pen and the pad of paper on the pew next to him. "Here's our ideas about the service. Let me know what you think."

When Rory got home, Teresa and Liz were returning from getting dinner, carrying bags from a local Chinese restaurant. They'd barely gotten inside when there was a knock on the door.

"Trent! What are you doing here?" Teresa said.

"I want to talk, for real this time."

"Go ahead, eat your dinner," Teresa said to the other two women. "This could take a while."

Rory and Liz carried the food into the kitchen, leaving the couple alone in the living room. They ate their dinner to the murmur of voices from the other room. They were finishing when Teresa entered the kitchen, suitcase in hand.

"You're leaving?"

Rory set her chopsticks down on the table.

"I don't know what's going to happen, but we're going to try to work things out." She put the key to the house on the kitchen counter. "Thanks for everything."

Rory gave her a hug. "I hope things work out for you. Let me know if you need anything."

The three of them walked to the front of the house, where Teresa's husband was waiting for her.

"Do you think they'll make it?" Liz asked as they watched the couple get in their respective cars.

"I hope so." Rory headed back into the kitchen and began putting away the leftovers. "Did you ever contact your friend at the police station about Lance?"

"The police confirmed he was in San Diego that night, though they can't account for every minute of his time."

"Then he could have driven back that evening."

"They obviously don't think he did it if they arrested Dawn instead. What did Tripp say when you saw him?"

Rory told her friend about their conversation at the church.

"Not a good situation for either Tripp or Kit, I think." Liz poked her head in the refrigerator. "Are there any of Teresa's cookies left?"

"I thought you were full."

Liz pointed at her stomach. "Didn't you know? I have a separate stomach just for dessert."

Rory shook her head and shoved the cookie jar across the counter. "Be my guest."

Chapter 27

Wednesday morning, Rory dropped Kit's belongings off at a local charity, keeping a couple of his books for herself to remember him by. After making sure nothing of his was left at her mother's store, she exited Arika's Scrap 'n Paint and headed down the sidewalk. When she passed Beach Healing and Acupuncture, she exchanged waves with Asia, who was updating the display in the store's window.

As Rory walked down the block, she sensed someone watching her. She looked behind her, but all she saw were customers going in and out of stores or studying window displays. As far as she could tell, no one was paying particular attention to her. She continued on her way, but couldn't shake off the feeling of being followed.

She took her cell phone out of the pocket of her jeans, pausing every few feet to take a selfie. After snapping several pictures, she stopped at a light to check the photos. All she saw in the background was the same unrecognizable brown blur.

As soon as she crossed the street, Rory increased her pace to put distance between her and her shadow and ducked into the first alleyway she came across. She crouched behind a dumpster, her gaze trained on the entrance, and waited to see if anyone would stop.

Moments later, a woman dressed in brown paused at the mouth of the dim alley and peered into the shadows. She was taking a step forward when someone jumped her from behind and pushed her to the ground face first, pinning her arms behind her back.

"Gotcha!" Asia said.

Rory stepped out from behind the dumpster and stared open-mouthed at the clerk from Beach Healing. "Asia, what are you doing?"

"Capturing your stalker, of course. You must have known someone was following you."

Rory gestured toward the woman who was wriggling on the ground, trying to get out of Asia's fierce grip. "Let her up."

The clerk dragged the other woman to her feet and stood behind her, holding onto her wrists so she couldn't get away.

"Marcia?" Rory stared in surprise at the woman she'd met at the gym. "Why were you following me?"

"He's mine, you know." Marcia jutted her chin at Rory. "Now that grandma's gone, Lance is mine." She twisted around, trying to get free, but Asia held fast.

"There's nothing going on between the two of us," Rory said.

"You can't fool me. I saw how he treated you at the gym, pretending not to know you, then taking you out in the hallway so he could be alone with you."

"Really, there's nothing going on. I barely know him."

"Then why do you have his number in your phone?"

"How do you...?" Rory thought back to Sunday evening in the bar when her phone hadn't been in the box as she'd expected. "Oh. You took my phone."

"Borrowed it when the bartender went into the back room. The place was so busy no one noticed. You really should lock it, you know. Otherwise anyone can get at the information."

"You sent that note too, didn't you? And that was your silver SUV following me." When Marcia didn't respond, Rory continued, "Did you kill Willow so you could have Lance to yourself?"

A look of horror came across the woman's face and she stopped wriggling. "No! I would never do that."

"Where were you the Friday Willow died?"

"I was in San Diego, on a mini-vacation. If you don't believe me, you can check with my hotel. If you'll tell your goon to stop manhandling me, I'll show you proof."

"Let her go," Rory said to Asia.

She let go of her grip and stepped back, eyeing the other woman warily.

Marcia picked her purse off the ground, pulled out a piece of paper and handed it to Rory.

Rory stared at the date on the receipt for a hotel in San Diego. "This is the same hotel where Lance was staying."

"I know. I saw him there. Imagine my surprise. We even had dinner in the same restaurant down the block."

"Was it a surprise? Or did you follow him down there?" Asia said. "Were you stalking Willow's boyfriend too?"

"I like to keep track of him, that's all. Make sure he's okay."

"What time did you see him on Friday?" Rory asked.

"He had dinner by himself. Finished around eight, then he went to a local bar. He was there until at least midnight. Got so drunk I doubt he even remembers where he was that night. I watched to make sure he got back to the hotel safely before I went to bed."

If he was in San Diego until midnight, he couldn't have driven back and killed Willow, Rory thought. And neither could Marcia, though that still left his other fans. One of them could have been as rabid about him as the woman in front of her.

Rory was thinking over this new information when a deep voice said, "What's going on here?"

The three women turned toward the alley entrance, where Detective Green stood looking at them.

"What are you doing here?" Rory said.

"Someone called the police station and mentioned your name. Said you were in trouble. Something about someone following you. Is one of you going to tell me what's going on?" He looked at each of the women in turn.

They stared at each other, then all started talking at once.

"I wasn't stalking her," Marcia blurted out.

Asia pointed to Marcia. "She was following Rory down the street so I called you and followed her."

"I thought someone was following me so I ducked in here," Rory said.

The detective rubbed his temples as if he felt a headache coming on. "Let me get this straight. You..." he pointed at Marcia, "...may or may not have been following her." He gazed at Rory. "And you..." he pointed at Asia, "...followed Marcia here." He stared at the three of them. "Was anyone hurt? Does anyone want to lodge a complaint?"

All three women shook their heads.

"Okay. I'll let you go for now, but stop following people around. If I ever hear one of you is harassing someone again..." He left the threat hanging and waved his hand in dismissal. Asia and Marcia exited the alley and turned onto the sidewalk, going in opposite directions. When Rory started to follow them, he said to her, "Stay right there. I want to talk with you." He paced in front of the alley and finally said, an exasperated expression on his face, "When you thought you were being followed, why didn't you call me?"

"My cell phone battery was dead, and you know how hard it is to find a pay phone these days."

"Uh-huh."

A faint cock-a-doodle-doo came from the pocket of her jeans. Rory looked around as if trying to find the source of the sound while she casually put her hand inside the pocket to stop the crowing.

He raised an eyebrow. "Are you going to answer that?"

"What are you talking about?"

Moments later, three quacks sounded, a few seconds apart.

"Someone really wants to get hold of you." He ran his hand through his hair. "What am I going to do with you? Next time you think someone's following you, call me." Another quack. "You'd better find out what they want."

Detective Green walked out of the alley, mumbling to himself.

Rory checked her phone. One missed phone call and four texts, all from the same person. She dialed the familiar number. "What's going on?"

"Candy, she needs to talk to us," Liz said.

"Shoot! We forgot to tell her we didn't need her help anymore."

"Forget about that. She says it's urgent. Meet me at the park next to my office right now."

A short time later, Rory and Liz stood on the sidewalk in front of the park where they had agreed to meet Candy. Perched on a slight hill, it sloped down toward the street below. With an unobstructed view of the ocean, the park was sandwiched between a deli on one side and Liz's real estate office on the other, a green oasis in the middle of the concrete block. A half dozen benches were scattered across the grass, all facing the ocean. At this time of day, only two of them were occupied.

"Why aren't we meeting at Candy's office? It's not far," Rory said.

"She said something about it being more private here."

"Hard to believe this is better than her office. Seems she has more control over whether anyone's listening to us there."

Liz shrugged. "Maybe she's practicing her clandestine-meeting skills. There she is."

She pointed to a woman with a bubble haircut sitting on a wooden bench in the middle of the grassy area.

As they approached the bench, Candy raised her newspaper so it obscured her face and pretended to be reading. As soon as they sat down beside her, she said, "You didn't tell me you were getting me involved in a murder investigation."

"What are you talking about?" Rory said.

"Don't look at me when you talk," Candy hissed. She placed a folder on the bench beside her and slid it over without looking at them. "Look inside."

Liz picked it up and opened it, displaying its contents so Rory could see. At the top of a stack of papers was a grainy photo of a woman with a name written below it.

"That's Willow," Rory said. "Why does it say Angel Portrero?"

"Willow Bingen and Angel Portrero are the same person. Angel disappeared off the face of the earth six months ago. No one she knew in Santa Barbara has seen her since. She changed her name and job and moved down here."

"How did you make the connection?" Rory leaned her head toward Liz, pretending to direct her comments toward her instead of the other woman on the bench.

Candy let the paper drop to her lap for a fraction of a second before she remembered she was supposed to be covering her face. "I went looking for a picture to show around. Wasn't easy since she had no social media presence. Finally found one of her on one of her old coworker's Facebook pages."

"What about Zoe and Christopher? What did you find out about them?"

"Didn't get to them. I stopped as soon as I realized Angel was the same person who had been murdered recently. You're going to have to continue on your own. I'm not interfering with a police investigation. I can't jeopardize my license. Everything I found is in the folder. Something hinky's going on. When I contacted the people she used to work with at the hospital, they clammed up, said she was laid off, but wouldn't say anything else. There's something fishy about her departure, something they wouldn't tell me. Maybe you'll have better luck in person. I've got to go." Candy folded her newspaper and stood up. "Wait five minutes before you leave. Good luck. Next time I'm charging you."

The two women watched the private investigator walk across the grass, then split up the stack of neatly printed pages to go over.

"She was a nurse in the ICU. Laid off like Candy said." Rory flipped to the next page. "Looks like she left the profession after that. There's no record of her working at a hospital anywhere. That's odd. What do you have?"

"Transcriptions of interviews with coworkers. Nothing jumps

out at me, but something about the answers makes me wonder if they're hiding something." Liz handed the pages to Rory who read them, then nodded in agreement.

"I wonder if the police know about all this," Rory said as she handed the pages back to Liz, who stacked them neatly and placed them back in the folder.

"Didn't you say Dawn told them her real name. They would have found out, wouldn't they?"

"Angel wasn't the name Dawn mentioned."

"Three different names. What's that about?" Liz said.

"Sounds like she changed her name every time she ran away from something. From Laura to Angel when she left her family and from Angel to Willow when she left Santa Barbara."

"You could call Dashing D to make sure they know about this third name, but I wouldn't want to get Candy in trouble. She hasn't had her license long," Liz said.

"We don't have to tell him where we got the information. We could just tell him the name and let him draw his own conclusions."

Rory made the call, steeling herself for an interrogation, but when Detective Green answered he didn't seem surprised by the news.

"What did he say?" Liz asked after Rory hung up.

"He knew about her changing her name to Angel Portrero. Said they already looked into her past life and didn't find anything of interest."

"They might not know the connection between Kit and Willow. That they knew each other before."

"It might not be important. I'll call him later and tell him. I think we should get more information first. I wonder why Willow chose Portrero as her new last name."

"I can't call her Willow or Angel. Too confusing. I'm going to use Wangel from now on. Portrero could be her maiden name. From what you told me that Dawn said, the woman didn't want to have anything to do with her kids or her husband. She probably changed it back as soon as she could."

"True. And she might never have changed it when she got married. I'll have to ask Dawn the next time I see her. The police are probably too busy to follow up with this Angel angle. Maybe we can help." Roy looked at the time on her cell phone. "It's still early."

"Are you thinking what I'm thinking?" Liz said.

They looked at each other and chorused, "Road trip!"

Chapter 28

On the two-hour drive to Santa Barbara, Rory brought Liz up to date on her encounter with Marcia that morning.

"She certainly has an obsession with Luscious Lance," Liz said. "I wonder if he knows she followed him to San Diego. Or how she even knew he was going there."

"She probably heard him talking to one of the other trainers at the gym. I doubt he noticed her. He would have given her name to the police to verify he was in San Diego all night if he had."

"That's if he even knows her name." Liz frowned. "We're at a dead end. Lance and Teresa have alibis. Dawn was there that night. Maybe she's lying and she really did do it."

"Kit was there too. I wish he'd been able to tell us what he saw. There's still the possibility one of Lance's fans or one of Willow's tenants did it. And, remember, there's the blackmail angle." Rory slowed down to let a car into the lane in front of her. "Hopefully, we'll learn something in Santa Barbara that will give us a fresh clue."

"You know what we need? Music. It always helps me think." Liz turned on the radio and began dancing in her seat to the beat.

Rory looked over at her passenger and smiled. "I'm glad you're not driving."

"I can drive and dance. I do it all the time."

"Remind me to stay off the road when you're on it."

When Rory pulled into the parking lot of the hospital where

Angel had worked, Liz consulted the notes Candy gave them. "We're supposed to talk with a Dan Dominick. This says he's a nurse, but doesn't say what area of the hospital he's in."

"I hope he's here today. I didn't think about calling ahead."

The volunteer at the information desk directed them to the floor where Dan worked. Before long, the two exited the elevator on the correct floor and followed the signs to the telemetry unit.

"We're looking for Dan Dominick. We were told he works on this floor," Rory said to the first hospital employee she saw.

The woman pointed toward a middle-aged man in navy blue scrubs walking down the hall toward them.

"Dan?" Rory said.

The man smiled at them. "That's right. How can I help you?"

"Do you have time to answer some questions about Wil—Angel Portrero? We understand you worked with her."

At the mention of the woman's name the smile disappeared from his face.

"Does this have something to do with that phone call the other day? That PI?"

"That's right. We're associates of hers. We're following up," Liz said.

"I was sorry to hear Angel's dead, but whatever you need, I can't help you. I told that PI everything I know." He started to walk away.

"Please," Rory said. "Just talk to us for a few minutes. Candy will dock our pay if we don't bring back a full report."

"Tough boss, huh? I've had my share of those." He checked his watch. "My break's coming up soon. Meet me in the cafeteria in ten minutes."

Rory and Liz headed for the cafeteria where they bought a late lunch and settled down at a table for four. Liz took a pen and a pad of paper out of her purse and placed them beside her tray.

A short time later, Dan slid into an empty chair and placed a coffee cup on the table in front of him. "I haven't got long. What do you want to know?"

"You worked with Angel before she moved down south, right?" Rory said.

"That's right."

"We understand she left in a hurry."

"She got laid off. I already went over all of this with your boss. Cindy, right?"

"It's Candy. We're just verifying everything for the report," Liz said.

His eyes narrowed. "You're from the L.A. area? One of those beach cities? Seems a long way to come to verify information. What are you really after?"

Rory looked around. Even though no one was within earshot, she leaned forward and lowered her voice. "Candy had the feeling there was something about Angel leaving you weren't telling her."

Dan took a sip of coffee and looked down at his cup in contemplation as if considering his next move. He put his elbows on the table and leaned forward, looking each of them in the eye. "You can't tell anyone other than your boss where you got this, okay? You can't mention my name at all."

Rory and Liz nodded their agreement.

"You're right, I didn't tell Candy everything. The layoff was a cover, a convenient way to hide the real reason Angel left."

Rory sucked in her breath in anticipation, silently willing him to continue.

"Maybe I shouldn't tell you this."

"Please, it's important." Liz laid her hand on his arm and batted her eyelashes.

"Drugs went missing." He stopped when a woman in scrubs walked by and looked at them curiously. His eye began to twitch, and he waited to continue until she sat down at a table out of earshot. "You can't tell anyone I'm talking to you."

Liz jotted something down on her notepad. "We won't. What kind of drugs?"

"Antibiotics, painkillers, all kinds of things. Enough to open your own pharmacy."

"And you think she stole them?" Rory asked.

"Not me. The hospital administration."

"Was she addicted to something?" Liz asked.

"I never saw any signs of it. I got the impression she stole them to treat people on the QT. People who couldn't afford it or didn't want to come in for treatment."

"Like the homeless?" Rory asked.

He shrugged. "Maybe. Anyway, the administration started an investigation when they realized the drugs were missing and caught her red-handed."

"Why didn't they just fire her?"

"Didn't think it would look good for the hospital. A layoff was on the books anyway, so they avoided any problems by letting her go. That's all I know."

"Why didn't you tell this to Candy over the phone?"

"We were told never to talk about it. I like my job. I want to keep it." Dan stood up. "Remember, you didn't hear any of this from me."

"What do you think of that?" Liz asked after he left. "Wangel almost sounds like a saint, stealing drugs to help people in need. Sounds a little like your Tripp."

Rory blushed. "He wouldn't steal drugs. He'd find a way to get them legally. And he's not *my* Tripp."

"You're still going out, aren't you?"

"It's early days." Rory put down her fork. "Let's get back to Willow. I can't call her Angel, it just doesn't seem right. I don't see how what she did here could have anything to do with her death."

"Unless she was doing the same thing down in Vista Beach," Liz said.

"She wasn't a nurse anymore and didn't work at a hospital so she wouldn't have the same kind of access to drugs. It's odd though," Rory said thoughtfully. "Her attitude toward the homeless."

"What's so odd about it? I'm sure there are a lot of doctors and nurses who try to help them. It's in their DNA."

"That's not what I'm talking about. When I left Kit's bike in my mom's store, Willow was there. She said some derogatory things about the homeless. Plus Veronica told me she started a petition to make the city ban them from the streets. I wonder what happened to change her mind. I can't believe it was her thinking they'd stolen her glasses. And we still don't know why she switched to herbal medicine."

"That's obvious. She was blackballed after she was let go. Probably couldn't find a job as a nurse anywhere after that. There's lots of money to be made in alternative treatments." Liz sat back in her chair. "I guess that's all that we can learn here. Do you want to stop off at the outlet mall on the way home?"

They were in the parking lot, standing by Rory's car, when the same nurse who had been eyeing them in the cafeteria walked toward them.

"I heard you talking to Dan about Angel. I don't know if there's been a funeral yet, but I want to contribute money toward flowers." Without telling them her name, she shoved a folded bill into Rory's hand and walked toward the hospital entrance.

Rory stared after the woman. "She didn't even give me a chance to thank her."

"That was odd," Liz said. "How much did she give you?"

Rory unfolded the bill to find a note tucked inside. "Ten dollars. And there's a note." On the piece of paper was a name and address in the Santa Barbara area. Underneath that was "He didn't tell you the whole story. She'll tell you the truth," with the first word of the second sentence underlined.

Rory handed the note to Liz. "Looks like we have a stop to make before we head home. The outlet mall will have to wait."

Chapter 29

Rory entered the address from the note in the navigation app on her phone and followed the directions. She parked her sedan on the palm-tree-lined street in front of their destination and peered through the window at the single-story stucco house. An iron fence with broken and rusty spikes surrounded the tiny front yard full of drought-conscious landscaping.

Liz double checked the address on the piece of paper. "This is it, all right. What's the plan? Should I play real estate agent? It's not my usual territory, but I could easily be scouting the neighborhood for a client."

"I think we need a more direct approach. We'll ask about Willow and see where it takes us." Rory opened her car door. "The woman who gave us the note must think this Delores is willing to talk."

"The direct approach. I like it."

Weeds encroached on the plants, tickling their ankles as they walked up the path to the front door. The eight notes of Westminster chimes sounded faintly through the wood door when they rang the bell. After standing on the doorstep for a considerable length of time, they came to the conclusion no one was home. They were turning away when the door finally opened, revealing a woman with gray hair using a walker. She peered at them through glasses so large they swallowed her face.

"I've already found Jesus," the woman said and started to close the door.

"We're not here to talk religion," Rory said.

"Or sell you anything, Mrs. Waitman. You are Delores Waitman, aren't you?" Liz said in her sincerest tone of voice.

The door slowly opened again. Delores peered at them curiously.

"We want to talk to you about Angel Portrero," Rory said before she could close the door again.

Surprise turned to disbelief then anger on the older woman's face. She studied them, her gaze checking out every inch of them, sizing them up. "What paper are you with?" she finally asked.

"We're not reporters. We just want to ask you a few questions," Rory said.

"I don't have anything to say."

"Wait," Rory said. "A nurse at the hospital sent us."

"Who?"

"She never gave us her name, just handed us a note saying you could help us. Show it to her." Rory nudged Liz, who handed the note over. As soon as the woman saw the handwriting, the belligerence went out of her face and she said in a more welcoming voice, "Come with me."

They followed her down a dark hallway into a comfortable room filled to the brim with furniture. Knickknacks and framed photos covered every horizontal surface. Delores carefully rolled her walker through a wide path between pieces of furniture, the other two following close behind. Rory scrunched in her shoulders, afraid she would knock something down. She breathed a sigh of relief when they navigated the area safely and were standing in a sitting area that contained a couch and chairs.

"Have a seat." Delores indicated a loveseat upholstered in a velvety fabric. "Would you two like iced tea or lemonade?"

"No, thank you, we're fine," Rory said.

"We wouldn't want you to go to any trouble," Liz added.

The two took their places on the sofa while Delores settled

down in a recliner and placed her walker to one side. No sooner had they all sat down when a black cat came out from behind a chair and eyed the newcomers curiously. After sniffing everyone's legs, the cat gracefully jumped onto Rory's lap, giving Liz a brief glance before resting her head on her paws and closing her eyes.

"You must be good people. Maleficent doesn't cotton to just anyone. Why did Janet send you? What did you want to know about Angel?" The woman practically spat out Willow's former name. Sensing her displeasure, the cat opened its eyes and stared at Delores.

Rory stroked Maleficent's fur and before long, the cat closed her eyes again and went back to sleep. "We were asking at the hospital where she used to work about why she left. They said she stole drugs from the dispensary so they quietly let her go. Janet told us to ask you about it."

"Angel. I lost my son because of her. Some angel she turned out to be."

"Was your son homeless?"

"Homeless? Where did you get that idea? He lived here with me, not because he couldn't afford a place of his own, but because he was a good son and liked taking care of me and my house. I'm afraid the place isn't as well kept up as it once was." She gestured toward a photograph on the table beside the couch. "That's him, right before he got sick. As you can see, he wasn't homeless."

Rory picked up the silver frame and held it so Liz could look at it. The photo inside showed a tall middle-aged man dressed in casual clothes leaning against a classic 1960s Mustang. "Handsome," she said, returning the frame to its place. "Sorry for your loss. We understood that she stole drugs to treat the homeless."

"Balderdash! Who told you that? Not Janet. She knows better. Angel didn't use them to treat people. She used them to kill people."

Rory stared at her, unsure if she had heard correctly.

"Close your mouths. It's not a very attractive look on someone your age," Delores said.

"She was an angel of mercy?" Rory asked.

"Some mercy. She killed people who were nowhere near death. She killed my Reggie. He had cancer. The treatment was working. His doctors were optimistic. Sure, he was in pain, but it wasn't anything he couldn't handle. *She* decided it was time for him to go. It wasn't. It wasn't his time!" She pounded the arm of the recliner with her right hand. "You can't convince me otherwise."

"How did she kill him?"

"Injected morphine or something like that in his IV."

"Did you tell someone at the hospital?"

"All they were concerned about was keeping their names out of the papers. They said there was no proof." She leaned forward. "There were others, you know."

"Others?" Rory and Liz said at the same time.

"How many?" Rory asked.

"A half dozen at least. Those are the ones I know about. There were probably more."

"Did the police get involved?"

"The hospital was too concerned about their reputation. Not exactly a good thing to have an angel of mercy on staff. Like you said, they quietly got rid of her. Hid it by doing it as part of a layoff."

"What about you? Did you go to the police?"

"No proof, they said, but I know it was a cover-up, plain and simple."

"The hospital must have security cameras."

"Not in the rooms. Privacy concerns. All of the footage from the hallways was lost or damaged, some excuse like that. They fired her, but didn't report her as far as I know. I called the other hospitals in the area and complained about her. I figured if I made enough of a racket, no one would hire her. None of them did, then I lost track of her. I figured she moved someplace else. I wish I could have done more. That was a while ago. Why are you asking about her now? Did she kill someone else?"

"She's dead," Liz said.

"Good. There is justice in this world." Delores nodded her head in satisfaction. "She can't hurt anyone else. I hope her illness was long and painful."

"She was murdered," Rory said quietly.

"Murdered? You don't look like you're from the police. Did she harm one of your relatives?" Delores looked at them thoughtfully. "No, you seemed too surprised when I told you about my son."

"We're working with a private investigator south of here in Vista Beach, following up for her," Rory said, opting to continue with the cover story they had used at the hospital in case the woman checked up on them. "Thank you for your time." She gently pushed the cat off her lap and stood up. "We can see ourselves out."

"Nonsense." Delores positioned her walker in front of her and pushed a button on the recliner. It tilted up, making it easier for her to stand, and she walked them to the front door.

They were standing on the porch when the woman said, "Thank you."

"What for?"

"For telling me about her. I'll rest easier now knowing she's no longer able to hurt anyone else. I hope she's spending eternity writhing in hell for what she did."

Rory and Liz didn't say anything until they were in the car.

"Do you think it's true?" Liz settled into the passenger seat and clicked her seatbelt in. "That Wangel killed patients?"

"I don't know why Delores would lie about it." Rory started the car and pulled out onto the street.

"Maybe she doesn't want to believe her son died of cancer."

"The hospital did fire Willow."

"Laid her off. For stealing drugs."

"So what was that about her helping the homeless?" Rory headed toward the freeway on-ramp.

"Probably a cover story so no one would figure out the true reason she stole the drugs."

"Do you think Zoe could have been one of her victims?"

"Not sure the timing's right. Hold on, I took some notes." Liz dug around in her purse and produced a notepad. "I wrote down the date on Zoe's death certificate. And here's the date Wangel was fired from the info Candy gave us. No, Angel was no longer working at the hospital when Zoe died. And, according to the death certificate, she died there."

As they headed back home, Rory thought about what they'd learned. If everything Delores had told them was true, their suspect list for Willow's murder had now become much longer and she had no idea how to discover the identity of a single one of them.

"You did what?" Detective Green's mouth hung open in disbelief.

Rory shrank down in the chair as she questioned the wisdom of telling him about the previous day's road trip. "Sorry. I guess I wasn't thinking," she said in a small voice.

"Why do you insist on putting yourself in danger? For someone so intelligent..." He paced from one side of the interview room to the other. "You see these gray hairs?" He pointed at his hair, which she noticed for the first time did have a few strands of gray in it. "I didn't have them when I first met you."

She shrank down in her seat a little more. "Sorry?"

He placed his hands on the arm of her chair and leaned down. His eyes met hers and he said in measured tones, "You're not a cat. You don't have nine lives. Stop acting like you do."

"Okay," she whispered.

He straightened up and gestured toward the door. "Go. You're giving me a headache. Try to stay out of trouble for more than five minutes, please."

She scampered out of the room as fast as she could.

"What did he say?" Liz stood up from the chair in the police department lobby where she had been waiting.

Rory grabbed her friend's arm and pulled her toward the exit. "I'll tell you outside."

Only after they were two blocks away from the police station did Rory speak. "He wasn't happy."

"He'll get over it. Is he going to look into those people who died?"

"I think so."

"Then that's all we can do."

Later that day, Rory walked around the corner of her house into her backyard. She was heading toward her back door when she spotted Mrs. Griswold standing on the grass, peering at one of the windows of Rory's single story house. The older woman checked something off on a clipboard she held in her hand.

"Mrs. Griswold, can I help you with something?" Rory said.

"There you are. I'm glad to see you've been taking precautions. So far you're the only one on the block who has all of your windows shut and locked."

"You're checking everyone's windows? Why?"

"Those burglars are still out there. I want to make sure we're not inviting targets for them." She pointed to the light over Rory's back porch. "Does your light work?"

"I'll make sure I turn all my outside lights on tonight."

Mrs. Griswold nodded her head in satisfaction. "Good. Too easy to hide in somebody's backyard around here when it's dark. I keep on petitioning City Hall for streetlights, but no luck so far. Did I tell you? I caught a Peeping Tom hanging around recently. Caught him in Willow's backyard, peeking into her kitchen window. Had a dog with him too. Found poop all over my yard. People really need to clean up after their animals. It's an epidemic these days."

Rory pulled up the photo of Kit and Buddy on her phone and showed it to her neighbor. "Is this him?"

"Yep, that's him, all right, and the dog too. You know him?"

"I did. He passed away recently."

"Sorry to hear that, but it's one less problem for me to worry about."

"Did you call the police when you saw him?"

"Of course. I take my job as Neighborhood Watch block

captain seriously. An officer came out and talked to him. Didn't arrest him though. Let him off with a warning. That was a couple weeks ago. Mrs. Quakenbush told me he was back though, the night Willow died. In Willow's backyard again. Ran off when he saw Mrs. Quakenbush."

"She told me that too. Why didn't you tell me this before?"

"You didn't ask. I told the police when it happened, that's the important thing." She glanced down at her clipboard. "Better get going. I've got to finish checking the rest of the houses on the block. I'll make another round after dark to make sure everyone's got their outdoor lights on." Mrs. Griswold stared pointedly at the porch light over Rory's back door.

As she watched her neighbor walk through the side gate onto Seagull Lane, Rory wondered why Kit had been in Willow's backyard twice and if it had anything to do with her murder.

Chapter 30

Rory entered the sanctuary Friday morning minutes before Kit's funeral was scheduled to begin. A dozen people sat in the pews near the front of the church facing a closed casket flanked by two funeral wreaths of white roses and carnations accented with eucalyptus.

As she walked down the aisle, Ben, the homeless man she had met in the library, tipped an imaginary hat to her. She smiled in return and slipped into a pew next to Liz and her parents.

"I'd almost given up on you," Liz said in a quiet voice.

"Sekhmet kept me up half the night. As soon as I fell asleep, she would meow in my ear and nudge me awake again. I think she's finally realized Willow's not coming back."

"She'll calm down soon."

"I know, but it makes me sad to see her wandering around the house looking so lost."

Rory's gaze swept the sanctuary, taking in the librarian who had befriended Kit as well as several of the church volunteers who handed out lunches on Fridays. As far as she could tell, no member of the police department numbered among the mourners.

"Looking for Dashing D?" Liz asked. "Don't look so surprised. I've known you a long time. One of my friends at the station told me he had to go to a parole hearing today."

Moments later, Reverend Paulson stepped to the front to start the service while Tripp slid into a pew in the first row. When the minister called on Rory to speak, her legs wobbled as she walked down the aisle. Her voice choking up occasionally, she shared memories of the time she had spent with Kit and how devoted he had been to his dog. Tripp gave her a reassuring touch on the arm as she returned to her seat and he stepped to the front. Several more people spoke, including two people Kit had done odd jobs for, who praised his work ethic.

After the final hymn was sung and the service was over, everyone helped set up tables and chairs in the parking lot while one of the Friday volunteers put out the food provided by a local deli. The homeless who showed up for their sack lunches today had the option of joining the mourners for a sit-down lunch in honor of Kit.

Rory was talking with the librarian when she heard a "Psst!" followed by a louder "Rory!" coming from behind her. She turned to see a wildly waving Veronica standing next to the food table. Beside her was a nervous-looking man with a ponytail. Rory excused herself and headed toward the pair.

As soon as Rory was close enough, Veronica grabbed her arm and dragged her off to one side, out of earshot of the rest of the group.

"What's going on?" Rory said.

"This is—" Veronica looked over at the nervous man who was saying "No names, no names" over and over again in a low voice. "Doesn't matter what his name is. He's part of my army. You know, the one I told you about the other day."

"Your informants."

"That's right." With a flick of her hand, the reporter urged the man with the ponytail forward. "Go on, tell her what you saw."

His lips quivered and he looked uncertainly at Veronica, who nodded her head in encouragement.

"I was at," he said, followed by several unintelligible words.

Rory leaned forward, but couldn't make out anything else he said. "I'm sorry. Could you speak up?"

"...really odd." Ponytail's voice grew stronger as he gained confidence. "I mean, usually it's pretty quiet in that area. Even though the beach is real close, there aren't many people walking along that part of the street." A faraway look came into his eyes as if he were remembering something, then he continued with his tale.

Rory listened carefully, but couldn't figure out what he was trying to tell her.

Veronica nudged him. "Cut to the chase. We don't have all day."

"Sorry." He blushed. "Okay, where was I?" He looked down at his shoes as if gathering his thoughts. "I was walking downtown, minding my own business when I saw something odd. Really odd. You know the street, don't remember its name, the one at the top of the hill going up from the pier?"

He waited until Rory nodded before continuing. "This woman walked by wearing like, this flowy dress thing in really bright colors. It went down to her ankles."

"Brown hair? Really thin?"

"That's right."

Willow, she said to herself.

"She was coming out of this alley. Odd place for a lady like her to be. I mean, it's dark in that alley. It runs between these buildings, only trashcans and the like in there. Not many people walk down it. The street's not that far away and all." He glanced at Veronica. "Right. Get to the point. Anyway, she looked angry, like real angry. I stayed away from her, kept my eyes on the ground and walked straight ahead. Didn't want to set her off. After she passed by, I looked back and saw this guy I know, Kit. Oh, this was his funeral, wasn't it? Anyway, he was coming out of the alley with his bike and his dog. Sort of staggered a bit, then headed down to the beach."

"When was this?" Rory asked.

"Last Friday. Two weeks ago around this time."

Her ears perked up. The day she found Kit on the beach.

"Was I helpful?" Ponytail said.

"Very." Rory pulled a bill out of her pocket and handed it to him. "Thanks. Make sure you get some food before you leave."

As she headed back to the tables, she thought about what he'd told her. First, she had learned from her neighbor that Kit had been at Willow's house the night she died, then from another neighbor that he had also been hanging around her place weeks before that. Now, this man had told her about seeing Willow and Kit in the area where he'd been attacked. From the sound of it, Willow must have been the one who had hit Kit.

When everyone had eaten and the leftover food, tables and chairs had been put away, she looked around for Tripp. Not finding him in the sanctuary or outside, she headed down the familiar corridors of the building next to the church toward his room.

When she reached her destination, she found him rummaging through dresser drawers. "Where is it?" he said to himself loud enough so Rory could hear. When she knocked on the door, Tripp looked over and smiled. "Did you need something?"

"Just wanted to make sure you were okay. And give you this." She held out a padlock key and a piece of paper with the location and entrance code for the locker on it. "It's the key to the storage locker Kit rented. The details are on the paper. It's mostly boxes. I think there are some things that belonged to your sister in there. We saw her wedding album."

"You looked through it?"

"It was before we knew his full name. We thought we might find something to help identify him."

He placed the paper and key on the nearby dresser. "Thanks."

"I almost forgot. I have a box of papers in my house too. I'll bring them over later." Rory stood awkwardly, unsure what to do next. "When's Kit going to be buried?"

"This afternoon."

"Do you need me to go with you?"

"No, thanks. I think I would rather do it by myself. I'll call you, okay?"

"Sure, I understand." She thought about asking if he knew anything about Kit's relationship with Willow but decided the time wasn't right. She gave him a reassuring hug and headed home.

Chapter 31

"Where are you taking me so early?" Rory slumped down in the passenger seat of Liz's car and closed her eyes. "It's my birthday, and it's Saturday. I should be able to sleep in. At least you could have brought me a diet Coke."

"Believe me, it'll be worth it. I'll get you a soda afterward."

Less than five minutes later, the car stopped. "We're here."

Rory opened her eyes to find they were in an almost deserted parking lot next to the beach. The only other vehicles in the lot were two firetrucks parked near the exit. "What are we doing here?"

"You'll see."

Liz led the way onto the sand and swept her arms in front of her. "Happy Birthday!"

"Oh my." Rory sucked in her breath and stared open-mouthed at the scene before her. Eight muscular men dressed in black shorts and black t-shirts with the Vista Beach fire-department logo on them ran in pairs back and forth across the sand. "What is this?"

"What does it look like? A bunch of fire-department hotties training, of course." Liz spread two beach towels on the sand and curled up on one of them. "Running on sand is very challenging. Gets you in shape really fast."

Rory sank down onto the other towel.

"Almost forgot." Liz jumped up and went to her car, returning with a twenty-ounce bottle of diet Coke and a bear claw with a candle in it. "Breakfast and a beverage for the birthday girl. Sorry I don't have any matches. Pretend the candle's lit and blow it out."

"Thanks." Rory grinned and took the cold bottle of soda and pastry. She closed her eyes and blew out the imaginary flame on the candle.

"What did you wish for?"

"To find out who killed Willow so we can get Dawn out of jail. I'm not sure where to go from here. We know Willow hit Kit, but I have no idea why or if it has anything to do with her death. I feel like we're at a dead end."

"No, no, no. No sleuthing on your birthday. I know it's important to you, but you should take the day off."

"You're right. It can wait until tomorrow." Rory ate her breakfast and returned her attention to the training session going on in front of her. "How did you know about this?"

"I know people."

"Don't they mind us watching?"

"It's a public beach."

When one of the men spotted the two spectators, he nudged his running partner. They broke off from the pack and headed across the sand.

"Hi, Liz," one of them said when he stopped in front of them.

At her nod, both firefighters dug roses out of their pockets and presented them to Rory.

"Happy Birthday," the first one said.

"Sorry they're plastic, but it's the only thing that would hold up," the second one added.

She blushed and took the flowers. After she thanked the men, they jogged back to their group. "How did you manage that?"

A smug smile on her face, Liz said, "I told you, I know people."

"You are the best friend." Rory gave her a quick hug.

Moments later, at a word from their leader, the group ran toward their firetrucks. Soon they were gone and the two women were alone on the beach.

"No one's ever going to top this as a birthday present." Rory folded her towel and followed Liz back to the car. "Where are you taking me now?"

"Someplace fun. You'll see."

Rory spent the rest of the morning with Liz, then headed downtown for lunch with her parents. She was making her way along Main Street, when she sensed someone following her. She looked around half expecting to spot Marcia lurking nearby, but didn't see her or anyone else acting suspiciously. She shook off the feeling and continued down the sidewalk.

She rounded the corner and joined the crowd walking down the steep hill toward the ocean. Two teens carrying surfboards weaved their way uphill, forcing those going in the opposite direction against the buildings.

Rory moved to the right and stopped at the steep staircase going down to the restaurant below. She was about to start down when she felt pressure in the small of her back. The next thing she knew she was falling forward. As she tumbled down the stairs, she grabbed for the railing, but it was too far away. Her eyes widened when her head came within inches of striking one of the concrete steps. She flung her arms in front of her face to protect herself, landing at the bottom on her left shoulder. Groaning in pain, she looked up to the street level. All she saw were pedestrians passing by.

Her parents and restaurant staff crowded around her and helped her up. As soon as she told them what happened, the manager called the police. After the uniformed officer took her statement, Rory's parents helped her up the stairs. She was easing her bruised body into the passenger seat of her parents' car when Detective Green arrived. He put his arm on the top of the car and leaned down to study her face. "What happened? Are you okay?"

After Rory told him everything she knew, he looked at her parents. "Did you two see anything?"

They shook their heads.

"Are you sure it wasn't an accident?" He nodded toward a teen carrying a surfboard up the hill. "It's crowded. Someone could have accidentally hit you with a board. Did you see anyone carrying one when it happened?"

"I suppose it could have been something like that, but it felt more like a deliberate push." Rory winced as she shifted in the seat, trying to find a more comfortable position.

"Go ahead. Get yourself checked out. I'll talk to the officer who took your statement and see what he found out."

After a doctor examined her and bandaged her shoulder, Rory headed home to rest.

When Liz came to pick her up for dinner that evening, she found her still in a t-shirt and jeans.

"Why aren't you dressed? What happened to you?" Liz gestured toward the sling around Rory's left arm.

"Sprained shoulder." She led the way into the living room and sat down on the couch beside Sekhmet, explaining how she'd been about to go down the stairs to the restaurant where she was meeting her parents when she felt pressure in the small of her back. "Someone pushed me, I know it."

"You were lucky it wasn't worse. What did the police say?"

"No one saw anything. The sidewalk was crowded. The police think it was an accident. Wrong place, wrong time."

"Wouldn't be the first time. But if you say someone pushed you, I believe you." Liz stood up. "Come on, I'll help you get dressed."

"I can't wear that dress. It's too hard to get into."

"We'll find something else. Come on. You need to eat. I bet you didn't get lunch."

After looking through the closet, Liz selected dress pants and a short-sleeved blouse, topping it off with the turquoise necklace Rory had bought herself as a present. On the way to dinner, Liz pulled into a parking spot in a residential area of the city.

Rory peered through the side window of the car. "This is my parents' house. What are we doing here?"

"I'm dropping off some flyers for a friend of theirs that's looking for a house here in town. I thought it would be nice to invite your parents to dinner with us since you missed lunch." Liz grabbed a stack of papers from behind her seat.

The two walked up the path to the front door of the Andersons' home. Rory opened the door and stepped into a house that seemed unnaturally dark and quiet. Even though the sun hadn't yet set, with all the blinds closed, the house was dark enough that when Liz dropped her flyers, it was hard to see them on the wood floor.

Liz gathered up as many of the scattered papers as she could and squinted in the low light. "I think one of them landed over there, but it's so dark it's hard to tell. Go and turn the lights on for me, would you?"

"Mom? Dad?" Rory called out as she stepped from the entryway into the living room and fumbled for the light switch on the wall.

When the overhead lights came on, a chorus of voices shouted "Surprise!" and confetti flew through the air toward her.

Rory blinked in the bright light and took a step back, then a smile slowly spread across her face. A banner with "Happy Birthday Rory" on it stretched across one wall of the living room. Balloons were tied to chairs that were scattered around the floor. In front of her stood a group of her friends, many of them people she met through painting and her mother's store as well as others from church. Tripp smiled at her from the back of the group.

"Happy Birthday, dear." Her mother stepped forward and gave her a hug, followed closely by her father, who echoed the sentiment and bent down to kiss his daughter on the cheek.

"You should have seen your face." Liz grinned.

"You dumped those flyers on purpose, didn't you?"

Liz shrugged while everyone crowded around Rory and wished her a happy birthday.

Moments later, Arika clapped her hands. The chatter of voices stopped, and all of the guests directed their attention to Rory's mother. "There's a buffet on the dining room table. Grab a plate and help yourself. Birthday girl goes first, of course."

Tripp piled Rory's favorite foods on a plate and carried it into the living room for her. The two claimed a spot on the sofa and quietly talked.

When the doorbell rang a few minutes later, she answered it, surprised to find Detective Green standing on the porch with a colorfully wrapped package in his hands.

"Sorry I'm late. Happy birthday." He handed her the package and she invited him inside. "How's the shoulder?"

"It hurts, but nothing a little rest won't heal. Did you find out anything more?"

He shook his head. "No one saw anything. My best guess is it was an accident."

"Thanks for looking into it. Can I open this now?" Rory nodded at the box.

"Go ahead."

She tore the wrapping off the package to find a flat box of Frango mint chocolates. She looked up in surprise. "I love these! How did you know?"

"Your mother helped me pick them out. Sorry I couldn't get the hexagonal box. I guess you can only get that in Seattle. The only one I could get online is this one."

"The packaging doesn't matter. This is perfect. Thank you." She leaned over to give him a kiss on the cheek, then thought better of it and gave him a one-handed hug instead.

Rory pointed him toward the food and settled back down in her spot on the couch, Liz sitting on one side of her, Tripp on the other. Music quietly played in the background through the speakers placed throughout the house. The crowd spilled out into all the downstairs rooms and out onto the patio. After she ate, Rory took selfies with a number of her friends who posted the pics on social media. At one point, she glanced across the room and noticed Detective Green talking with her father. She smiled at the two of them, their heads close together so they could hear each other above the chatter.

"Okay, everyone, it's time to dance!" Liz turned up the music and began swaying in time to it. She grabbed Rory's good arm and pulled her into the entryway, the nearest open space in the house. Soon they were joined by others. When the music slowed down, Tripp asked Rory to dance. As he held her in his arms, he said, "I have something for you."

He pulled a colorful envelope out of his pocket. She opened it to find a gift card to the skate rental place where they'd had their second date. "I thought we could do it again some time."

"I love it, thanks." Rory was kissing him on the cheek when her mother clapped her hands and said, "It's time to cut the cake. The birthday girl is needed in the dining room."

As they were walking through the living room, Tripp's cell phone rang. "Sorry, I've got to take this. Go ahead. I'll be right there."

Rory headed into the dining room where a cake, at least three layers tall, sat on the table with her name written on the icing.

"It's beautiful," she said. "Did you bake this, Mom?"

"Teresa took care of it. It's from that new bakery downtown, Ingersoll's."

Rory turned to the wedding planner, who stood to one side, a sly grin on her face.

"That's why you insisted I come with you to taste those wedding cakes. There was no client, was there? It was all a ploy to get me to pick out my favorite flavor."

"There was a client, all right, but I figured I could kill two birds with one stone."

Everyone gathered around the table while Swan lit the candles. After all the guests sang "Happy Birthday," Rory held her long hair back and closed her eyes to make a wish. She was about to blow out the candles when she heard a voice behind her say, "What did I miss?" Rory turned and spotted Candy standing at the edge of the crowd. She waved, then returned her attention to the cake, her long hair falling in front of her face.

The next thing she knew her face felt hot and a foul smell assaulted her nostrils. Everyone shouted and someone shoved the cake aside and patted her hair between their hands.

After the excitement was over, Rory stared into the concerned eyes of Detective Green. "What happened?" she said.

"You're not having a good day. Your hair got a little too close to the flames," he said. "Sorry for being so rough, but I needed to put it out. Are you all right?"

"My hair was on fire?" She looked around the room and everyone nodded in agreement. "I had no idea. I didn't really feel anything. My face got a little hot, but that's all. Then there was this awful smell." Rory touched the right side of her head, bringing a strand of her hair to her nose, and sniffed. The horrible smell still clung to it.

"It was good you were so close," Tripp said to the detective. He turned to Rory. "That was an urgent call from the clinic. Someone didn't show up for work so I need to take a shift. I'm afraid I'm going to have to leave. Walk me to the door?" When he opened the front door, he paused with his hand on the doorknob. "Sorry I wasn't there when you set your hair on fire and that detective came to the rescue."

"Jealous?" she said.

"Maybe." He grinned and kissed her on top of the head. "Duty calls. Get back to your party. I'll call you later."

"Thanks for coming and for the present," Rory said and shut the door.

When she got back to the dining room, her mother took charge.

"We've got to get that smell out. Swan, why don't you cut the cake while I help Rory with her hair," Arika said. She ushered her daughter into an upstairs bathroom and a little shampoo later, the smell of burning hair was gone. Rory studied her face in the mirror. Her hair on the right side of her head was noticeably shorter and its edges had a ratty look to them.

Arika stood behind her daughter and patted her on the shoulder. "It's easily fixed. I'll make an appointment with my hairdresser for tomorrow."

"I didn't think she worked on Sundays."

"She'll do it. It's an emergency."

"Maybe it's a sign I should cut my hair. Liz will be pleased. She's been trying to get me to make a change for months now."

"It could have been worse. You're lucky Martin acted so quickly. Let's get you back to the party. Everyone's waiting for you."

When they returned to the celebration, Liz walked up to Rory and whispered, "Did someone push you into the cake?"

"No, this time it was all me. I got distracted and forgot about my hair."

"Why don't you take Martin a slice of cake. I think I saw him going into the backyard. It's the least you can do," Arika said.

Rory found him alone on the patio sitting in one of the wicker chairs, shoulders hunched forward, staring at something in his hands.

"Martin? I brought you some cake." She set the plate on the table next to his chair. "For my knight in shining armor. Thanks for...you know." She gestured toward her freshly washed hair.

He looked up and smiled. "Always glad to help a damsel in distress."

Rory settled down on the chair beside him and took a bite of the chocolate cake with raspberry filling.

"That's nice." He pointed with his fork to the tear-shaped necklace she was wearing. "New? I don't remember seeing it before."

"It was a birthday present."

"Tripp?"

"No, I bought it for myself."

"I thought maybe he'd give you a ring."

"Like an engagement ring? Lord, no. We've barely started dating."

"But I saw you tasting wedding cakes the other day..."

"That's what you've been thinking all this time?"

He shrugged his shoulders. "There is such a thing as love at first sight. And I didn't see you much when I was dating Mel. I have no idea who you've been seeing."

Rory nodded toward the photo he still held in his hands. "Who is that?"

He tilted it so she could see. A smiling Detective Green had his arms around an attractive woman about his age. "My wife."

"She's beautiful. I'm sorry for your loss."

"Thanks." He cocked an eyebrow. "Mel told you?"

"She didn't give me any details. Just that you lost her a while back."

He carefully put the photo in his wallet, picked up the cake and took a bite. "This party reminded me of her. We had one right before I lost her."

"What happened? You don't have to talk about it if you don't want to."

He sat back in the patio chair and stared at the plants on the other side of the yard. "Do you know anything about the job I had before Chief Marshall hired me?"

"I've heard rumors." Rory remembered Liz telling her when they first met the detective about how the police department he'd formerly belonged to had been corrupt and that he'd helped bring the problems out into the open.

"The police department I was a part of lost its way. Not everyone, mind you, but enough. Bribes, letting evidence 'get lost' in certain cases...that kind of thing. My wife got caught in the middle."

"Oh, no," Rory said in a hushed tone of voice.

"My partner was one of those who'd been taking bribes. He didn't appreciate my helping to bring the problems to light. He tried to kill me, but he ended up shooting my wife instead." He looked down at his half empty plate.

A tear trickled down her cheek. She rested her hand on his arm in sympathy. "I'm so sorry. I can't even imagine what that was like. Was it his parole hearing yesterday? Is that why you didn't go to Kit's funeral?"

"He didn't get it." He smiled sadly at her. "Sorry to be such a downer on your birthday."

"Don't worry about it, I understand."

"Rory," her mother's voice called from the doorway. "Some of the guests are leaving. They want to say goodbye to you."

Rory wiped another tear from the corner of her eye. "I'm coming," she said and hurried into the house, leaving Detective Green to finish his cake in peace.

Chapter 32

The next day brought cool temperatures and overcast skies to the residents of Vista Beach. The heat wave that had consumed everyone's thoughts for over two weeks had now become a distant memory.

After church and her emergency hair appointment, Rory settled down for a little quiet time. With Sekhmet curled up next to her on the sofa, she picked up the copy of *The Phantom Tollbooth* she'd found in Kit's belongings, a story she remembered reading as a kid. She immersed herself in the tale of a young boy named Milo and his magic tollbooth. She got so caught up in the story, she soon forgot all about Kit's death and Willow's murder.

When she turned the last page a couple hours later, she noticed a piece of paper sticking out from between the endpaper and back cover of the hardback. She carefully pulled away the paper from the inside cover to find a letter Kit had written to his wife, dated after she passed away. She was going to put it back where she found it when Angel's name caught her eye. In the letter, Kit asked why Zoe had killed herself and vowed to make Angel pay for providing his wife the means to do it.

Rory tucked the letter back inside the book, set it down on her lap and thought about what she had read. Now that she knew Kit had a reason for wanting Willow dead, or at least punished, she reviewed everything she'd learned about him and his relationship with the herbal healer. How he'd been seen in her backyard twice and had a physical confrontation with her in the alley the morning of her death. Rory slowly put the pieces together in her mind.

When Mrs. Griswold saw him at Willow's house two weeks before, he was probably trying to talk with her. Willow must have finally agreed to see him, picking the alley as an out-of-the-way spot. When she couldn't reason with him, she hit him to shut him up. That must have been the last straw for Kit. When he recovered enough, he left the hospital, went back to her house to confront her once more and grabbed the knife off the counter and killed her. When Mrs. Quakenbush saw him, that must have been when he was dumping her purse in the bushes, trying to make it look like an intruder had broken into the house.

Rory Facetimed Liz to run over the scenario with her to see if she thought it made sense.

After Liz gave the new hairdo her seal of approval, she said, "You look worried. What's going on?"

Rory read the letter to her.

"I can see why you think Kit killed her. Are you going to give it to the police?"

"I have to, but Martin won't be happy after what he said to me the other day."

"You didn't break in somewhere and find it. It was in a book you happened to be reading."

"Kit had motive and opportunity. Mrs. Quakenbush saw him in Willow's backyard that night. And the means was right there on the kitchen counter. In the letter, he sounds mad at Willow for giving his wife something to end her suffering. They probably argued and he grabbed the knife in anger. I'm not sure there's enough proof though."

"You need to give it to Dashing D, anyway. It might convince the police to drop the charges against Dawn. Reasonable doubt and all that."

"I know. But before I do, I'm going to check Willow's backyard one last time. See if the police missed anything. And I want to break the news to Tripp. He and Kit might not have been that close, but this does involve his sister. I don't want him to hear about it from the police."

A short time later, Rory slipped through the gate into Willow's backyard. Her gaze swept the area from the grass to the plants surrounding the house to the steps up to the back deck and the French doors leading inside. She ignored the lawn, figuring anything left on the grass would have been noticed long ago, and searched the plants, starting with the one she'd found the credit card under. She separated its leaves and stared down at the ground, but all she saw were weeds and dirt. In a neighboring azalea, a glint of gold on the ground caught her eye. She reached down and brushed away spent blooms that had fallen off the plant. Underneath them, she found a tiny gold chain attached to a red rabbit's foot.

For a moment, she couldn't remember why the good-luck charm seemed familiar. Her heart broke when she realized where she'd seen it before. She retracted her hand as if the plant were on fire and stepped back.

Rory sat down on the steps and buried her head in her hands. Everything made sense now. She knew who had killed Willow, but she wasn't sure the charm was enough for the police. She needed to find more evidence to prove to them and herself that what she suspected was actually true.

A little while later, Rory drove her car into the church parking lot, easing into a spot in the far corner away from the dozen cars that were already there. She made her way into the church complex, pausing when she heard a chorus of voices raised in song coming from the direction of the sanctuary.

She checked the time on her cell phone. Choir practice was halfway over. She had at most half an hour for her search. As quietly as possible, she walked down the hallway toward Tripp's room and knocked on the door, prepared to make an excuse for visiting if he was inside. When no one answered, she opened the door and cautiously peered into a deserted room.

She slipped inside, eased the door shut behind her and turned on the light. A bedside lamp illuminated the small space, just large enough to accommodate a twin-size bed, three-drawer dresser and nightstand. A door on the far side of the room led into a tiny bathroom.

Rory began her search there, checking underneath the sink, inside the medicine cabinet and the toilet tank. When no new evidence of Tripp's guilt surfaced, she looked through the bedroom, finding nothing of interest in the drawers or closet. Crouching down on the floor, she spotted a backpack underneath the bed. She dragged it out with her good arm and placed it on top of the mattress. She was unzipping the main compartment when she thought she heard a noise in the corridor. She tiptoed to the door and peeked outside, breathing a sigh of relief at the empty hallway. She eased the door shut and returned to her search.

One-handed, Rory upended the backpack, dumping its contents onto the bed. A glint of gold caught her eye. She moved a book aside, revealing the proof she needed, a gold charm bracelet with an empty spot that had once held a sun.

Rory set the bracelet aside. She was returning the rest of the items to the backpack when she felt a prick in her neck and moments later, slumped to the floor unconscious.

Chapter 33

Rory woke to the gentle rocking of waves. Water surrounded her as she lay on a surfboard in the ocean, cords across her chest, waist and legs binding her to it. She peered into the darkness and saw, way off in the distance, the lights of houses along the shore.

"You're awake."

Rory turned her head toward the voice. Tripp was sitting on a surfboard next to hers, tying a rope to a white ball anchored one hundred yards off the shore. She remembered seeing the buoy when she went to the beach, but hadn't expected to one day find herself attached to it.

"What did you do to me?" She tried to raise her hands toward her aching head, but the ropes prevented her arms from moving more than a few inches. She patted the pocket of her jeans as surreptitiously as possible.

"Looking for this?" Tripp held up her phone. "Bye bye." He let go and the cell fell into the water. "Oh, and I can't forget this." He unhooked Willow's charm bracelet from around his wrist and dropped it. The ocean swallowed it up.

"Why are you doing this?"

"Can't have you telling the police about what I did. By the time anyone realizes you're missing I'll be long gone and your body will have drifted out where no one will find you."

"Where are you going? Back to Africa?"

"Maybe. There's nothing for me here now. I have no desire to rot in jail for killing someone who deserved to die, especially when I can help so many people who need it. This is your fault, you know. I thought you'd stop investigating after I pushed you down those stairs, but no, you kept right on going."

"I know Willow gave Zoe the means to kill herself. Is that why?"

"She didn't kill herself."

"What? But Kit thought—"

"I know what he thought, but he was wrong. She didn't kill herself. Willow did it."

"I don't understand. She gave her the means, sure, but I wouldn't say she killed—"

Tripp banged a hand against the buoy, sending the surfboard Rory was on rocking violently. "You. Don't. Understand. Willow played God. She decided Zoe's time was up. My sister didn't ask her for anything. She trusted Willow and thought she was taking something that would help her fight her cancer, not kill her. The last dose Willow gave her was laced with poison. The doctors in the ER tried to save her, but it was too late."

"Are you sure? How did you find out?"

"Willow told me herself. I went to her house to find out why my sister did it. Instead I found out...I never meant to do it, you know."

"What happened?" As quietly as possible, Rory worked on getting one of her hands free.

"I need to start at the beginning, when I came back from my latest trip to Africa. Like I told you before, I hadn't talked to my sister in years. When I got back, a friend handed me a letter from Zoe. She'd been diagnosed with cancer and wanted to see me before she died. She was still fighting it, but also preparing for the possibility she would lose."

He took a deep breath. "When I got to her place, she'd already passed. The police talked to me and told me they suspected Christopher—Kit—had helped her die. They couldn't prove anything and Kit was no longer in the area. He'd lost everything and disappeared. It took me a while, but I finally figured out where he was. I came down here and volunteered at the church, hoping to find him. Eventually, I did. When I talked to him, I accused him of helping her die. He told me Willow was the one who had given her the medicine, that it was an alternative treatment for cancer patients that had accidentally killed my sister. So I went to Willow's house that night to try to get her to stop giving out this herb to other people. She told me I didn't know what I was talking about. Told me that she decided my sister's time had come, that she didn't want to see Zoe in so much pain, so she gave her the herb laced with poison. She was so sure she'd done the right thing, she didn't show a shred of remorse."

"And your sister never knew?"

"No, she thought she was taking her usual herbal treatment. She never dreamed Willow would betray her like that."

"That's awful."

"Willow didn't admit it at first, but when she finally told me what she'd done, I couldn't believe what I was hearing. I snapped, grabbed a knife that was on the counter and stabbed her."

"Then you arranged it to look like an intruder had come in through an open window and killed her?"

"That's right. I took the jewelry she had on, then took the screen out of the window and ransacked the kitchen. I tossed her purse in the bushes after I took money and a few credit cards out of her wallet. I stuffed it all in my backpack and threw the jewelry and cards in a dumpster near the church, far enough away from her house the police wouldn't think of looking there. At least I thought I'd gotten rid of it. The bracelet must have fallen to the bottom of my backpack."

"What about the camera and the SD card? Were you the one who hired those kids to steal it? How did you know it was there?"

"I was at the bar when Lance was there. He was pretty drunk. Kept on talking about this camera and how he needed to get it back before the police found it. How it wouldn't look good for him since his prints were all over it. He'd planted it to check up on Willow."

"But the video would have exonerated him."

"He wasn't thinking straight and I wasn't about to point it out to him."

"But those women said he was there by himself—Oh. You made that up, didn't you? That's why you volunteered to talk to them." Rory felt the cord across her wrist beginning to loosen.

"I couldn't risk you finding out I'd talked to him that night."

"Then you went outside and hired the homeless kid."

"I changed my voice and made sure he couldn't really see me," Tripp said.

"What if the police had already found the camera?"

"If they had, they would have arrested me a long time ago."

"The key to the house. Where did you get it?"

"I took it off Lance's keyring at the bar. He didn't miss it since he'd been staying at his place in Hawthorne."

"You were the one on the bike then, who took the bag from me."

"I saw you pick it up after the girl had dropped it off." Tripp looked down at her. "Now you know everything. I'll leave you now. I've tied this pretty loosely." He pointed to the rope anchoring Rory's board to the buoy. "By the time you get free, you'll have drifted far enough out, you'll never make it to land. And don't forget the sharks. I hear they like the water around here." He lay down on his surfboard and paddled toward shore, leaving her alone in the ocean.

Rory yelled for help, but soon realized it was wasted energy. She was on her own.

She struggled with her bonds, finally managing to free her right arm. The surfboard rocked as she worked on the ropes. She'd barely gotten her legs free when it flipped over, slamming her injured shoulder against the water. She screamed and her mouth filled with water. As she fought her way to the surface, her flailing hands accidentally pushed the surfboard away. Clinging to the buoy, she coughed up water and caught her breath. Once she recovered, her gaze swept the area, looking for the board, but she couldn't see it in the darkness that surrounded her. Giving up on ever finding it, she got her bearings, spotting a string of lights in the distance, telling her in which direction safety lay.

Unsure if she could make it to the beach with her shoulder injury and her clothes weighing her down, she kicked off her tennis shoes and struggled out of her jeans. After taking a few deep breaths, she said a silent prayer, let go of the buoy and headed toward land.

Willpower drove her through the waves. Her body ached and she longed to rest, but she knew she was so exhausted that if she stopped to tread water, she might never start up again. She pushed through the pain in her shoulder, and after what seemed like hours, felt land beneath her. Lying face down in the sand, she let the ocean wash over her until she'd gathered enough strength to continue. She pulled herself to her feet and, in a dripping wet t-shirt and underwear, walked unsteadily across the deserted beach toward the lights of the nearest houses. In the parking lot next to the pier, she spotted a lone car. With her last bit of energy, she walked toward it and knocked on the driver's side window. The two people inside broke apart. Two pairs of eyes stared back at her through the glass. She mouthed the word "help" and collapsed onto the pavement.

Chapter 34

Rory's eyes fluttered open. Panic gripped her as she became aware of her surroundings and realized she was lying on a bed in a room that wasn't her own. It subsided as soon as she recognized the white walls of the hospital.

"You don't have to walk around town half naked to get my attention," a deep voice said.

She turned her head toward the sound. Detective Green sat on a chair beside the bed and smiled.

"Tripp."

The smile on the detective's face faded. "He's not here. Do you want me to find him?"

"No, you don't understand. He killed Willow."

"Tell me."

In halting words, Rory told him about her ordeal in the ocean and the discovery that had led to the realization that Tripp was a murderer. "The rabbit's foot is still under the plant by Willow's house. I never told him about it. But he tossed the bracelet in the water."

"Don't worry. We'll get him. Any idea where he was headed?"

"Africa, I think."

He patted her arm. As soon as he left the room, she drifted off to sleep. When she woke a few hours later, Liz was sitting by her bedside, reading a magazine. She put the magazine on her lap and leaned forward. "Thank God you're okay. We were really worried."

"Tripp?"

"Dashing D picked him up at the airport. His plane was delayed."

"Good," Rory said, closing her eyes.

A sling on her left arm and a tote bag in her right, Rory made her way down the hill toward the ocean. A giant inflatable screen was set up against the north side of the pier. People of all ages converged on the area and spread blankets on the beach facing the screen, waiting for the free Thursday evening showing of *The Wizard of Oz* to begin.

She stood on the walkway next to the sand and searched the sea of faces. As soon as she spotted Liz, she wended her way through the crowd and sank down onto the blanket next to her friend.

Sitting cross-legged, Rory looked around her. "Good spot. Exactly the right distance from the screen. When did you get here?"

"Half an hour ago. Candy is getting popcorn from the snack bar." Liz held up a large bag of M&Ms. "I've got chocolate."

Rory unpacked her tote bag. "I brought soda and chips. Is Doug coming? There's room for one more."

"I didn't want to invite him. I thought it might bring up bad memories since, you know..."

"You mean about Tripp?"

"The first date you had with him Doug was there too. I thought he would remind you of it. I wanted this to be fun for you." Liz placed a hand on Rory's arm. "How are you doing?"

"I'm okay. Maybe okay isn't the right word. I'm still mad."

"At least Dawn's free now. You should be happy about that."

"I know, I know. Let's talk about something else. Are Bethany and her family going to adopt Buddy?"

"Yes. He's a good fit for them and he seems to be adapting to his new environment well. What about Sekhmet? Have you found her a home?"

"I'm going to keep her. She really likes living with me. It's nice to have her around the house. She's good company." Her phone chirped and Rory looked down at its screen. "Veronica posted a new item on VBC. Looks like they caught those burglars, the ones that have been on that spree. At least we don't have to worry about that anymore." She offered a soda to Liz before opening one for herself.

As Rory took a sip, she spotted Dawn in the distance and waved her over.

"I can't thank you enough, Rory." Dawn stood next to the blanket and smiled down at them. "I owe you."

"I'm just happy you're okay. Did I see you at your mo—Willow's house earlier?"

"Chief Marshall wanted help packing up her things. I found her diary." She pulled a book out of her tote bag. "I'm beginning to understand her more. She was homeless right after she left us. Her time on the street wasn't pleasant. She was robbed and beaten. Everything she had back then was stolen from her. Guess that's why she seemed to have it out for the homeless."

"They're not all bad people." Rory nodded toward the diary. "Did she say how she made her money?"

"After she got back on her feet and became a nurse, she sold drugs she stole from the hospital, then invested what she made. I'm not sure how I feel about inheriting money made that way. My brother and I are thinking of donating most of it to charity." Someone shouted Dawn's name. She looked up and waved. "I'd better get going. I'm sitting with the girls from the store. Let me know if I can do anything for you. Take care and thanks again."

She'd barely left when Rory heard a deep voice behind her say, "Nice to see you all here." She looked up to find Detective Green dressed in a polo shirt and shorts standing on the sand next to them.

"May I?" He motioned toward the blanket. When she nodded her agreement, he sat down in the empty spot next to her.

"Nice night for it," he said.

She nodded and took a sip of her soda, unsure what to say.

He stared straight ahead. "I stopped by to make sure you're okay. The last week has been rough for you."

"Don't worry, I'm fine. My shoulder's healing. I'm still mad at Tripp for using me like that, only going out with me to see what was going on with the investigation, but I'm a big girl. I'll get over it."

"I'm sorry you had to go through that. Don't judge every man by what he did."

"I don't. How did you know I was going to be here?"

His gaze swept the crowd, which was growing as the time grew near for the movie to begin. "It was a good guess. Seems like everyone is here tonight."

Rory looked down at her soda. "I'm sorry I didn't call you about Tripp when I first figured out he killed Willow, but I wanted to be sure."

"You might have to testify against him."

"I know."

He looked at her with concern. "You okay with that?"

"We weren't going out that long. I'm fine." Rory drew a flower on the sand in front of her. "What do you think will happen to him?"

"He's got a good lawyer who's working hard to get him off."

She looked up. "But he confessed."

"Only to you. Not to anyone else." He touched her hand. "Don't worry, he won't get away with it. The rabbit's foot you found can be traced back to him and there's a strong motive. I'm sure he'll realize soon he's better off taking a plea deal."

Before Rory could say anything else, Candy arrived. "Here you go, popcorn for everyone." She passed out individual bags to the other three before settling down on the blanket on the other side of Liz.

Detective Green nodded his thanks and munched on his popcorn.

Rory whispered to Liz, "You're the one who told him I'd be here, aren't you?"

"Maybe," Liz said with an impish grin on her face. "Detective," she said in a louder voice, "Veronica posted on her blog that one of the officers in our police department caught those burglars, but she didn't say how."

"They ran a red light in the city. The officers who stopped them saw stolen items in the backseat and the two matched the description we had of the burglars."

"Seems stupid of them to run that light," Candy said.

"Criminals can be pretty stupid at times. That's how so many of them get caught."

"Did you ever find out why Willow came to town when she did?" Rory asked. "It seems odd after all those years that she would suddenly want a relationship with her children. From what Dawn told me, she'd never shown any interest before."

"The autopsy showed she had an advanced stage of cancer. Inoperable. She didn't have much longer. My best guess is she wanted time with her kids before she died."

"That makes sense. Did you tell Dawn?"

"I felt it important she know. Willow never told her about it."

Rory leaned closer to him and lowered her voice. "What's going on with the chief? Do you think he's going to be okay?"

"The results of his last test were good, so it's promising."

"I'm glad."

He started to get up. "I'll let you three enjoy the show."

Rory laid a hand on his arm. "You can stay if you want. I'd like that."

"Only if you go out to dinner with me tomorrow." He cleared his throat. "I'm asking you out on a date, in case that wasn't clear."

"I would be happy to go on a date with you, Martin."

Rory sat closer to him. He reached over and touched her hand. They intertwined their fingers and stared at the screen as the movie began.

Sybil Johnson

Sybil Johnson's love affair with reading began in kindergarten with "The Three Little Pigs." Visits to the library introduced her to Encyclopedia Brown, Mrs. Piggle-Wiggle and a host of other characters. Fast forward to college where she continued reading while studying Computer Science. After a rewarding career in the computer industry, Sybil decided to try her hand at writing mysteries. Her short fiction has appeared in *Mysterical-E* and *Spinetingler Magazine*, among others. Originally from the Pacific Northwest, she now lives in Southern California where she enjoys tole painting, studying ancient languages and spending time with friends and family.

Henery Press Mystery Books

And finally, before you go...
Here are a few other mysteries
you might enjoy:

PUMPKINS IN PARADISE

Kathi Daley

A Tj Jensen Mystery (#1)

Between volunteering for the annual pumpkin festival and coaching her girls to the state soccer finals, high school teacher Tj Jensen finds her good friend Zachary Collins dead in his favorite chair.

When the handsome new deputy closes the case without so much as a "why" or "how," Tj turns her attention from chili cook-offs and pumpkin carving to complex puzzles, prophetic riddles, and a decades-old secret she seems destined to unravel.

Available at booksellers nationwide and online

Visit www.henerypress.com for details

TELL ME NO LIES

Lynn Chandler Willis

An Ava Logan Mystery (#1)

Ava Logan, single mother and small business owner, lives deep in the heart of the Appalachian Mountains, where poverty and pride reign. As publisher of the town newspaper, she's busy balancing election season stories and a rash of ginseng thieves.

And then the story gets personal. After her friend is murdered, Ava digs for the truth all the while juggling her two teenage children, her friend's orphaned toddler, and her own muddied past. Faced with threats against those closest to her, Ava must find the killer before she, or someone she loves, ends up dead.

Available at booksellers nationwide and online

Visit www.henerypress.com for details

CROPPED TO DEATH

Christina Freeburn

A Faith Hunter Scrap This Mystery (#1)

Former US Army JAG specialist, Faith Hunter, returns to her West Virginia home to work in her grandmothers' scrapbooking store determined to lead an unassuming life after her adventure abroad turned disaster. But her quiet life unravels when her friend is charged with murder—and Faith inadvertently supplied the evidence. So Faith decides to cut through the scrap and piece together what really happened.

With a sexy prosecutor, a determined homicide detective, a handful of sticky suspects and a crop contest gone bad, Faith quickly realizes if she's not careful, she'll be the next one cropped.

Available at booksellers nationwide and online

Visit www.henerypress.com for details